DIRTY POOL

BETHANY-KRIS

Published by Bethany-Kris

www.bethanykris.com

ISBN 13: 978-1-988197-86-9

Cover Art © London Miller

Editor: Elizabeth Peters

For every reader who asked me for Michel and didn't give up until I wrote his story.

CONTENTS

ONE

Michel Marcello liked *pressure*. He worked best when someone was right over his shoulder, reminding him that time was ticking down. His greatest educational achievements came from times when his life was thick with tension, and he could lose himself in textbooks. His highest test scores came from moments when the pressure was so high that anyone else might have cracked under it.

Not him, though.

He just worked better.

Books weren't a problem for him—from the time he was young, he found learning was the easiest obstacle he had to face in his twenty years. It helped that he loved to learn, and took joy from understanding something that before, had been entirely foreign to him. It was like a new challenge. Something else for him to master.

But exams?

Fuck.

He found exams boring as hell.

Maybe it was because he'd spent the entire first year of pre-med learning everything in front of him, and he hadn't struggled with any degree of difficulty to write his final exam on biochemistry. Hell, that had been his favorite subject for the past year.

Around the halfway mark of the final exam, he was already sighing. And fighting a migraine from wishing he could read faster. It wasn't that he didn't know the answers—he knew them *too well*. It felt like he was just going through the motions, and the exam was never going to be done. His laziness was where he made mistakes despite being as book smart as he was lucky to be.

Except this was what he wanted.

More than anything.

To be a doctor had been Michel's dream from the time he was eleven. He'd been out with Dante, his father, when a new recruit for a gang from the inner city thought to earn his way in by attacking the infamous Marcello mob boss. Michel's dad, that was.

It was the first time that Michel truly understood what it meant to be a Cosa Nostra family, and the dangers that came along with it. Before that day, the mafia had never touched Michel in a *real* way. He heard the whispers in his family about what his uncles and father did, and he thought he knew what it meant.

He didn't know anything at all.

The stray bullets missed Dante.

They hit the enforcer protecting Michel.

Pandemonium followed utter chaos after the attack. He remembered his father shouting *no cops, no cops* as the bleeding enforcer was dragged into an alleyway. A car quickly pulled up less than a minute later, and they all piled into the back. It was in the backroom of a Brooklyn medical clinic that he watched a trauma surgeon hired by his father, to stay on call *just in case,* save the life of that enforcer.

And there Michel was—all of eleven, but almost twelve, tucked away in the corner of the room because his father was busy focusing his energy on making sure

1

his man was saved. He watched the whole thing. The blood … the man on the table, awake without anesthesia, and the doctor, who even terrified, did his *job*.

He did it with steady hands.

Michel aspired to be that man. He was sure some people assumed, in one way or another, he would take after his mafia Don father and join the family—impossible with his bloodline and history, although the Marcellos would have made room if he truly wanted to become a made man. Or even, maybe he would take after his mother; a Queen Pin who ran the majority of her drug dealing business out of California.

Both things fascinated him. He respected his parents, their lives, and the choices they made. He grew up in the illegal, underground world of the mafia, and surrounded by criminals. That was all he knew. Even his best friends—his cousins, John and Andino—chose to go into the family business as soon as they were old enough to join.

Him, though?

He was going to be a doctor. Specifically, a trauma surgeon if all went well. And it would go well because he would make sure of it. Nothing was going to ruin this for him, not even himself. He wouldn't let his boredom get to him, not now.

Michel stared down at the exam in front of him, and blinked at the next question. Like the others, he knew the answer, and quickly circled the appropriate dot on the answer card. The promise of a migraine was still fighting its way through the front of his skull behind his eyes even as he worked his way through the next two pages of the exam.

He glanced up, and checked the time on the clock at the front of the room. It rested just above the large white board that the professor liked to use to doodle on as he gave nonsensical lectures—yet another thing that gave Michel the fastest migraines of his fucking life. He was going to be glad to get this first year of pre-med over with, and move on to something a little more challenging.

According to that clock, though, he had another two hours of this. *Two goddamn hours*, and he was already a quarter of the way through this exam. The only good thing he could see about this situation was the fact he was soon going to be getting to the written portion of this exam, and his brain would have to work a little harder.

He just needed to get to that point.

Slipping his hand into his pocket, he pulled out a bottle of over the counter pain meds, and popped off the cap. He shook the bottle, and two pills fell into his palm. Next to him, the guy raised a brow at him as Michel tossed the pills into his mouth before grabbing the water on his desk to help swallow them back.

The student at the desk next to his shared a look with him that said, *I get you, man*. The guy looked like he was about to drown, and he could already see his failing grade staring back at him. Hell, maybe he could.

Honestly, all Michel needed to do was take a look around this classroom, and he could easily pick out probably at least twenty percent of the students that wouldn't make it to their second year. No one truly understood the hell of pre-med until they were in the thick of it, and there was no getting out.

They went in thinking one thing …

And changed their direction after year-one thinking another.

Not Michel, though.

He knew what he wanted.

This.

• • •

"Hey, Ma," Michel said, shifting the messenger bag on his shoulder as he left the exam room with thirty minutes left to go. He'd actually finished his exam an hour earlier than planned, but the professor required him to wait until that half-hour mark before he allowed him to leave the room, along with anyone else who was done early and felt like taking the risk of not double checking their answer cards and written portions. "You're calling a bit—"

"Well, how did it go?"

Michel laughed.

Of course, she knew.

Catrina remembered everything.

"The exam went well," he told her.

"Ah, *bambino*," Catrina replied, her Italian accent thicker than anyone else's in their family because Italy had been her birthplace and where she was raised. "I knew you would do well. My smart *ragazzo*, yes?"

Always his mother's baby.

"It was touch and go there for a while," he replied, "but I got through it."

"Was it really?"

Michel scoffed. "Not even close."

It was cake, honestly.

Catrina let out a soft sigh. "I figured as much, but don't you dare get comfortable or lazy, Michel. You need the best grades you can get if you want to see this through. When it comes to a residency—"

"They're going to look at everything. I know."

"Of course, you do."

Some people thought his mother was cold as hell in a lot of ways. He supposed she could be to people on the outside of their life. She had a persona to uphold, and she presented it first and foremost to people before they ever got a good look at who she really was behind her mask of a *mafia boss's wife* and *Queen Pin.*

To him, though?

She'd always been *just* his mom.

Well, sort of …

She'd adopted him, and so had his father, but he learned that in his teenage years after snooping through his parents' shared office. He hadn't meant to stumble on the falsified paperwork, but when he brought it up to Dante and Catrina, they didn't lie.

Catrina was, biologically, his aunt. Her sister had been pregnant, and died shortly after he was born because of the man who … impregnated her. Or *raped*, no one was really one-hundred percent sure on that, or they simply didn't want to tell Michel the truth.

Either way, that was how his mother and father became, well, his. People liked to assume, or those that knew the truth, that Michel *must* have some deep-rooted issues with his parents because he didn't biologically belong to them.

Those people were idiots.

Michel had no issues.

He didn't know anything but the man and woman who he called mom and dad. They were the only parents he ever knew, and the only ones he wanted to know, too. They gave him this amazing life. *They* gave him the ability to do whatever he wanted and make his own choices about what direction his life would go.

Without them, he would not be *him*.

How was that not a parent?

Catrina and Dante were the only people who raised him, and the detail that they didn't share, blood, never factored into what he knew to be true. He loved them *entirely*.

And they loved him.

So much.

Michel came out of the corridor exit, and right into the parking lot where his Mercedes waited in the warm summer air of Detroit. He stepped out of WSU School of Medicine and gave it one last look over his shoulder, a sense of pride thickening his blood with every step he took carrying him further away from the walls of the college that challenged him every step of the way for his first year of pre-med.

Yeah, some shit was easy.

Others?

Not so much.

But he liked it.

Respected it.

His parents taught him that, too.

"What are your plans for the summer, then?" Catrina asked, bringing him back to the conversation at hand. "Today was your final exam before break, right?"

"It was."

"*And?*"

Michel shook his head, knowing there was no way out of this conversation. "And I haven't decided yet what I'm doing with my break."

That was a lie.

He had decided.

He wasn't going home.

Catrina made a sad noise. "Well, okay."

He knew what his parents wanted—they missed him, and would like to have him home. In a way, he wanted to go back, too, but he'd heard the stories and rumors. Students that went back and got comfortable at home after their first year had a higher chance of not returning for the second. He didn't think his mother would appreciate him telling her that, though.

But he did miss them.

He missed his *family*. His cousins, aunts, uncles, and grandparents. All of them. Even his younger sister, as annoying as Catherine could be. Being an Italian through and through meant he grew up in a culture that took family seriously.

4

Large dinners, church every Sunday together, and time spent as a whole unit of one. The closest thing he got to being near his family in Detroit was the Marcello faction of the mafia in the city—the Vannozzo family served his needs when he needed something familiar around him.

They kept him busy sometimes, too.

At least, his dad didn't mind because Michel was around people Dante trusted, and had some control over being they were an extended arm of his father's mafia organization in New York. He wasn't really involved in the Vannozzo's business here, but they had been hinting lately that if he wanted to get back into a bit of dealing—like he'd done for years in New York throughout his high school years—that they would be happy to provide him with the shit to sell.

Michel was considering it.

He didn't know what his father would think of that now that Michel was in college, and he was supposed to be putting the *famiglia* ideals behind him for this doctor dream. He wasn't really interested in finding out, either.

Catrina hummed under her breath, drawing Michel from his thoughts as she muttered, "Yes, Dante, I'll tell him."

Michel chucked. "Tell me what?"

"Your father said you should come home."

He fiddled with the fob to his Mercedes as he stood beside the car, and then hit the unlock button. The car lit up on all four corners, the black paint job shining in the daylight. He didn't immediately jump into the vehicle, instead opting to finish his conversation with his mother first.

Now or never.

"I'm not going to come home for the summer," he said.

Catrina was quiet for a while, and he hoped he hadn't upset his ma. He loved her, but he also needed this time. As it was, he'd made the move to Detroit a whole year earlier than his first year of pre-med had started. He wanted to settle in, and get used to the city. He was going to be here for a while, right? He might as well learn to love it.

That meant *staying*.

Catrina relayed what Michel said to his father. In the background, he heard Dante reply, "Well, tell him to stay out of trouble."

"You heard that, then?" Catrina asked Michel.

He laughed. "I did."

"Do as your father says, Michel."

"When do I ever cause trouble, Ma?"

"Define *trouble*."

She wasn't lying.

Michel might not be actively *in* the life like they were, and yet, somehow he still managed to dip his hands in the waters. As his sister liked to say, there was no such thing as being a little wet where the mafia was concerned. One was either dry entirely, or soaked to the fucking bone.

He wouldn't look for trouble, though, but that didn't mean it wouldn't find him. This life was just funny in that way.

"Yeah, I'll try," he told his ma.

"You better."

● ● ●

Michel walked into *Bella*—the mob-owned, Italian eatery—and inhaled the scents of mozzarella and pasta. Spices and richness followed, clinging just as firmly to the air as utensils scraped against plates, and laughter lit up the restaurant. Nothing reminded Michel of home as much as a proper Italian restaurant did, honestly.

The fact it was mob-owned probably helped with that, too.

He bypassed the chick at the podium with a Bluetooth speaker in her ear and a tablet in her hands. She barely even glanced at him, recognizing his face and knowing better than to ask if he had a reservation. He didn't need one—he knew the owner.

Just because he threw all of his attention into that first year of pre-med didn't mean he hadn't taken the time to also *make friends*. In their life, it didn't matter that someone moved away from family and the business—that shit was everywhere. Michel was still the son of a mafia Don at the end of the day, and he needed contacts. Something his cousins had been quick to point out to him when they figured out he was dead serious about med school, and moving to Detroit.

So, he made friends.

Ones with *big* names.

His last name probably helped with that, too. Everyone who was *anyone* in the world of organized crime knew the Marcello surname without further explanation needed. He suspected his father had a hand in putting him in the path of Salvestro Vannozzo, cousin to the Vannozzo boss and a top Capo of the family in Detroit, because Dante wanted to make sure Michel had some kind of clout watching his back during his time there.

He wasn't complaining.

The Vannozzos reminded him of home, and that kept him from getting too homesick. He also wasn't exactly good with *normal*. He could have easily made friends with people at college, and maybe he should have just because, but those people didn't understand him. They didn't know what it was like to grow up the way he did, and they would never understand the way he sometimes talked in riddles, or his serious dislike of anything related to authority.

He *needed* like-minded people.

Salvestro and the rest of the Vannozzo men he made an effort to spend time with gave him exactly those things, and more. Because he came from a familiar background and family, with a last name that afforded him a great deal of respect, Salvestro and the Capo's men welcomed Michel in as a friend.

Of sorts ...

They kept their business guarded, to a point. He didn't fault them for that, either. He wasn't a made man—he couldn't know all the details, and he really didn't want to. He did get a firsthand look at some of their dealings, but that was far different from being a *friend of theirs* and just a *friend*.

One meant he was *in*.

One meant he was just okay.

Michel was fine with being just okay.

"And there's the doc!"

Michel chuckled at Sal's greeting as he stepped into the entryway of the private dining area of the restaurant. Sal preferred to do all his business and meetings out of the sight of the regular patrons. It wasn't good for business to scare people away with the mob details, after all.

"Not a doctor yet," Michel reminded his friend.

"Ah, *Dio vaffanculo*," Sal replied, flipping a hand in Michel's direction as he turned to the guy sitting across the table from him. Another familiar face to Michel here in Detroit. David Barese, a bookie for the Vannozzo family doing a good portion of his business in clubs that Michel liked to frequent throughout the city. "Listen to the shit coming out of his mouth, huh?"

David laughed, and passed Michel a grin. "You're always gonna be the doc to us, kid."

Michel bristled at the *kid* comment. He knew they were just fucking with him, and he enjoyed it, really. That was part of their life, and it meant he was welcomed here. They were treating him as one of them. In a way, they reminded him of his cousins, John and Andino.

"What are you doing today, anyway?" Sal asked, flipping through a deck of cards before laying out a spread on the table. "I thought you had *classes*?"

"Exams," Michel corrected, "and I finished my last one today."

"*Yes*," David crowed, "that means the doc is free for the summer. What are we going to do with him, Sal? Put him to work, do you think?"

Michel rolled his eyes as he came further into the room. He didn't pull out a chair to sit with the two men at the small table because he really didn't plan on staying for that long. He just wanted to see if David or Sal had any interesting plans for the weekend because he felt like celebrating his final exams. All year, he'd been careful not to indulge too much. Sure, he'd go out, but he wouldn't *really* party. No heavy drinking, and certainly nothing that was going to mess with his mind like a bit of smoke or a pill.

Well, school was done.

And these men knew how to party.

Sal passed Michel a look, considering David's statement for a moment before he asked, "Have you ever considered that, *cafone*?"

"Calling me a fool doesn't make me want to work for you because I *know* that's what you're asking without actually asking me."

The man smirked. "You know how it works. But seriously, have you thought about it? I mean, I talked to your cousin—John. I know you used to deal. Had a bit of a touch for it, according to him."

Michel ran his tongue along his teeth, and sucked in air to make a hissing sound at the same time. "I *did*."

"What else are you going to do for the summer?"

"Study. Find a woman to keep me entertained. Sleep until noon."

"*Study*, he says," David grumbled.

Michel flipped his middle finger up at the man, but David only shrugged and went back to the card game with Sal like nothing had happened in the first place. "But yeah, I considered it."

Sal nodded, looking at the cards on the table as he said, "I could set that up for you. *Just* for the summer, if that's what you wanted to do."

Do I?

That was the better question.

Michel had a bad habit of missing familiar things. Hustling for money—even if he did have more dollars in the bank than he would ever know what to do with—was one of those things that he found familiar, and *easy*. Like learning, or his family.

He also hated being bored.

This would help with that.

"All right," Michel said, "just for the summer."

"*Perfetto*," Sal praised, raising a brow to David who was smiling again. "Seems we've got a new recruit. What do we teach him first, huh?"

"Ah, I don't think he'll need much training. He is a Marcello, after all. It's in his blood. As long as he's not stepping on anyone's toes or working in the wrong places, he'll be fine."

Right.

In his blood.

Michel didn't correct them.

Blood never mattered to him, anyway.

TWO

"Did you check your sugars, lass?"

"My sugars are *fine*, Da."

"Gabbie—"

She popped the small sweet chocolate into her mouth, and turned to face her father, Charles, with a grin. "My sugars are *fine*."

Aye, she was going to suffer for that little treat later, no doubt. She would have to check her sugars simply *because* she broke her diet for one itty, bitty piece of chocolate, but it was worth it. The chocolate melted in her mouth, and slid down her throat like it was pure *heaven*. She didn't get sugar very much, if at all.

Her dad raised a brow, and fought the urge to smile. "When you act like this, you remind me so much of your mam, lass."

"Probably more today, huh?"

He nodded once, and reached out to tuck one of her stray red curls behind her ear. "Today more than other feckin' days."

Charles moved to stand beside Gabbie, and then turned to watch the rest of the people in his home gathering around the large table to get their plates ready. Every year on this day, they celebrated a woman who was no longer with them. Her mam. Gabbie didn't remember very much about her mother—Betha Casey passed on when she was still a young girl from an accident on the highway as she was driving home from a dinner with friends.

The absolute love of her father's life, next to *Gabbie*, he'd never remarried, and she was his only child. It showed, too. Like this conversation right *now*.

"No more sweets," her father grumbled, giving her a look from the side. "I don't want a call from the hospital because you didn't manage your—"

"I'm twenty years old. I can take care of my diabetes, Da."

Charles sighed.

Gabbie shrugged.

This was the same conversation they had more times than she cared to admit over the last few years. She understood, though. Her father's greatest fear was that he was going to lose her, too. She was the last person he truly loved in the world. It made him feel out of control because he couldn't manage her disease like he had when she was younger. She was the adult with the say so about her own body, what she did with it, and the things she put *inside* it. Like sugar.

He had to trust that she was doing what was right, and he simply didn't feel like she was doing what she needed to. She was used to him hovering, but lately, it just annoyed her more than it probably should.

As a child, she never understood why her father was quick to bark at *anyone* who dared to offer her something sweet. She'd been born insulin resistant, and while they were able to manage it for the majority of her childhood, as she slipped into her later teenage years, something changed.

Hormones.

Life.

Who feckin' knew?

9

She packed on the pounds—almost thirty in her senior year. People heard *type two diabetes* and automatically assumed someone was unhealthy because nobody developed type two unless they weren't taking care of themselves, right?

Wrong.

A very small percentage of people—Gabbie was in that lucky number—could develop type two diabetes because of other health problems, like being insulin resistant. She managed her diabetes with a very strict diet, exercise, and occasionally medications when she needed it.

She'd lost those thirty pounds, but because of the way her disease worked, she was borderline underweight. Something her doctor and father liked to remind her every time she had to step on a feckin' scale. She'd gone from putting on weight like crazy in a matter of months to struggling to gain any weight for several years.

Yeah, a struggle.

That was the best way to describe this disease.

"Could we not do this today?" she asked, glancing up at her tall father.

Charles stared back at her, unaffected.

She took after a lot of her father's features—from the red, unruly hair to the freckles that dotted the bridge of her nose and her cheeks ... her whole body, really. Even the shape of her green eyes, and the high line of her cheekbones matched her father's more masculine, stronger features. She was the softer, feminine version.

But her lips?

The small cleft in her chin?

The dimple in her left cheek?

Charles said that was all her mam.

"Today is supposed to be for *Ma*," she reminded her da, "not for you to hover and poke at me about what I'm putting in my mouth."

"But if I don't do it, who is?"

Gabbie sighed, and crossed her arms over her chest. The people at the table had yet to realize the man throwing this dinner party to celebrate the life of his dead wife had still not joined them to eat. Not that it was stopping them from digging into the food on the platters.

"That's the point, it's for *me* to worry about now."

"Can't do that, lass," Charles said, "that's not how a father's mind works."

She was about to open her mouth and argue further with her father—how was he ever going to learn to *trust her* if he continued to do this?—when someone at the table saved her from the trouble.

"Charles, are you bothering that lass of yours again?" Brennan asked.

One of the men at table grinned at Gabbie. Rather conspiratorially. Like he knew exactly what her father was doing, and he was going to try to save her.

Brennan Brady likely did know, too. Her father's right-hand man in the Irish mob, Brennan, had been in her life for as long as she could remember. The same way a lot of people at the table were all familiar, comforting faces to her. She hadn't truly understood that her father was an Irish mob boss until she was thirteen, and couldn't make friends at her private Catholic high school because the other girls' parents told them to stay away from her.

Rumors spread.

People whispered and avoided.

High school had been hell in that way.

She learned the truth, though, and that explained a lot about her father and the men that constantly came and went from her life and home growing up. All those late night meetings in her father's office, and the way *everyone* in her life hated and distrusted the cops simply because they *were* cops.

Besides, Gabbie quickly learned that in *their* life, she didn't need friends from the outside. She had all the people she needed—friends included—within her own family. They were the only people who truly understood what it was like to be in this family, after all.

What else did she need?

"Aye, *lad*," Charles growled, giving his friend a look as he stepped forward to finally take his seat at the table, "you mind your own broad at home, and let me mind mine."

"Let the girl *eat*," Kenneth, her uncle, and another man under her father in the organization said from his seat between his wife and adult children. "She'll mind her sugars, boyo. You make sure of it."

"Exactly." Her father pointed a finger at the two men, giving them a look that told them to shut up. "None of you have to do it—had it been up to you lot, she woulda been shoving all kinds of sugar in her mouth from the time she could *chew*. Shut the holes in your feckin' faces, and eat your food before I decide to kick the bunch of you outta my house."

Gabbie grinned, and shook her head.

What else could she do?

This was her father.

Her *life*.

It was never going to change.

"Are you going to sit, lass, or stand back there and glare at me head some more?" her father asked.

Gabbie scoffed. "I wasn't glaring at your head."

"Be a first, yeah?"

She took her seat at the table next to her father on the left. Across from her sat her cousins, Aine and Aidan.

"Not a *first*," she told her father. She made sure to give him the look that he liked to say reminded him of her mother when Betha was mad at him. "Eat your food, Da."

"Are you coming tonight?" Aine asked Gabbie from across the table.

Charles had a whole mouthful of food as he mumbled, "Going where?"

Gabbie gave her cousin a look, too.

A *shut your feckin' mouth* kind of look.

"Going *where*?" her father asked louder once he'd swallowed his food.

Grand.

This was just perfect.

Now, she was going to have to listen to her father bitch about all the sugar in liquor because her cousin couldn't keep her mouth shut about hitting up a new club that their family opened the week before.

"A club," Gabbie said, sighing.

Her father eyed her from the side.

"*I know*, Da. Check my sugars."

Charles' lips flattened into a grim line. "You're my only one left, Gabbie."

Yeah, she knew.

It meant a lot of things.

She was respected.

Adored.

Spoiled.

And entirely smothered.

"I won't drink," she told her father. "But I want to go have a dance, that's all. I'm done with classes for the summer, so I don't have to worry about getting up early, either."

College was no joke. Especially not for an aspiring criminal defense lawyer.

Charles nodded, believing her innocent smile. Men, even those like her father with darkness in his eyes that hid all kinds of secrets, were still the same in the end. All it took was a smile, and they were done for.

"Grand, lass."

No, she wouldn't drink.

Much.

She wouldn't drink *much*.

Couldn't she have just a little fun sometimes?

• • •

"Aidan, could you at least wait until I'm not talking to you to stare at a girl's arse?" Aine asked, her annoyance clear over the bass of the music in the crowded club. "You're such a cunt."

"Can you blame me? Did you see the arse on—"

Aine put her hand up in her brother's face, effectively quieting him without saying anything at all, and turned to Gabbie with a shake of her head. "*Men.*"

Gabbie grinned around the rim of her *one* drink she was allowing herself to have. It didn't have a high sugar content, and she should be fine. But that also meant it tasted like absolute shite. Win some, lose some.

"Want to dance?" Aine asked.

"Sure," Gabbie returned. "At least then, Aidan can find someone to take home without you ruining every single one he looks at."

Aine glowered.

Aidan laughed, and pointed in Gabbie's direction. "And that's why you're my favorite cousin."

"I'm your only cousin."

"Yeah, well ..."

Gabbie didn't get the chance to respond because Aine was already dragging her cousin out to the dance floor. They weaved in and out of the sway of sweaty, drunk bodies. She had to give her uncle's man credit for this new club—it was pretty grand. The music kept them moving, the employees, from the bouncers to the servers, kept everything running smoothly. The whole atmosphere of the club just screamed *fun*.

A party, really.

She needed that break.

Her black, slinky club dress fell a few inches above her thighs, and glimmered under the flashing lights attached to the ceiling. The swell of people on the dance floor seemed to grow as the song switched to something that had everyone jumping to the beat with hands in the air. Gabbie, having fun and really letting loose for the first time in God knew how long, spun a circle and by the time she stopped to take a breath … well, lost her cousin in the crowd.

Shite.

On another night, she might not have been too worried about losing Aine. Her cousin liked to pick up a guy and take him home sometimes, and Gabbie was more than capable of taking care of herself for the evening.

Except, she *was* trying to follow her father's rules. Even if she was twenty, and not a child anymore. It was always easier when she simply fed into her father's bollocks, and didn't try to fight him every damn step of the way. One of those rules was for her to stay close to a familiar face tonight since this club *was* mob-owned by one of her uncle's men, and that meant business could be happening in the shadows.

She'd not asked what kind of business because she knew better than to do that. It wasn't like her father would have answered her, anyway. Better to not bother in the first place, and save herself the lecture.

Pushing up to her tiptoes in the high heels she'd put on earlier, Gabbie scanned the crowd. All she could see, however, were swaying bodies and sweaty heads. It probably didn't help that she was directly in the middle of the club and there was literally *so much* going on in every corner that everything drew in her attention.

Feck.

She decided to head for the bar—the same place she had left with her cousin. No doubt, if Aine wasn't there, then Aidan would be somewhere in the fray probably still trying to pick up someone to take home with him.

Gabbie didn't find either of her cousins at the bar. Oh, it was packed full of people waiting for drinks, and shouting for the bartenders to hurry up, but there were no Caseys in sight. She smiled at the female bartender when she brought over a glass of water for Gabbie—likely recognizing her face—she pushed it across the bar with a wink.

"Taking a break?"

"Trying to find the other two I came with," Gabbie replied, laughing.

"Oh, they'll be back around. No worries there."

Probably.

Sometime.

Instead of going to look for one of her cousins, she figured it was better for her to stay in one place. That was better than the three of them moving around the large venue trying to find one another, right?

She was just taking a sip from the glass of water when a man slid in beside her at the bar. He didn't look her way, instead his attention focused in on the woman behind the bar working at their end. In a way, she thought it was a shame he didn't look at her, so she could get a full-on view of those handsome features, but she was *loving* his slightly turned profile.

Strong jaw.

White teeth bared in his grin.

Brown eyes.

His tanned skin looked almost golden under the lights of the club, and his dark, curly hair tousled down a bit near his ears like he'd been running his fingers through it. The strands couldn't be contained if the way they fell into his eyes were any indication. He filled out the pair of dark slacks covering a fine arse, not to mention the way the side of his shoulders and part of his back looked covered in a button down, red silk dress shirt.

God.

She loved a man that could fill out his clothes, and she adored it even more when he had wide shoulders, and a back that *begged* for fingernails to dig in.

"Lambay, three fingers," the man told the bartender.

Gabbie arched a brow, her mouth working before her brain did. "An Irish whiskey, huh?"

Before the bartender even replied to the man to confirm his order, his gaze turned on Gabbie. She swore in those few seconds, as his profile turned into the full view of his face, the club faded into the background.

It was just her and him.

Green eyes meeting brown.

His profile didn't do him justice. *At all.* The curve of his lips when he smiled went a little deeper, showcasing dimples on each cheek. Thick, dark eyebrows lifted slightly, one arching a little higher than the other at her question. Perfect white teeth flashed in his grin, and those intense eyes of his drifted over her quickly, drinking in the dress that looked painted onto her body before his gaze snapped back up to her face.

He really was a handsome lad.

Sexy.

"I prefer it," the man said, his tone like brown sugar. Dark, deep, and sinfully rich. "If there's anything the Irish know, it's their liquor."

Gabbie flashed him a smile. "Tell me about it; personal knowledge. Isn't it obvious?"

There was no hiding the lilt in her tone—the hint of an accent that, despite her efforts to try and subdue it, was still there. An *Irish* accent.

The man winked, unashamed. "Can't tell at all."

She laughed. "You're a horrible liar."

"I never really need to lie, though."

Huh.

"Gabbie," she said.

He put a hand out when she offered hers, and the second his fingers wrapped around hers, she swore the heat that sparked between the two was enough to make her draw in a sharp breath. She couldn't tell for sure, though, because she was a little too focused on the way he was looking at her.

He liked what he saw.

So did she.

"Michel," he replied easily.

Gabbie wasn't innocent when it came to men, but she also wasn't very forward. Growing up as the daughter of an Irish mob boss meant almost *everyone* knew who the feck she was in these parts. Just her last name was enough to send a man running away from her lest he find himself in hot water with her family or da.

This man, though?

He was still there. Either he didn't know who she was, or he didn't give a feck. She liked that far more than she should.

She *really* liked the way he was looking at her in that moment, too. Grinning in *that* way. Like he was the cat looking at a saucer of cream, and he was ready to lap up every single drop of it. She wasn't going to lie and say she didn't like it because she sure as hell did. He wasn't too bad to look at, either.

"I was going to look for my cousins," she said, "but I was thinking maybe another dance would be good."

Michel make a noise under his breath, and glanced over his shoulder. "Shit, I … I'm supposed to be working right now."

"You work at the club?"

And he didn't know who *she* was?

Unlikely.

He shook his head, saying, "Not exactly."

What did that mean?

"But you know what," Michel said, grabbing the tumbler of whiskey when the bartender slid it over to him, "fuck work. I found something better."

Gabbie drew her bottom lip between her teeth, asking, "Oh, did you?"

"Looking at her, yeah."

He offered his hand, and she took it again. The same heat from earlier sparked through her hand, and up her arm. This time, though, it traveled through her body and straight down to the spot between her thighs. She couldn't take her gaze off Michel, either, or the way he tipped that glass up to swallow the three fingers of whiskey in one go.

He didn't flinch.

Didn't make a *sound*.

She knew that liquor was harsh.

And damn, she liked that, too.

Michel wet his bottom lip, taking away the remaining whiskey with a single, sexy sweep of his tongue. She had the greatest urge to reach up, and see what his lips might feel like when they were pressed against her fingertips.

Or even better, against her *mouth*.

"A dance?" he asked.

Gabbie nodded. "You got it."

She slipped off the stool at the bar to follow him, her fingers weaving in with his as she stayed close to his back. She *really* liked that view—the way his muscles moved under the silk, and the way the lights shadowed his features when he glanced back at her.

Then, the crowd swelled.

Someone hit Gabbie from the side, sending her to the floor. Michel swung around, his strong arms already reaching out to catch her, but he was just one second too late. She hit the floor alongside someone's glass that shattered as soon as it hit the tile.

"*Gabbie*," she heard Michel say.

Concern wrote heavily across his handsome features, and the first thing she wanted to do was apologize for ruining … well, whatever this was. Although, he simply looked like he was more worried about getting her up from the floor. He called her name again, but it sounded faint. It was too far away even though he was right above her.

She knew why, too.

The pain in her arm.

The blood dribbling to the floor.

Feck.

Blood always made her—

Everything went dark.

THREE

"Here, lad, a blanket."

Michel took the item from the Irishman lingering near the doorway, and used it to act as a pillow. "*Grazie,* and you are …?"

The guy, whether it was the fact Michel thanked him in Italian, or asked his name, tipped his chin up a bit. Almost like he wasn't going to reply to Michel's question at all, but then he did, muttering, "Aidan Casey."

Casey.

That name sounded familiar, but it wasn't really bringing anything to the surface for Michel. It felt like something he should know—if this was New York, he'd already know who the fuck the guy was just *because* he had to if someone was important. He wasn't as accustomed to those rules in Detroit.

"He's me annoying cousin," Gabbie mumbled.

Michel's attention went back to where it was needed, and honestly, where he wanted it to be the most. Gabbie, just waking up from her spill, blinked up at Michel. With her head elevated on the blanket, she was now angled just enough to stare straight at him.

He smiled.

"Your what, again?" he asked.

Just to see …

"Me cousin, you wagon."

Michel's smirk deepened a bit—he'd been insulted before, but he couldn't remember a time when he'd been insulted by a beautiful woman, who was also Irish, in a slang he didn't understand for the life of him. "You know your accent gets a little deeper when you're confused, right?"

Gabbie's brow dipped in the sweetest way, and her green eyes lifted to meet his again. "Probably. I'm not thinking about it as much then."

"Blood makes you pass out, huh?"

A small sigh passed her lips, and she made sure to avoid looking at *anywhere* but her arm. "Maybe it does when it's my blood, yeah."

"*Maybe,*" Michel joked. Over his shoulder, he said to the cousin in the doorway, "There's a first aid kit somewhere in this place, I imagine. Could you find it for me?"

"Aye, mate."

Gabbie blinked up at the ceiling and then turned her head a bit to stare sideways at the line of stalls with narrowed eyes. "You brought me into the *bathroom?*"

"Apparently, someone was getting the shit beat out of him in the office, if what it sounded like was to be trusted," he replied, trying not to grin at how disgusted she looked at the idea of being on a bathroom floor. "And this was just cleaned, so it seemed better than leaving you out on the crowded floor for everyone to stare at you once you woke up."

Her pixie-like, button nose scrunched up before her gaze came back to him. It kind of struck him how *delicate* her features were. From the soft line of her chin, to her cheekbones. The spattering of freckles on her nose and cheeks continued down her throat, and disappeared below the plunging neckline of her dress.

He had the strangest urge to find out if those freckles just … kept going *everywhere*. He bet that would be a game of Connect the Dots that would not soon be forgotten.

"I figured the bathroom was the right choice, all things considered."

Gabbie frowned. "That's fair."

Yeah, he thought so.

He'd been focused on getting her on the dance floor, and then seeing if he could convince her to let him take her home. And then some drunk fool in the crowd had to go and fucking *ruin it*. Michel didn't think now was the right time to continue that conquest with Gabbie, but he wasn't going to pretend like she wasn't checking him out right then, either.

"Have you gotten your fill of looking at me yet?" he asked.

Her gaze snapped away from his throat where he'd left the top two buttons of his silk shirt undone. "You're awfully full of yourself, lad."

Michel smirked. "And yet you like what you see, *bella principessa*."

"Was that … Italian?"

"It was, now let me look at your arm."

Gabbie immediately turned her head away when he lifted her arm. The cut wasn't so bad—at least, not as bad as he thought out on the dance floor. It wasn't going to need stitches, and he'd grabbed what looked like a clean rag from a passing server to press it against the wound and staunch the blood flow. Now, it was barely bleeding at all.

"Not too bad," he said, "maybe a Steri-Strip or two."

"A what?"

"A kind of band aid."

"Oh," Gabbie whispered. "So, no hospitals?"

Michel gave her a wink, replying, "No hospital."

"Good. I don't feel like listening to my da bitch tonight."

He thought to ask her about her father—and why the man would bitch at her for an accident—but a man darkened the doorway of the bathroom. Passing a glance over his shoulder, he didn't recognize the guy at all.

"What?" Michel asked sharply.

"You the doc? I was told to find you—my friend said I could cop from you tonight if you were still around. Somebody saw you come back this way with the girl."

Fuck.

All over again, Michel was reminded of why he came to this damn club in the first place. *Work.* A week of dealing for the Vannozzo Capo, and already, Michel was learning this was not like his previous trips down this path. Apparently, Sal just gave his name to *anyone* who asked for it, and his phone number, too. Along with that goddamn nickname of *doc*, like it was a joke for them, but it annoyed him more than anything else.

Michel was more than capable of finding his own customers. Or, that's how he always used to do it when he worked for his cousins and family back home. Here, they didn't give a shit who he was dealing to as long as he was getting rid of product.

A phone call from someone who wanted to score some coke sent him to *this* club, and after he'd made the exchange with the customer who hinted he probably had more people to buy, he headed to the bar. Gabbie distracted him from going back to the customer to finish any more transactions.

"Well, doc?" the guy asked.

Michel grunted under his breath, not bothering to hide the fire in his gaze as it turned on the man again. At the same time, the Irishman from before—Gabbie's cousin—came back to the doorway with another guy he didn't recognize. "Not tonight."

"Damn."

"Bye," Michel barked.

The guy headed out of the doorway, but the other two men standing there hadn't missed the majority of the conversation. He felt the way their eyes turned on him like they had something to say, but with Gabbie on the floor, they kept their mouths shut.

He didn't know what it mattered.

Gabbie, on the other hand, asked, "Doc, huh?"

"Something like that," he muttered.

"Here's the kit, *doc*."

Michel gritted his teeth, both annoyed and ready to get the hell out of there. A heavy weight had come to sit in his stomach, and he wasn't sure why. Maybe because he'd felt out of place in this club from the moment he stepped inside it— the large Irish flag hanging over the DJ booth had been enough to say this club might not be a safe place for him to deal. The guy getting the shit beat out of him in the office was another clue.

But really, Gabbie just heard someone ask him for drugs ... if she understood any kind of street slang when it came to dealing—and who didn't understand it? That, more than anything, bothered him. If she wasn't running from him before, she sure as hell would be now.

In the doorway, the two men muttered back and forth in a language Michel couldn't understand. Gabbie stared at them, her brow drawing inward like she was trying to distinguish what they were saying but they talked fast.

Then, they left.

"What was that about?" Michel asked, jerking a thumb over his shoulder.

He went to work opening the first aid kit as her attention came back to him. Even though he wasn't looking at her, he could still *feel* the way she looked at him. It was visceral, really. Like her stare was pinning him in place, and he couldn't escape from it. Strange, though, because a part of him didn't want to escape it, either.

"Territory," she said quietly, "They were talking about territory."

Bad sign number three.

Michel was putting shit together, and it spelled bad things for him. Right then, though, he was more focused on making sure Gabbie was good before he had to make a quick, safe exit from this club.

If he was in Irish territory—there was a major Irish family in Detroit—then he was not safe here. *At all.* It was common knowledge in the criminal underworld that Irish and Italians did not get along. They were famous for their feuds that

19

lasted years, and were some of the bloodiest ever seen on the streets. He did not want to be a casualty if that was the case here, too.

"Let me get this cleaned up," Michel said, not wanting to get lost in his thoughts again.

Gabbie stayed quiet as he worked on fixing her arm as best that he could. He used the alcohol wipes to clean the wound, and felt a stab of pain in his chest when she hissed from the sting. He made quick work of using a couple of Steri-Strips to close the wound, and then a large band aid overtop just to be safe.

Running this thumbs along the outer edge of the band aid, a warmth spreading fast and furious from her skin to his. He swore it traveled right up his arm, and straight down into his gut. He didn't miss the way goosebumps bloomed on her skin from his touch, either.

Damn.

"Do you feel that, too?" she asked softly.

Michel met her gaze. "Feel what?"

"The *warmth.*"

Why lie?

"I do," he murmured.

Gabbie's tongue peeked out, and wet her lips. He'd be a horrible fucking liar if he said he didn't watch her tongue glide across her lips and wonder what she might look like doing that while she was on her knees with his cock in her hands.

Yeah, he was so fucked.

"Oh, there you are! Aidan came to find me."

At the feminine voice in the doorway behind him, Michel was quick to help Gabbie up from the floor. Once she was on her feet, and seemed steady enough, he could have let her go. Instead, he kept one hand at her lower back, and another on her arm as they turned to face the red-headed woman in the doorway.

Gabbie pushed her mess of red curls out of her face, and passed a nod to Michel. "I had a doctor to help me."

Michel chuckled. "That's not entirely true."

She just smiled, and winked, knowing she was teasing him. Then, her attention went back to the woman. "Sorry I ruined our night."

"It's fine." The woman still stared at Michel, but quickly went back to Gabbie. "I have a car ready if you're—"

"I think I might have Michel here take me home, actually."

His fingers tightened on her arm—the uninjured one.

"Oh," the girl said, eyes widening.

Gabbie laughed. "I'll see you tomorrow, Aine."

Aine grinned slyly. "You got it."

Michel waited until the girl was gone from the bathroom doorway, and the two of them were alone again before he spoke. "So, we're just going to pretend like you didn't hear a guy ask me to sell him drugs, then?"

Gabbie peered up at him—green eyes glittering, and sin curving her lips sexily. "My father is Charles Casey, so if you think *that* bothered me … you're messing with the wrong lass, Michel."

That name …

Charles Casey.

It rang a bell, too.

Just not a loud enough one to make him think this was a bad idea. Oh, he was pretty sure taking Gabbie home was going to get him in some kind of shit, but hey … if it was worth it, then that's all that mattered to him.

He'd figure out the rest tomorrow.

"I guess we'll take my car, if you don't have one," he said.

Gabbie arched a brow. "I guess so."

• • •

Michel stayed a step behind Gabbie as she walked over the white pebble walkway leading to the stairs of a brick brownstone. She kept peeking over her shoulder every few seconds to make sure he was still there, and each time, he grinned back at her. There was something about the way her cheeks reddened—making her freckles stand out all the more—that did good things for him.

And his cock.

The thing was … Michel would always be a gentleman first. He didn't know anything different, and he suspected his father and mother would be *highly* disappointed in him, otherwise. So, it didn't matter what his cock thought about the way Gabbie's ass looked being hugged by that short, shimmery dress. She could change her mind at any time about inviting him home with her, and that was all there was to it.

At the buttery brown door of the brownstone, Gabbie fiddled with her keys, and glanced up at the brass numbers attached to the brick.

"Nice place," Michel noted. "Quiet."

It was.

Even the street seemed like it was lights out for everyone around. There wasn't even a jogger coming down the street, or someone to walk a dog. That was uncommon for a city. Someone was always around, it seemed.

Gabbie shrugged one delicate shoulder under the jacket Michel had offered for her to take when it seemed like it might be getting cold. "Da rents this place for me—closer to the college. I wanted to be in a dorm, but he decided differently."

He didn't miss the bitterness in her words. His parents hadn't exactly decided where he was going to live, but his mother had been quick to veto *every* apartment. The dorms were no-go for Michel from the jump because he liked his space. Eventually, he settled on a bungalow tucked away between the city park, and a row of brownstones.

Gesturing at her door, he said, "So, what happens now?"

She arched a brow. "I thought that was obvious."

Michel grinned, letting his tongue peek out to touch the corner of his upper lip. "I never *assume*, Gabbie. You could have changed your mind between the club and here. It's better to ask."

"Well, I haven't changed my mind."

"Oh?"

Look. There was his cock again.

Ready to go.

21

"Good," Michel murmured, shifting so that his shoulder rested against the brick as he looked down at her. "Then, I suggest you get the door unlocked, so we can get off your front steps. Otherwise, I can't be held responsible for what happens out here where anyone can see after watching the way your ass looks in that dress."

She drew in a quick breath. He didn't miss the way her pupils blew wide, either. Those fingers of hers curved around the keys in her hand, making them jangle in the darkness. He wouldn't pretend like that didn't have his cock perking all over again, straining against the line of his zipper to remind him he hadn't gotten what he wanted yet.

Which was to be buried balls deep in this woman.

Soon.

Michel simply winked, and nodded at the door again. "Whenever you're ready."

Gabbie turned to the door with the key already ready to slide in the lock. "You sound *confident*."

"That your neighbors are going to know my name by the time I'm done with you here? Probably."

Her first step inside the brownstone nearly missed the ledge leading into the house from his statement as she pushed open the door, but Michel was quick to catch her with one arm sliding around her waist. He took that chance to press a kiss against the back of her neck, too, as he dragged her closer to his chest at the same time. She fit into the fold of his body *perfectly* as he learned forward.

The first taste of her skin wasn't nearly enough for him, either. Gabbie's head fell to his shoulder as he slammed the door shut behind them, and they moved further into the hallway. She dropped her clutch, and his bag went with it. The fucking jacket he'd given her to cover up with was in the way, and all that served to do was send a shot of frustration racing through his gut.

He wanted *more*.

Another taste.

And the jacket was stopping him.

Gabbie sighed a happy sound when Michel dragged the jacket down her arms roughly, not caring a bit that he'd probably wrinkled the blazer something terrible when it fell to the floor. He had other things to think about now. Like all the freckles dotting the line of her shoulder, and disappearing down her throat to the deep V neckline of her dress. There were too many, and he couldn't possibly kiss them all, but fuck him if he wasn't going to *try*.

He started with her shoulders, his tongue striking out to get a taste of her skin with every kiss he dotted along her body. A shiver raced through Gabbie when his hands drifted over the shimmery, slinky dress. He wanted to *feel* her curves—find where his hands fit, and where she liked to be touched the very most.

Sliding his hands lower as his teeth grazed the racing pulse point on her throat, he asked, "Are you wet for me already?"

Gabbie let out a quiet sound. "You should definitely find out."

He agreed.

Letting his hands rove down over the hemline of the dress, he pulled the fabric up as his palms slid higher. There was no mistaking the way her legs trembled the closer his fingers drifted toward the apex of her thighs.

That heaven.

He bet it would taste like that, too.

Heaven, but sin.

Now, he just wanted to know if his theory was correct. *But first …* His knuckles skimmed over the hood of her sex, the lace-trimmed cotton of her panties soft against his skin. The next stroke went a little lower, right over top of her clit. Her hips jerked a bit from the touch, and he grinned against her skin.

"*Sensitive*," he told her. "This is going to be fun for you, then."

"I feckin' hope so."

Michel laughed, dark and husky. His throat just felt thick, now, because he felt like he'd been playing with her for too long. Teasing, and testing the waters just to *see* … and now he wanted something more.

A lot more.

"Where is your bedroom?"

"Upstairs," Gabbie murmured.

"Undress as you go."

He loved that she didn't even *question* that demand. There was no hesitation in her decision to leave his embrace, and move forward. Peeking over her shoulder as she headed for the stairs at the end of the hall, he realized there wasn't actually very much that she had to take off. The dress dropped to the floor first, leaving creamy skin to his appreciative gaze. Those freckles of hers were *all over*. He didn't know what to look at first on her body.

How about the curve of her waist, and where it melded into hips that swayed with each step she took? Or even the roundness of her ass that had his hands clenching at his sides with the need to dig his fingers into that supple flesh—or *fuck*, even his teeth? Maybe the two dimples at her lower back, or the way her eyes glittered when she peered back at him again?

There was a lot about her to discover.

So much.

Michel didn't move until all he could see of Gabbie as she walked up the stairs was her legs from the calves down. She stopped for a second, and he wondered what in the hell she was doing. Then, he watched her legs shimmy a bit before those lace-trimmed, cotton panties dropped down around her ankles. Stepping out of the fabric, her walk continued.

His pants became *tighter*.

Yeah, fuck.

Michel went after her, and he wasn't quiet about it because he could hear Gabbie's sexy laughter echoing from the upstairs as he climbed the stairs as fast as he possibly could. He made sure to pick up those panties she left behind, too.

All the while, he shredded his dress shirt, and unbuttoned his slacks before pulling the zipper apart, too. He kicked his shoes off outside of a bathroom—the same spot she had apparently dropped her bra to the floor.

The next room was a spare bedroom.

The one at the end?

That's where he found Gabbie.

Naked on the end of the bed, red hair spilling over her shoulder, she sat there with her head cocked to the side like she was waiting for him. A sinful smile curved her lips as she tipped her chin up—a silent *challenge*, he thought.

Her words confirmed it. "Still want to find out if you made me wet?"

A harsh sound ripped from Michel's throat—he wasn't even sure where it came from, but it felt raw coming out. "You have no fucking idea."

She widened her legs for him, her heels resting to the edge of the bed. *No shame*, he thought, and he loved that. He didn't have time to chase a woman's insecurities, but especially not when it came to her body. All women were beautiful, and all women were different. He got off on a woman who knew that about herself, and wasn't afraid to show off everything she had.

And right now, Gabbie was flashing him a pink pussy that glistened under the dim lighting in the bedroom provided by the lamps on either side of the bed. She wasn't entirely bare—a small patch of trimmed hair above her pussy led down to the promise land. His mouth *watered* because what did she taste like?

Tart, and hot?

Sweet, and heady?

He wanted to find out.

Michel stalked closer.

Not yet close enough, though.

"I want a taste," he said, "but I can't promise how long that's going to last before I bend you over and take what I *really* want."

Gabbie eyed the panties hanging from his fingertips. "And what did you bring those for?"

"Maybe I'll stuff them in your mouth to make you taste yourself while I'm fucking you. Or hell, maybe I'll wrap them around your hands to keep them still. All that matters right now is that you say *yes*."

Again, she didn't hesitate.

"*Yes.*"

Michel moved forward until he was standing at the end of the bed just in front of her. Gabbie's gaze drifted over his naked chest, and down his torso until her stare lingered at the black waistband of his boxer-briefs peeking out over the edge of his opened slacks. She liked what she was looking at, and he felt that in his *bones*. That grin of hers deepened, and Michel chuckled.

"Stroke my ego more, please."

Her stare snapped back up to his. "I thought you looked good with your shirt on, but ..."

Michel leaned forward, then, his hands landing to the bed before his mouth found hers. There was a hunger in their kiss—a *need* he'd not felt in a long time. He found her kiss was as addicting as anything that felt good for you, but was probably also bad. Her fingernails dragged down his chest as his tongue slashed against hers before he nipped the bottom of her lip. It was her sweet gasp that sent him spinning, and moving faster.

Once he got her back to the bed, his hands were already at her thighs, widening them more. He gave her no warning before he was right where he wanted to be, and *so was his mouth*. His lips encased her clit, first, teasing and coaxing the throbbing bud with gentle flicks of his tongue before he'd suck on it again. Her trembling increased when one of his hands slid down, and he pushed a thumb deep into her sex to massage the wet, swollen flesh as he worked her clit with his mouth.

Once he found the spot that really had her arching on the bed, and made her fingers twist into his hair as her hips grinded against him, he kept that up. A steady, firm beat with his thumb, and the same pressure with his tongue until she was gasping.

Almost there.

And *shit*, did she ever make beautiful noises.

Loud cries.

Shaking moans.

More.

His name sounded the very best, though.

"Michel, I'm gonna—"

He knew it already, even if she hadn't been able to finish before the orgasm came down on her. If it were possible to watch someone break all apart before your very eyes, that was the beauty of Gabbie when she came.

Michel pulled away from her, the heady and tart taste of her still lingering on his lips as he found the condom he always kept in his pocket *just in case*. Tearing the foil packet apart, he let her resituate herself on the bed to come and help him tug his pants down until his erection was straining against the line of his underwear. Her fingertips drifted over his length as he sifted his fingers through the mess of her curls.

"Get on your knees," he heard himself say.

Was that even his voice?

It sounded too ... *hoarse*.

It made sense, though. There was a desperation coursing through his body like he'd never felt before, and he was not going to abate it until she was shaking underneath him while his dick was coated with her cum.

Simple as that.

Gabbie's gaze flicked up to his, but just as quickly, she did as he told her. He got rid of the pants and boxer-briefs before sliding the latex down his length. She was too high up on the bed for him because he wanted to be *steady*. As much as he could to fuck her as hard as he could. Plucking up the panties he'd discarded before he went in between her thighs to get a taste, he also wrapped an arm around her legs to drag her back to the edge of the bed.

"What—"

She looked over her shoulder, but he already had those panties waiting for her. He decided, after hearing those noises she made, he didn't want to gag her. Not this time, anyway. Capturing her wrists with one hand, he used his other to wrap those panties around her wrists just tight enough that when he or she pulled, it was going to sting, and there was no way she'd get free. But it wasn't going to leave marks.

Her skin was too pretty for that, anyway.

"Oh, my *God*," Gabbie mumbled when Michel fitted in behind her, and wrapped two fingers around the panties holding her wrists at the small of her back, too. "I can *feel* you."

Just for good measure, he grinded the length of his latex-covered erection against the crack of her backside, feeling the way she pushed back against him. All it took was the slight shift of his hips, and the head of his cock rested against her slit.

Gabbie stilled, and dragged in a shaky breath. *"Do it."*

Michel's grip tightened on the panties, and his other came to gather her hair in his fist so that he could see her face as he fucked her, too. One flex of his hips, and he was buried deep into her pussy. She flexed all around him, every tight muscle hugging him all the way in, and then grabbing tighter when he pulled back out.

"Fuck," Michel swore, the words ripping from his chest.

She echoed the sentiment.

But breathy, and higher.

His hips snapped back against her ass again, and he felt that in his marrow. The way her body took him in, and stretched open. He couldn't help but watch her pussy take his cock, and when he pulled back out, how she coated him.

The pace between them became brutal, and frantic. Her fingernails dug into the side of his hand where he was keeping them pinned at her lower back. The line of her delicate shoulders strained the harder he fucked her, and she backed into every thrust.

She took him *so well.*

Perfect, really.

He didn't know when her cries melded into something more frantic, but he loved that, too. Every single sound that came out of her just urged him on more until he could feel that tightening in his spine, and the heat in his balls. Gabbie trembled through a second orgasm, her head falling down as she sobbed into the sheets. The sight alone was enough to push Michel over the edge, and two thrusts later, he was spilling into latex.

Silence echoed in the dark bedroom.

For all of five seconds.

Gabbie shook with her laughter as she turned her head on the bed, and eyed him over her shoulder. He was still trying to catch his fucking breath. "Can we do that again?"

Michel smirked. "Maybe."

But *hell yes*.

They stayed like that for a bit, his cock still semi-hard inside of her still flexing pussy. Gabbie let out a soft exhale before asking, "Why do they call you *doc?*"

Michel groaned. "Most of them don't know why they say it—they've just heard it, and ran with it."

"But those who do know?"

"I just finished my first year of pre-med."

Gabbie smiled a brilliant sight. "A *doctor.*"

"Someday, yeah."

"Huh, I could see that. You'd look good in a lab coat." *Crazy woman*, he thought, but he liked it. Her randomness kept him on his toes. She sighed another one of those happy sounds, and her ass wiggled against him. "Don't leave as soon as you wake up; I make a mean breakfast."

Michel wasn't the type to even stay the night, but hell, if she *asked* ... "Agreed, *donna.*"

FOUR

The smell of turkey bacon egg muffins baking in the stove had Gabbie's stomach twisting with hunger. That was the thing about this disease of hers—very rarely did she get to a good place with her weight. She was either tipping the scales of too much, or too little. And when she was in the underweight category, like now, eating and making sure it was the right foods was almost constant.

Her entire day could sometimes revolve around what she was going to eat, when she was going to eat it, and recording everything about it from the calories to her sugars before and after eating. It was made harder when she had to go out to eat because everyone else wasn't like her. They didn't have to watch everything they put into their mouth because it wouldn't send their sugars out of control like it did hers. Not to mention, not every place in town was exactly diabetic friendly.

It never ended.

Wiping her hands on a dishtowel to rid any remnants of the juices from the apples she'd cut up, she grabbed the glucose monitor she'd left on the counter the night before for easy access. Turning it on, the machine beeped as a score of zeroes for the day crossed the screen, ready to record the fifteen checks, at least, she would do throughout the day. Quickly, she scanned through the last three days of her testing to see if there was any pattern the device wanted her to know about that she should monitor.

Usually, it leveled out during her exercise periods—twice a day, once in the afternoon, and then again later in the evening when she was alone. She did a mixture of yoga, and HITT training with high intensity aerobics to counteract the amount of calories she had to consume daily, and added in a high protein and fiber diet to help, too.

She slipped one of the one-time use lancets from the bottom of the machine after she'd inserted a test strip into the top of the device, and pricked the tip of her finger. A good drop of blood came out, and she turned her face away as it still made her queasy after all these years, and placed the strip where it needed to go to do its thing for the machine.

A few seconds later, the machine beeped again.

Gabbie read the number.

A little high, she thought.

Not too high, but edging there. Getting a bit too close. She set the items aside on the counter. If her father was standing over her shoulder to see the number, he'd probably tell her to cut the apples from her breakfast, despite the high fiber content, and just go with the wheat toast, fake cocoa hummus, and turkey egg muffins.

She still needed the fiber, though.

And to go grocery shopping.

Something else she did *way* too often.

"You're diabetic?"

Gabbie's head snapped up fast, and she found a sleepy, but still quite sexy, looking Michel standing in the entryway of her kitchen. He hadn't bothered to toss any clothes on, instead making due with his boxer-briefs from the night before. It allowed her a glorious view of the railroad path of abs leading down his stomach, and the way the band of his underwear rested on the hard cut V of his groin. The dark dusting of hair that led from his navel to under his shorts made her think what it might be like to drag her fingernails across his lower stomach as she sucked his cock.

And *wow*.

That was enough of that.

She was wet again.

Grand.

"I am," Gabbie said. "Type two."

Michel's brow dipped for a second, and he gave her a look. "Developed later, then?"

"Around sixteen, almost seventeen when they diagnosed me with type two. I was born insulin resistant, so I was used to having to manage my diet and whatnot, anyway. Something changed—"

"Hormones, *life*," Michel interjected.

Gabbie laughed. "Yeah, *something*. And I had a sudden weight gain …" She trailed off, quite aware of the way Michel's gaze traveled down her body and then slowly came back up to her face. The intensity of his stare was enough to make her shiver right there on the spot, but the idea that he might be disgusted at the thought of her a little heavier made her stomach twist painfully. "I know, hard to tell, right? Thirty pounds added onto this doesn't exactly sit well."

"Actually, I was thinking you probably looked good like that, too, and it was a shame I missed out."

Heat bloomed in her stomach.

She was sure it colored her cheeks, too.

"Charmer," she replied.

Michel winked. "I state *truths*."

"Mmhmm."

He crossed the kitchen, and picked up an apple slice on the table as he passed. It wasn't until he was standing right in front of her, and popping that piece of fruit in his mouth that she looked up to meet his gaze again. He looked *far* too good chewing on that fruit and looking at her like he would rather it be a part of her that he had in his mouth.

Goddamn.

"I stayed for breakfast," he murmured.

"It's not done yet."

"Is it going to be good?"

"I have to eat a lot, and it has to be *healthy* things, so I make sure everything that goes into my body is an experience. You're the lucky lad that's going to get to share that with me this morning."

Michel grinned lazily, his thumb coming up to press against the seam of her lips. She heard his silent question to open up, so she did just that. He popped just the tip of his apple-flavored thumb in her mouth, and she sucked on the tip, letting her teeth drag along the pad of his skin before he pulled it out and dragged it down her chin.

"How long?" he asked.

Gabbie blinked. "For what?"

"The food."

Heat curled in her belly.

Anticipation.

That look in his eye, she knew it.

It was the same one from last night.

"About five more minutes for the bit in the oven," she whispered.

"Enough to see what I can do with my hand, then."

"Oh, I *really* want to see that."

Michel had her pushed up against the counter before she even blinked. His hand skimmed her inner thigh with a slow touch—feckin' torturous, really.

"Open up a little more," he demanded.

She did, widening her stance enough that his palm cupped her thigh close enough to the apex of her thighs that she could feel his warmth radiating. A tremor worked its way through her body as his fingertips danced along her skin, and he flashed his teeth in a wicked smile.

"What do you like, huh?" he asked. "I didn't get to play very much last night."

Her breath hitched when his knuckles grazed her bare sex—she hadn't even bothered to toss on panties, simply an over-sized shirt because it would do the job. "What do you mean?"

"Do you like a couple of fingers toying with your clit? A thumb pressing hard circles? Do you need to have something inside you to get you off? What does it the *fastest*, Gabbie?"

She wet her lips. "A-a mixture."

Michel nodded, and then cupped her sex with his palm. His fingers drifted over her clit, tapping a quick beat to the throbbing nub and he bent down lower to put them eye level. "How about you show me, then? Show me what *you* do, and we'll see how fast you can come when it's me doing it, too."

How was she supposed to deny him when he was looking at her like *that*? All intense, and ravenous. It made her feel like she was the only person in the world that he could see. It was a lot to take in, and it only served to notch up her desire even more.

"Come on," Michel said, "before the timer on that oven goes off, and I want to eat."

"Your attention switches that fast?"

"Food and sex …" Michel grinned. "Equally good things."

He wasn't wrong.

One of her hands dipped between her thighs to sit overtop his. She used the pad of two of her fingers to press against *one* of his—slow circles at first, she moved his fingers with hers, showing him exactly the way she liked to get off when it was just her to do the job. That grin of Michel's turned all the more sinful when Gabbie's breaths came out faster, and her lips parted. The right pressure on her clit, and those circles could get her off faster than *anything* else.

"My turn," Michel said darkly.

He snatched her hand away to pin it to the counter while the one on her pussy kept working that same, steady beat. He was fast learner, it seemed. It didn't take long at all for Gabbie's peak to climb higher, and she felt the orgasm rushing in just as the oven started to beep to signal the food was done.

Bliss raged on.

Michel didn't let up for a *second*.

"The food," she gasped, "... I have to get it out of the oven."

Michel's dark laughter filtered into her senses as his lips crashed down on hers. There was something primal in his kiss—so feckin' hungry, and ready to eat her right up. Gabbie was almost willing to forgo the food on the off chance she could get him back to her bed *as soon as possible* but Michel was the smart one between them, clearly.

He pulled away from the kiss, and dropped a soft one to the tip of her nose. "You need to eat—we can play after."

"Okay."

His wink about undid her again.

They were halfway through the food on the table when a ring started to echo somewhere down the hallway. Michel's head popped up from his plate, and his gaze narrowed. "Is that my phone?"

Gabbie shrugged. "It isn't mine."

"Give me a sec."

"Sure."

He disappeared from the kitchen, and into the hallway. She listened as his footsteps quieted when he neared the end of the hallway—her bedroom. He didn't seem to care if she heard him pick up the call, though.

"*Ciao*, Michel here."

Gabbie tore off a piece of whole wheat bread, and smeared a bit of hummus on the top before popping it into her mouth.

"Shit, I *knew* I recognized that last name," Michel said, his voice coming closer to her now. Silence echoed his statement before he quickly added, "No, no. I'm not going to find myself in any more shit, thanks." Footsteps followed Michel's words, and then an annoyed, "Yeah, yeah, I get it. Wrong place—I was just answering *your* people who wanted to cop, Sal, so who's problem is this really, anyway?"

And then just before he came back to the doorway, she heard him say, "So I stepped on someone's toes, *fine*. I'll make sure next time, I don't do that. What do you want from me right now?" Another stretch of silence answered that question before Michel muttered, "All right, I'll be there and we can figure it out."

Gabbie swallowed her bite of food as Michel came back to stand in the doorway. Only now, he had his clothes in one hand, and his phone in the other. She knew it then, without him needing to tell her, that he wasn't going to be staying with her for much longer.

Shame, really.

"Something wrong?" she asked.

Michel let out a bitter laugh. "Yeah, something's wrong. Casey, huh?"

She arched a brow. "Casey, *aye*."

"I'm not familiar with all the ins and outs of the families in Detroit that ... control the cities and outer limits, you know?"

"You should learn then, Michel."

"Apparently." He scrubbed a hand down his jaw, glancing away as he asked, "You told me your father's name last night … it just got mentioned again."

Gabbie almost grinned. "Head of the family—*the boss.*"

Michel nodded. "My father, too, but in New York. *Marcello.*"

She blinked, stunned.

Everyone knew the Marcellos. Anyone who was familiar with the criminal world, anyway.

Michel's gaze drifted back to her, but now, he just looked amused. "Wrong place, wrong time last night, that's all. I have to go—someone's in a fit, and I need to handle it before they handle me."

Selling on someone else's territory could do that. Gabbie didn't say it out loud, though. She doubted Michel needed the reminder seeing as how he looked like he knew exactly the kind of shit he'd stepped in now.

"I'd like to see you again," she said.

She wasn't one to be forward.

Right now?

After last night?

And this morning?

Hell, yeah.

Michel smirked. "Would you?"

"Why not?"

"Not sure it'd be smart, is all."

Gabbie made a face. "Who said anything about being *smart*? My phone is on the table—plug your number in, and text yourself from it so I have yours, too."

She didn't offer it like a suggestion. A demand. Michel chuckled as he did what she said. They'd figure out the details another time. That's what *later* was all about, right?

• • •

Gabbie's morning routine went on as normal once Michel was gone. She even managed to clean up the kitchen *before* she had to check her sugars again after eating. She was considering doing a quick warm-up exercise that would get her prepped for the gym, so she didn't have to bother with one when she got there later in the day, but the ringing cell phone in her bag stopped her from rolling the yoga mat out.

She didn't bother to check the caller ID before putting the phone to her ear after grabbing it. "Hello?"

"Gabbie, sweetness."

Despite it being *way* too early to deal with any kind of grumblings from her father, she had to smile at his greeting. Usually, he left her mornings alone, and didn't bother her until later in the day when he would then want to know *every single detail* about her day, and more. His hovering could get to be a bit much, but she was his only child, and she had simply resigned herself to this.

"Hey, Da."

"How's your morning going?"

"Fine."

Not a lie.

It had been damn fine.

She didn't think he wanted the details, though.

"How do you feel about breakfast with me and Brennan, then?"

"Well, I—"

"Oh, that wasn't a request. We're outside. I will see you in five minutes. I'm sure you're up and about by now."

Her father wasn't joking.

He hung up the phone before she could explain that she had already eaten, and wasn't in the mood to entertain him and his best friend for the entire morning. She had better things to do, for one, and she still needed a damn shower.

She also knew Charles.

If she wasn't outside in five minutes, ready to go and do whatever he wanted for the morning, then he would quickly make his way inside her house. Then, he would *take* her out of it like she should have just done in the first place.

Might as well make it easier on herself.

Gabbie tried to be as fast as she could to pull something more suitable on than black leggings, and a baggy T-shirt. She was still trying to pull her hair into a manageable ponytail when she stepped out of her house. Locking the front door, she eyed the car idling at the curb next to her driveway.

Charles waited just long enough for her to lock the door before he started honking the Lexus's horn for her to hurry up. She glared at her father sitting in the passenger seat, where he leaned over to keep his hand pressed against the horn of the steering wheel until she had opened the back door, and slid into the vehicle.

"Do you mind?" she asked.

"Mind what?"

Charles sounded so confused.

Gabbie just gave him a look. "I do have neighbors, you know."

"A whole lot of eejits, too."

"First of all, my neighborhood is *fine*."

"I know, I picked it."

As annoying as that was. She couldn't even pick the place where she wanted to live because her father had to do that for her, too. She loved him, but he needed to back off. Just a wee bit, that was all.

Gabbie sighed. "I think the man honking the horn at nine in the morning might be the one doing something wrong, Da."

Charles shrugged his broad shoulders under the navy blazer he wore, and shot her a grin over his shoulder. "Boss's right, no?"

"I already ate breakfast," she said, wanting to change the conversation.

"Well, you can keep us company. Brennan doesn't mind, do you, mate?"

Brennan passed Gabbie a look, and smiled. "Never."

She opted to say nothing because at this point, there wasn't anything worth saying. The car pulled away from the curb, and she settled into the back seat after she buckled up. Her father and his right-hand man conversed back and forth, their conversation switching from their mother tongue to English in a blink.

Gabbie found that *most* difficult to follow along—she understood Gaelic well enough, but only when someone was speaking slowly. It was harder for her to distinguish the many topics they bounced between when they used both Irish and English to bark at one another, though. Yet another thing that she never understood between her father and his best friend. They yelled at one another more often than they *talked*.

Then, her father glanced into the mirror again, catching her gaze. "How did last night go, lass?"

"Grand, Da."

"Oh?"

"Aye."

She was not about to go into every little detail of her night. She'd managed to pull on a long sleeve sweater that hid the cut on her arm, although she was sure at some point, someone at the club who witnessed the accident would mention it to her father. If he didn't know about it now, then she wasn't going to bring it up.

Plus, Michel ...

She didn't think Charles wanted to know that.

"Anything interesting happen?" her father asked.

Gabbie arched a brow. "No."

"Hmm."

"Any drinking?"

She sighed. "I'm not even twenty-one, they won't serve me."

Lies.

They would and did serve her at some of the mob-owned joints she attended simply because they knew who she was. Plus, she seriously believed they were scared of what might happen if they refused the Irish boss's daughter something she asked for.

And, if she went to a club that wasn't mob-owned ... well, she had a nice little fake ID provided to her by Aine that worked to get her whatever she wanted. None of those details were important for her father to know, or this discussion.

What were a few white lies?

They wouldn't really hurt, right?

"No problems at the new place?" Charles asked.

"None that I noticed."

Except a gorgeous Italian selling drugs in your territory. She kept that thought to herself because she wasn't sure if her father even knew about Michel being at the club to deal. There was only one major Italian crime family in Detroit—the Vannozzos. They didn't particularly get along with her father's organization, but over the years, they'd accepted that they would just keep a healthy distance.

Gabbie wasn't sure, and she didn't think she could ask her father without raising his suspicions about why she was asking, but she was sure the Vannozzos were a brand of the Marcellos in New York. She didn't actively seek out information about the criminal world her father was so involved in, but she wasn't dumb or deaf, either. She heard when people talked, and she had been around long enough to hear conversations on that topic.

Was that it?

Had Michel came down from New York, and while doing his pre-med, decided to keep himself entertained by messing with the Vannozzos?

"I heard the club was quite full last night," her father said, dragging her from her thoughts.

Gabbie nodded. "A wee bit. Not too bad, though."

He didn't seem very serious about his line of questioning, and if he knew that she was lying, then he didn't show it. His face remained passive even as he probed her a bit more about her night, and what her plans were for the day after they went to breakfast.

Did her father know about the night before?

All the details?

She couldn't be sure, but she wasn't going to offer them willingly. As it was, he already worried about her and hovered far too much. She allowed him so much control over her life—although, *allowed* implied she got some kind of choice—and sometimes, she just wanted to feel normal.

"You know I love you, Gabbie," her father murmured from the front. "If I don't look out for you and make sure you stay out of trouble, then nobody will."

He said things like that a lot.

She figured he did that for himself.

Gabbie couldn't *forget.*

"I know, Da."

"Good. Remember that, lass."

FIVE

Michel stuffed his hands in his pockets and checked the street for oncoming cars before deciding it was safe to pass. Across the way, a barber shop waited for him to enter. Next to the door, a barber's pole moved around in slow circles, the white and red lines almost melting together the longer he watched it spin.

Why Sal wanted him to come here, he didn't know. He'd never been to this business before, not when Sal preferred to meet up for business or with his friends in one of his many restaurants. But this was the address where Sal made it clear Michel would find him—and frankly, it hadn't been a request.

Okay.

So, he fucked up a little.

Michel still figured it was partly Sal's fault for not making sure he had someone to fall back on for business here. He wasn't new to the game—although in New York, there was no such thing as territory lines for him; he could have gone out and dealt *anywhere*. Nobody would say shit to the son of Dante Marcello.

It was not the same here.

Maybe he forgot.

A foolish mistake, really.

The quiet downtown Detroit street was left behind as Michel entered the barber shop. The first person he found in the old school-styled shop was Sal reclined in the barber's chair with a towel around his throat, and a black cape tossed over his front. A man much older than him—if the graying of his hair and lines around his face was any indication—wielded a single blade razor a little too close to Sal's throat.

Michel never understood a man's desire, but especially not a man in this life, to allow someone to put them in a chair, tilt them back, and give them the power to *kill* them with one slice. Because that's literally all it would take. His father once explained to him that it was all about the trust with one's barber.

It was an *experience*.

Yeah, whatever.

He'd shave his own fucking face.

He found Sal first, sure, but the other men in the barber shop were obvious, too. The two men sitting in the waiting area, their backs against the wall—never a window—while they watched the Capo getting shaved in the chair. Michel recognized them, too.

Low fucks, really.

Cole Toscano—one of Sal's few enforcers that he kept close enough for the guy to make a regular appearance whenever Michel was around. And Brock Tocci, who was nothing more than a foot soldier for the Vannozzos.

The two didn't even pass Michel a look when he entered. Not that it offended or surprised him any because it didn't. They didn't have any control over him being that he worked for Sal directly at the moment, and he didn't have shit to say to them, either.

"*Merda*," Sal cussed, finally noticing Michel in the doorway. The Capo's dark gaze turned on him for a brief second as the razor hovered just below his right ear.

35

Michel thought it was probably the coldest the man had ever looked. He realized then that the friendship he gained with Sal and others really only went as far as Michel's ability *not* to cause trouble for them. "Took you long enough to get here, didn't it?"

"I came straight over," Michel returned.

Sal scowled, not looking as though he believed that for a second. "Sure, sure. Take a seat, Michel, and we can chat."

The only available chair was next to the fools in the corner, and Michel was not going to sit beside them like they were familiar in any sort of way. Maybe it was his raising, but he'd never known it to be okay for someone like him, with his last name and standing, to lower himself for the comfort of others.

"I'd rather stand."

Sal's gaze narrowed briefly before he muttered, "Your choice."

Sure.

Then, the man in the chair waved a hand at the man holding the razor to his cheek, his mouth barely moving at all while he spoke. "Meet my father—*Senior*. Or, that's what we call him to distinguish as we own the same name."

Michel nodded at the older man. "*Ciao*. Nice to meet you."

Senior arched one, white brow high as he looked Michel over. "I cannot say the same at the moment, Michel Marcello. Hasn't that father of yours taught you anything yet about the world *outside* of New York, or did he just plan for you to learn it as you fucked up?"

"Easy, Papa," Sal said, chuckling. "He's a young one, isn't he?"

Michel tried not to be annoyed.

And failed.

"I didn't realize I was on Irish territory until it was too late last night," he quickly explained. "And I was only doing what *you* told me to, Sal. Answer the calls, go to the buyer, and do the drop. That was it."

Sal grunted under his breath. "Never place blame on someone else when it's far easier to simply accept what you can change about your own errors."

Oh, great.

Were they having a whole *thing* here?

A moment together?

Michel had a man in his life who liked to spout Yoda shit at him like he was supposed to give a damn. His own *father*. He was far more likely to listen to Dante than Sal, anyway, not that he figured that would be very good to say out loud at the moment.

"I know I fucked up," Michel said simply.

Senior let the razor glide down the side of Sal's face, and was the next to speak, saying, "Detroit is not like New York, Michel. There, I doubt you have to consider your actions, or how they will affect other men around you like you will here. I understand that you come from a family and a man where your last name is enough to allow you to sit at the table with the rest of them, but it will not work that way here. Your father, nor your last name, will keep someone from killing you because you've caused us an issue."

Sal's finger pointed upward at his father. "What he said."

"I don't expect where I come from to do anything for me here," Michel replied.

Because he really didn't.

"And I'll be more careful," he added.

Sal sighed, and waved a hand, stopping his father from continuing the shave. Senior stepped back from his son, allowing Sal to sit up in the chair. He tugged the towel away from his lower throat, although his face was still only half shaved. He didn't seem like he gave a damn about it when his gaze landed on Michel again.

"We have had problems with the Casey family for *years*," Sal explained, "because those Irish bastards are the stronghold here. We have only recently managed to get to a peaceful place with them, and do understand that we cannot afford to go back to war with them. And we won't."

"Not for you, anyway," the enforcer in the corner muttered.

Sal jerked a thumb in the idiot's direction. "What he said."

Michel nodded. "I got it."

"Good. Make sure of it."

Not waiting to be dismissed—he wasn't a made man, and in all reality, Sal wasn't as much his boss as just a guy supplying him—Michel turned to leave. It was Sal's voice over his shoulder that stopped him from going one step further.

"Did I hear you got close to Gabbie Casey in the club last night, too?"

Fuck.

"Where did you hear that from?"

"Word travels, Michel."

"You shouldn't listen to everything you hear. If you believe everything, then you'll stand for nothing, Sal."

The man grunted, but Michel didn't turn around to look at him. It was far easier to see the truth when someone was looking at his face. Or, that's what his father always liked to say, anyway. Michel didn't know if it was entirely true, but he wasn't about to test the theory out right then, either.

"Just stay the fuck away from the Irish," Sal said, "and make sure you keep your head down, too. No more trouble, Michel."

He lifted a hand over his shoulder. "Understood."

• • •

"You the doc?"

Michel glanced away from the bartender he'd been chatting with for the last half hour. Apparently, the man had never been to New York, and Michel thought that was a fucking shame. Now, standing just a foot away from Michel's back waiting was yet another customer. The bartender, knowing what Michel was doing in this club, turned away to leave him to his business.

He appreciated it.

Because *finally* … someone figured out it was better to just place him somewhere to sell their drugs. This club just happened to be mob-owned on the Italian side of things, so of course the employees knew to mind their business when the time called for it.

Of course, he was trying to follow the rules and stay out of trouble. He was only doing his business where he was supposed to be doing it, or where he had been told to work. That way, no one could say shit if something happened.

And yeah, he was keeping his head down. He hadn't approached the Irish, and he had not crossed paths with even one since the weekend before. All good things, he was told. No one was too pissed off about what happened which meant he was expected to just keep moving and doing his thing like nothing was wrong.

Which meant ... no Gabbie.

That didn't mean he liked it.

Michel would be a damn liar if he said the phone in his pocket wasn't burning a hole just sitting there. It would only take a single call—he had her number, right? One call, and he'd get to see her again.

He resisted the urge to do exactly that as he turned on the stool to face the waiting customer. Given that he sold outside of a regular, safe place—like his small bungalow, or something—everything he had on hand in his messenger bag was already weighed, and prepackaged. It made for easy, and fast, exchanges out in public.

Two hands meeting.

Cash sliding into his.

Drugs moving to the buyer.

"I am the doc," Michel said, trying to keep his tone level. He still hated that fucking nickname, but it seemed like it grew on everyone else before it ever worked for him. Now, everybody who met up with him to buy simply asked if that's who he was, and then they knew they could get their shit. "Who sent you over?"

The guy looked to the side, and stuffed his hands in his pockets. He didn't answer right away which made Michel stiffen a bit on the stool. The man nodded, and then looked back at Michel with a shrug.

Something's wrong.

Michel knew it.

His first thought wasn't *cops*, though, because he knew better than that. He was a small-time dealer doing this on the side when he was bored. It wasn't even about the money because he'd have to move a hell of a lot more product to really make a difference. It was highly unlikely that he had even got on any cop's radar as of yet.

"Uh, was just told you were the doc if I wanted to pick up some—"

Michel held a hand up to stop the guy from saying more. He didn't miss the way the man's eyes shifted to the side again, in the same direction as before. What was over there in the crowd that seemed so interesting, anyway?

Fourteen.

That's how old Michel had been when he sold his first pill to some football player in his private high school full of rich kids that had more money than they knew what to do with. From that first sale, he'd learned a lot. His last name afforded him a bit of respect at home because fucking *nobody* wanted to mess with a Marcello, regardless of how much money they had in their bank accounts.

Still, he *learned*.

And fast.

If something felt wrong, then chances were, it was. He didn't ignore his gut—nothing good came from him suppressing his instincts. Bad shit always happened then, and he wasn't willing to risk that this was one of those times.

"Someone over there where you're looking?" Michel asked the man.

Instantly, the guy's gaze came back to him. His eyes were a little too wide. There was something staring back—worry, maybe?

The man blinked, and it was gone. A smile quickly replaced his concern, but none of that mattered to Michel. He'd seen what he needed to the first time around, and that was enough to tell him that he needed to get the fuck out of there.

Someone was over in the crowd.

Someone was watching.

Cops.

Someone wanting to jump him.

Junkies thinking he'd be an easy victim.

Who knew?

Michel wasn't about to find out.

He was quick to push off the stool, not even bothering to give the guy a second look as he grabbed his messenger bag from the bar. Slinging the bag over his shoulder, Michel nodded at the bartender who, clearly having heard the conversation, was already reaching for a phone to call for someone to meet Michel in the back.

Because yeah, they'd planned for this.

That's why he liked this club.

"Another time, man," Michel told the guy who'd approached him as he started walking away. "I'm all out tonight."

"Hey, wait—"

Michel tossed a hand up over his shoulder, but kept walking toward the back of the club. There should have been an enforcer or two in the back alley behind the club. That's where they were usually located, anyway. He didn't feel at all nervous as he headed for the hallway that would lead to the bathrooms, and two exits. He couldn't help but glance over his shoulder, though, just to check …

Sure enough, three figures cut through the crowd.

Coming right for him.

Fuck.

Michel picked up his steps as he slipped into the shadows of the hallway. He didn't bother to check behind his shoulder again as he came up to the exit. Another few steps, and he'd be fine because the enforcers would be waiting out back.

Or they should have been.

Michel found an empty alleyway when he stepped out of the exit. The door shut behind him far too quickly—it was only an exit, there was no way to get back *in*. He didn't really have time to question *why* the enforcers weren't back here, not when someone was already following him and he just had to get away.

Panic welled in his chest fast and swift, like a current within the ocean ready to drag him under and drown him. He had what, maybe thirty seconds?

Or less.

Those three people coming after him had been pretty close. Maybe twenty seconds, then. He thought about the knife in his bag, and the small switchblade he kept in his pocket. A gun would have been better, but he'd never been one to carry a weapon like that. His mother liked to say guns were heavy, loud, and hard to hide.

She wasn't wrong.

Michel darted down the alleyway, already pulling the switchblade out of his pocket and flicking the button on the side. The blade popped out as he heard the door open behind him, and footsteps echoed down the alley as his walk turned into a jog.

He didn't know these fucking alleys.

This wasn't *New York*.

Nothing about this place was like his home.

Michel had never been more aware of that than as he turned a corner in the back, and came to a goddamn dead end. "*Shit*."

"There's the feckin' cunt!"

Of course.

Of course, it was the Irish.

Michel turned around with the blade in his hand, but he came face to face with three assholes each holding guns.

"Hey, you're the *doc*, aye?"

Michel swallowed hard. "That's what they call me, anyway."

Why lie?

"Grand. We got a feckin' job for you."

What?

• • •

"The boss can't find out!"

"He *won't*. That's why we grabbed a doc, boyo."

"Yeah, but—"

"Shut yer feckin' face, huh?"

"A right wagon, you is."

Michel ignored the arguing men behind him as they shoved him down the hall. Where the third asshole had gone, he wasn't exactly sure. He figured now also wasn't the time for him to worry about it. Not considering the other two still had guns, and one was digging hard into the spot right between his shoulder blades.

Was it a hair trigger?

Was the guy holding it drunk?

There were a lot of variables here.

None to his favor, either.

"Walk *faster*," the guy at his back barked.

Michel tensed. "I don't even know where I'm going."

"The last door on the left."

He eyed the dimly lit hallway. He certainly hadn't driven around the city enough to know where exactly he was, but he suspected the shipping district only because they had brought him to a warehouse. Nothing good happened in warehouses.

Ever.

The last door on the left in the hallway was literally the *only* door on the left, but Michel didn't think it was particularly important to point that out to the fucks behind him. He didn't think it would work out well for him to explain their obvious stupidity all the way around the board, but he still had to resist the goddamn urge.

"Open the door, ya cunt."

Michel let out a heavy breath, and looked upward, silently asking God for the strength to get him through this without a bullet in his skull. That would be great. He pushed the handle on the metal door down, and opened it up.

At first, he didn't notice anything strange about the room given it was dark. A bit empty, maybe, and the smell ... a wet, musky scent that had his stomach turning. He fixed that easily enough by breathing through his mouth.

Then, he was shoved inside.

And a light was flicked on.

Michel was barely able to catch himself before he fell to the floor, and *finally* he figured out why these idiots had brought him here. He found it in the corner, on a dirty blanket with a pillow propping it higher.

Or rather, a man.

A *bleeding* man.

From his chest, it looked like.

Michel sucked in another breath, his panic welling higher as all the pieces of this crazy puzzle started to properly fit together. One after another, it all clicked in his mind, and he didn't know what to do. That night at the club with Gabbie, there had been quite a few people around when the guy wanting to cop drugs had called him *doc* as he helped her in the bathroom. It was possible they mistook that nickname because he'd been the one to tend to Gabbie's cut on her arm, and they just didn't know any better.

Rumors traveled fast.

They spread, and grew into a bigger lie.

A part of him wanted to laugh.

Another wanted to scream.

"Stray bullet caught him downtown," the Irishman with the gun at his back said. "Thought you might be able to help us out with this problem, and get it out. That'd be mighty grand of you, doc."

Holy fuck.

Were they serious?

"I'm a pre-med student," Michel muttered under his breath.

"*What?*"

He kept staring at the man on the blanket with the pillow under his head. Even the pillow was bloodstained, and the blanket? *Ruined.* He didn't need to be a doctor to tell them that just based on their friend's shallow breaths, and gray pallor ... there was no way he was going to make it through the night if they didn't get him to a hospital.

And *soon.*

"I'm not a doctor," Michel said clearer.

Not much louder, though.

"What the feck did you just—"

"I'm not a doctor!"

Did they hear him yet?

Was it clear enough yet?

They took him based on something they *heard.* They grabbed him because of a fucking rumor and a *nickname.* He was the one they brought here to save this guy, really? Because the most he knew how to do was fix a bad cut with some crazy glue if he really needed to.

And they wanted him to dig a goddamn bullet out of some Irishman's chest?

Michel started laughing, then.

But it was desperate.

And oh, so strained.

"I'm not a doctor," Michel mumbled, shaking his head but not able to look away from the man dying in the corner. "I can't help you. You took the wrong guy."

SIX

"And you're *set*, then?" Charles asked his daughter. "You're absolutely certain you're continuing this path for college?"

Gabbie smiled at her father. "I'm going to be a lawyer."

Once, her father had offhandedly mentioned that it had been her mother's dream to be a lawyer. Then, she fell pregnant shortly before a rushed wedding, and that dream was pilfered away as family and becoming a mother was more important to Betha.

Gabbie never felt like she simply *took over* that dream for her dead mother, but rather, continued it. She genuinely liked law, and she was a good student. For the most part, she found college easy, and while it would be quite a few years before she would ever stand in a courtroom to defend someone, that was okay, too.

"Mmm. A *defense* lawyer, lass."

"Was that what Mam wanted to be, too?"

Charles chuckled lowly and picked up his glass of the black stuff. Taking a hearty swig, he set it back to the table a little harder than necessary. "No, she had simpler dreams. She wanted to help children and be their voice. But as you know very well, she had a child of her own that needed to come first, and what do I always say, hmm?"

"Charity starts at home."

He smiled. "Exactly that."

Gabbie didn't agree with her father on that sentiment, especially not considering how well off they were when it came to stability and money. The thing was, the mindset her father sported was one he'd grown up with, and it was hard to remove that kind of outlook from someone who had never known anything different.

She wouldn't be the one to try, either.

Wanting to change the subject, because she didn't feel like yet again justifying to her father why she wanted to become a lawyer, Gabbie waved a fork over her plate. "How's the food?"

His green eyes met hers. "It's always lovely, lass."

"Have to ask."

He wouldn't say it—because if he did, then he would have to admit he didn't practice what he preached to her constantly—but he didn't like whole wheat *anything*. Which meant the casserole she'd come over to make him for supper was not his favorite thing. Oh, sure, she added enough spices and flavor to the dish that one really couldn't tell whether or not it was whole wheat pasta, but he *knew*.

He knew because she was eating it, too.

It had to be whole wheat.

Then, Charles rested back in his chair after discarding the napkin he'd been using to tuck into his shirt as he ate. That was her first sign he was just about done eating, and soon, he would dismiss her. It was a regular thing for the two of them to spend a wee bit of time together throughout the week.

Usually, she came over to cook dinner.

Sometimes, they went out.

She loved her father for that, in a way, even if sometimes it did feel like he was smothering her too much. He did make *every* effort to remind her that she was one, if not *the most*, important thing in his life. He cleared his schedule, shut off the phone, and took a few minutes just to chat with her.

Sure, he chatted in his way.

That usually meant questioning her.

Driving her *nuts*.

But he loved her, too.

"I know you think I'm a shite, Gabbie," her father said.

She glanced up from her plate, and met his gaze across the table. "I do not."

"You do. You think I control too much, and I ask too many questions. You believe I don't listen to you when you speak, or when you tell me what you want."

"Because sometimes you don't, Da."

He shook his head, laughing under his breath as he muttered, "And maybe that's true, but ..."

A smile graced her lips. "I'm the only one you have left, right?"

Wasn't that what he always told her?

Wasn't that always his excuse?

Charles' own smiled faltered a bit. "You are, but I don't give you enough credit, I think."

Gabbie blinked, surprised at that admission. "How so?"

"You indulge me all the time. Whatever I ask, you do it with a smile. You never make plans with your friends when you think they might take time away from me—do you even have friends?"

"A handful."

Not many, though.

Mostly, family.

Her father nodded. "I see. Because of me?"

"Not really."

"Then, why?"

"Is this really the conversation you want to have when we're supposed to be having a nice dinner together?"

Charles gave her a look that said he didn't appreciate her comment. Gabbie only shrugged in response because honestly, what else did he want her to do?

"I'm just curious ..." He trailed off, glancing at the clock on the wall like he found it interesting even if it wasn't. "I wonder if being this man—and your father—has ever affected you in those ways. Do I prevent you from being whatever you want to be?"

"No."

That was the truth.

It was that simple.

Gabbie would be or do whatever she wanted, regardless of what her father thought. And she knew that *because* he loved her as much as he did, that he would eventually concede to her desires, and let her do what made her happy.

Was he overbearing and fickle?

Yes.

That changed nothing.

He was still her da.

He still loved her.

"All right," her father said gruffly, picking up his napkin again. "Thank you for indulging me yet again, I suppose."

Gabbie laughed lightly. "Someone has to keep you on your toes, or make sure you stay in line."

He pointed a finger in her direction. "*That* ... well, that is also true. Eat your food, lass. And it is good, even if you do think I hate whole wheat."

She blinked again.

Charles smirked. "I know everything, Gabbie. Even when you think I don't."

Huh.

She didn't quite know what to make of that, so she happily went back to eating her food while her father watched her from the other side of the table. Eventually, he went back to his dish, too.

Charles didn't even glance up from his plate when the front door of the large home opened, and slammed shut. Mutterings echoed down the hallway as footsteps followed the familiar voice. Gabbie recognized the young man who came to stand in the doorway of the dining room—although, for as long as she had known Timothy, she didn't think she had ever seen him looking *this* disheveled and panicked.

There were very few men in her father's organization that he allowed a presence in his life. Timothy was one of them, although she didn't know that he held an actual position in the Irish mob. He was still working his way up. He certainly showed up around her father often enough which told her that Charles liked the guy.

Maybe like a son he never had.

Who knew?

Charles had once tried to set her up with Timothy, too, but that didn't work out well. The guy was a couple of years older than her, but didn't hold her interest at all when he was too busy trying to lick her father's boots to get his *in* to the mob.

She was secondary.

Gabbie wouldn't come second to *anyone*.

Still, her father was unbothered in his chair. He didn't look up once as Timothy shifted from foot to foot and fidgeted with his hands like he was waiting for his boss to *acknowledge* that he was standing ten feet away.

Charles was funny like that.

And he *hated* being interrupted.

"Did you not knock?" Charles eventually asked.

"I—"

"The answer is *no*, lad, you did not."

"Sorry, boss, but—"

"Go back to the door and knock, Tim."

"But—"

"If it is important enough for you to interrupt my meal with my daughter, then you will do what you need to in order to have me speak to you or even *look* at you, boyo."

"Fine. *Feck.*"

Timothy disappeared from the entryway, and his footsteps echoed all the way back to the front door. It was only after the front door slammed shut did Charles finally look up from his plate, and simply to pass Gabbie a smile as he waited for his man to do what he'd been told.

A knock resounded.

Charles sighed before bellowing, "Come on in!"

Timothy grumbled his whole way down the hall, and once he was standing in the entryway again, he raised his arms wide as if to ask *better?*

"What can I do for you tonight?" Charles asked, going back to his plate of food. "Because I am sure you lot were told to keep out of trouble."

"Uh …"

Charles glanced up again, and slowly, turned to face his man when Timothy struggled with his words. "What is it?"

"Something happened, boss."

"Something like *what?*"

"We fecked up."

"*How?*"

"Italians."

Gabbie stiffened in her chair.

So did her father.

"How so?" Charles asked, his tone dropping with a sharp edge. "And choose your words very carefully—it will determine how the rest of this evening goes, ye eejit."

"Someone took a slug to the chest. Word went around about the *doc*, you know? Kevin had the bright idea we could fix it, and not have to bother you with it. We took him out of a club downtown, and—"

"Is he alive*?*"

"Outside, boss."

"Feckin' hell. Useless, all of you are a bunch of useless *cunts*. More trouble than you're worth, I say." Charles was up from the table in an instant, and dropped the napkin down without a word to Gabbie, but she understood well enough. Dinner was over, and while he wouldn't explicitly tell her so, he still expected her to leave the house. "Bring him around back, and take him downstairs, then. Be quick about it. *Go.*"

Her father left the dining room.

She didn't move an inch.

Only one person had ever been called *doc* around her.

Michel.

• • •

Out of all the things Gabbie had learned being the daughter of an Irish mob boss, the *most* important had been to never step in on her father's business.

Ever.

If something was happening in the house, which didn't occur often, then she was to leave, if she could, or hide herself away. She could count on one hand the amount of time her father's line of work had stepped into her daily life and became vividly clear to her just *what* being the boss of an illegal crime family truly entailed.

Be safe, he'd tell her. *Turn your cheek*, he'd say. *We don't talk about the business, lass. What did you see, huh? Nothing, Gabbie. You saw nothing.*

Still, as she crept down the stairs leading into the basement of her father's house, she couldn't convince herself to go back upstairs. Even knowing it could get her into a world of trouble, and she would likely never hear the end of it from her father, she continued taking the creaky steps one at a time.

Because *what if?*

If it was Michel down there with Charles and his men ... what did that mean? Would they kill him? Why had they even taken him?

She just had to check.

If it wasn't him ... then it didn't matter.

If it was—what could she even do?

Gabbie didn't know, but she had to at least try.

Besides, she might like to see him again.

That was kind of hard to do if he was *dead*.

The basement of her father's large, three-level home was the only place that wasn't *finished*. The bare cement floor was cold under her sock-covered feet, and the walls were still damp from moisture. Above her head, pipes and wiring lined the ceiling and she felt cramped at how low the beams for the first floor were to her when she stood straight.

She never understood why her father didn't finish his basement like every other area of his home, but she figured it out quickly enough when through the maze of two-by-four boards sticking up from the floor to connect to the ceiling, she found her father and his men.

Three of Charles' lads stood a bit back from her father. Charles, on the other hand, was kneeling a bit, and from her position, she could see that he'd crossed his arms over his broad chest as he spoke to the man on his knees below him.

Michel.

Gabbie dragged in a quick, quiet breath at the sight of him. His clothes were dirty, and his shirt had been ripped. The side of his face looked bruised, and dried blood smeared along the corner of his busted mouth.

Oh, God.

"Do you want to tell me, lad, why you keep showing up in my life?" her father asked Michel.

Michel glanced up, and a slight smirk worked its way over his bruised lips. "Circumstance, I guess."

"Oh, is that what it is?"

"I'd say so."

"That circumstance is going to get you killed. I hope you understand."

Michel didn't even flinch. "I was in my own territory tonight. I made sure of that."

"And yet, here you are in *my* basement."

"Because *your* men—"

Charles struck out at Michel then, the back of his hand coming down hard to slap across the side of his face. The sound of skin connecting with skin echoed in the quiet basement, and Michel's head snapped to the side from the force of the slap.

Blood trickled from his mouth before he spat it to the dirty floor. Then, still as calm as ever, or making a good show of it, he looked back to Gabbie's father with an arched brow. *Waiting*, but not saying anything more.

"I can't have the Italians causing me issues," her father explained, "and you seem to be one that keeps coming up lately. Do you know how I prefer to correct problems in my life, you wee shite?"

Michel said nothing.

Smart, really.

"I remove them—*permanently*," Charles uttered.

Her heart clenched.

Charles stood straight, and his head just grazed one of the beams on the ceiling as he did so. She didn't know what did it—what made her open her mouth and speak. Maybe it was the man on the left who stepped toward Michel like he was going to grab him, or perhaps it was the one on the right who took the gun from his mate's hand.

Either way, she spoke up.

"Daddy, please don't hurt him."

Charles' back stiffened before he swung around so fast that he was a blur to her eyes in the dimly lit basement. All but a single bare bulb in the corner gave them a bit of light, but when her father's gaze landed on her, there was no hiding the fact that she was standing there, a witness to the death he was about to deliver.

"What are you doing down here?" he snapped at her.

Gabbie's gaze darted past her father to the man on the ground. Michel stared back, a sort of wonderment in his eyes, but a wariness, too. She understood that, and didn't blame him given his current predicament.

"I know they call him the doc, right?" She looked back to her father, ready to beg if that's what it would take. "I had to check and see if it was him. He helped me the other weekend at the club—I didn't want you to worry. I fell, and cut my arm. He bandaged it up, and …"

She held off from saying the rest. It probably wouldn't help to say they'd had sex.

Charles' jaw tightened, flexing with his irritation. "You think I don't already know that, lass?"

"You know everything, that's what you like to say."

"Why not tell me the next day when I asked you about your evening, then?"

"I told you—"

"You didn't want me to *worry*. Utter shite, that is. Try again."

Gabbie looked Michel's way again, but not for long. Just enough that she could see he still wasn't relaxed, and the men around him had not backed off at all. "I didn't think you would approve, and I didn't want a lecture."

"I see."

"Please, don't hurt him."

Charles cleared his throat, but didn't look away from Gabbie. She knew, then, that she was going to get what she wanted from her father if only because *she* asked him for it. He wasn't able to deny her a thing, not when she truly wanted something.

"This could cause a problem, boss," Timothy said next to Michel—he was the one holding the fucking *gun*. "The Italians won't take kindly to us picking up one of their people, and smacking him around a bit."

"I'll make sure they don't retaliate for it," Michel spoke up, his voice hoarse.

"You think they'll listen to you?" Charles glanced over his shoulder with a scoff. "I know all about *you*, Michel Marcello. Here, you are not worth very much, are you? But it may be *just enough* to cause me a lot of problems."

Gabbie's heart picked up speed again, just enough to make her feel like she couldn't breathe. Maybe this wasn't going to go the way she hoped for it to. She didn't know how else to help Michel, though.

"Da, *please*," Gabbie whispered. "He helped me. Can't you give him one more chance for *that*?"

Charles scowled as he turned back on her, and something she didn't recognize flashed in his eyes before he nodded once. "Take the young man to the Italians, and drop him off where they will see him, and can tend to him. Drop him off *alive*, lads. We'll see if he can keep his word on the rest."

Then, her father waved a hand and arched a brow. "Fair, or no?"

"Thank you," she was quick to say.

Charles pointed at the stairs. "Now *go*."

She did.

And she didn't look back, either.

Just in case …

Gabbie did all she could.

SEVEN

"Boss said he needed to be alive!"

"Aye, but he's still a piece of Italian shite, Kevin."

That was the last thing Michel remembered hearing before something hit the back of his head, and everything went black. He didn't even get the chance to cover his head—not that he would have done that when his hands were important tools to becoming a *surgeon*.

The next thing he knew, he was staring up at *darkness*. It took Michel entirely too long to realize what was happening, or where he even was. It was the muffled sound of an engine revving, and the slight swaying in the tight, cramped space that told him exactly what was going on, and where he found himself.

In the trunk of a vehicle.

Perfetto.

Michel was seriously starting to regret taking on the agreement to hustle for Sal over the summer, but he knew he was fucked now. He gave the man his word, and he would be expected to follow it through regardless if he wanted to or not.

That's just how it worked.

Michel blinked back into consciousness slowly, his stomach threatening to revolt. Bad sign number one, he thought. There was a good chance he was concussed, and the last thing he needed for that was to be passed out, for fuck's sake.

He remembered being dragged from the basement of Charles Casey's home, because apparently they didn't even trust him to walk on his own two legs. Before that, he could vividly see Gabbie in his mind—*God*, she was kind of like an angel in the darkness. *His* saving grace, in a way. Had she not come down into that basement, he seriously doubted that he would have made it out of there alive.

Did she even know that?

Jesus.

He was never going to forget how her voice sounded when she spoke up, and asked her father to spare him. Soft, sweet, and oh, so clear. Her words were smooth, but *scared*. A lot like the way she stood there, her hands shaking at her sides although he didn't think that she knew it. She was just doing what she thought was right. Asking for him to be let go was right to her, even if she was terrified to ask for it.

The rest didn't matter.

Except it mattered to Michel.

He owed that woman his life.

Cazzo.

He was brought back to the present when the vehicle jumped a bit—a speed bump, maybe? Michel's hands came out fast to steady his body so that he wasn't tossed around like a ragdoll in the damn trunk.

Fucking Irish.

They didn't screw around. The Irish were known for their violence—*savagery*, really. They didn't give a single fuck about anything, and their actions often showed it. He knew better, because he'd been told more than once growing up, that they didn't mess with the Irish. No one wanted to start problems with an Irish family unless they wanted to suffer for it.

And here he was.

Doing exactly that, idiot.

Michel hated the uncertainty of his current state. That he didn't know where in the hell he was, or where they were taking him. Sure, he remembered what Charles had told his men to do, but that didn't mean they would listen.

Killing an Italian would be nothing to them. He wasn't even a made man.

Fuck.

He missed New York.

Why didn't he just pick a medical school there again?

Michel fought his hazy mind as his eyes grew heavy again. If he was concussed, there was no damn way he was going to let himself fall asleep. He wasn't sure how much longer he was in that trunk while the vehicle swayed and jumped as he was driven to … who knew?

Finally, though, the car did stop. Michel perked up, his fists balling at his sides just in case he might need to fight when, or if, they opened the trunk again. He could taste the remnants of dried blood in his mouth, and his face ached like nothing else.

As did the back of his head.

There was a ringing in his ears, too. Not to mention, his body felt taut and tense. Like his back was sore, and his legs were far too cramped. He was sure he'd taken a few kicks to his ribs given how each breath he took in hurt like nothing else.

They hadn't held back.

Once the idiots at the warehouse figured out he couldn't save their friend—who died on that bloodstained blanket before they could even *leave*—it was all downhill from there. First, they argued about what they were going to do with him.

Kill him, or not?

Two settled on beating the shit out of him while the third man called someone to ask for an opinion on what to do. Apparently, they could take him without permission, but they didn't think killing him without an explicit okay would be the proper thing to do.

Right.

Goddamn fools.

Then, the trunk opened all at once. Bright light spilled in from the outside, making Michel momentarily blind. He blinked, his hands coming up to cover his face to shield from the light so that he might be able to see what was happening.

A street light.

That's what caused the flood of brightness.

"Out you go, you feck."

Michel barely heard the statement before one too many pairs of hands were on him. They grabbed hold of his legs, arms, and clothes before yanking him out of the trunk. He was dumped to the ground unceremoniously, followed by a bout of raucous laughter. He was so glad that his predicament was a source of humor for them.

Yeah.

"Ring the feckin' doorbell, and leave him. They don't need a message—he'll tell 'em."

What?

Michel was still trying to not throw up. Now that he was out of the darkness, the world had stopped swaying around him, and he was on solid ground with a little bit of light to see, his head wouldn't stop spinning. His gaze was fuzzy, and that ringing in his ears had picked up so much that he couldn't really hear anything without it sounding funny. And why did the back of his head now feel like it was literally *pulsing?*

He couldn't remember a time when he had gotten the shit beaten out of him so thoroughly. He had to give the Irish *that*, if nothing else. In the end, they might have let him go, but he heard their message to him loud and fucking clear.

Stay away.

That was not the hell he wanted.

Even as he thought that, Gabbie's image filtered into his mind. Her sly little smile, those spattering of freckles, and the green of her eyes glittering as she looked his way over her shoulder. All memories of her that he didn't realize his mind had grabbed onto until that moment, and he was struck silent from the weight of it.

Yeah, he should stay away.

This was a good reason why.

Who knew if he would, though?

A car revved somewhere near his head.

Too close.

Less than five seconds after tires squealed against the pavement, Michel heard another voice. A familiar one.

"Michel? *Fuck*, Michel!"

Footsteps pounded against cement.

He was rolled to his back.

Above him, he found Sal's worried eyes looking down at him. A new pair of hands were touching him, now, checking him over. This time, though, the hands were a hell of a lot kinder than the ones that had beaten the hell out of him.

"Who did it, huh?" Sal asked.

His eyes had to be swelled *badly*.

He could only see a slit of Sal in front of him.

"Doesn't matter," Michel managed to say.

Sal scowled. "*It does*. I know who it was—the only ones that had any reason. The Irish, yeah?"

"I made a deal. We don't answer."

"Michel—"

"*Don't answer them for it.*"

That was important.

He needed to get it out before he couldn't. And also, he thought to add as his tongue felt too thick in his mouth, "And don't tell my father *shit*, Sal."

He didn't want Dante to worry. Didn't he have to learn to handle himself? He couldn't have his father coming down here to cause issues just because Michel got in a little bit of trouble. That's not how this was supposed to work.

"You're a shit, you know that?" Sal asked.

Michel would have laughed.

Except he couldn't.

The whole world went black again.

• • •

"No work tonight, huh?" Sal crossed the VIP floor, leaned across the booth as he took his seat, and clapped Michel on the cheek. He grinned as the music in the club turned up a notch. "After last week, I think you earned some time off."

Michel chuckled, and shoved his friend's hand away. "At least I don't look as bad as I did."

"But do you look any *better?*"

He gave Sal the finger from across the booth.

Fucker.

"I wondered why you called me in if not to work," Michel said, relaxing a bit in his seat. That wasn't particularly easy to do lately. Despite the fact that the Irish hadn't bothered him in a week, and he heard nothing from that side of things, he still found himself constantly looking over his shoulder. "Are we just drinking?"

Sal nodded, and waved two fingers at the server who was designated to the VIP section of the club. "And celebrating, Michel … four shots, tequila for all of them."

Michel's brow lifted.

What were they celebrating exactly?

"Tequila—do you want me to be alive in the morning?"

Sal laughed. "It's good for the soul. Teaches you the meaning of life, *cafone.*"

Michel doubted that.

Tequila reminded him of death in the mornings.

Except he knew better than to refuse a made man when one offered him a drink—that was considered a great offense to their hospitality, whether you were also made or not. So, Michel said nothing else and took the two shots of tequila when the server brought them around. He wasn't even legal to be sitting in this bar still being only twenty, but that never seemed to matter to anyone in these mob-owned joints.

Story of his life.

He tossed back those two shots for himself, doing his best not to immediately throw it right back up because *holy fuck, tequila was awful.* That was the only thing his mind could scream as the liquor burned the whole fucking way down his throat.

"Another—"

Michel stopped Sal before he could really get going. There was no way he was going through another round of shots with that garbage. He'd watched Sal drop back a quarter of a bottle of tequila on a good night, and Michel was simply not that brave.

"So what are we celebrating, anyway?"

His question did the trick to distract the man, anyway.

Sal grinned his way again. "I had to wait, you see."

"Wait for what?"

The man shot him a look.

Michel stared right back.

Clearly, he was missing something here, but he didn't have the first clue what it was. For the most part, he spent the last week with his head down, and hidden within the safe walls of his small house. Not that a locked door would stop anybody from getting in if they really wanted to grab him and pull him out, but what else could he do?

So, he stayed in.

Made no trouble.

Said *nothing*.

He took the time to heal because clearly he fucking needed it. Most of the bruising was now a faded yellow and brown. All of the swelling in his face was gone. He didn't wake up sore, and still tasting blood in his mouth from the Irish beating.

All good things.

Michel was seriously hoping that was the end of it, too. He wasn't willing, in any way, to go another round with the Irish. He knew better than to hound on the issue, or spread the story around about what happened.

He didn't even complain about it just in case someone took it the wrong way, and thought that he wanted them to answer the Irish back with something to make it clear where he stood. He didn't want to make anything clear except to say what was done was fucking *done*.

His mother and father called earlier in the week, and he didn't even say a damn thing to them about the attack. It wouldn't do anything good for him, the Italians here, or the Irish, for that matter. There was no point in making a fuss, not unless he wanted a bigger issue to be caused over it all.

Let it be done, he figured. They made their point, and he heard it loud and clear.

That wasn't cowardly.

That was *smart*.

Michel was all about being smart.

Or … *trying*.

Sal clearly had other plans if his next statement was to be trusted. "See, the Irish have been toeing the lines we made for a while now. We made peace to keep the streets clean. Too many innocents were getting caught up in the mess, but … we can't let this go. If we were to let this go, Michel, then what might they try next? That doesn't make for good business."

All of the sudden, that tequila Michel had just swallowed threatened to make itself known again. It was about to spill right back out of his mouth, and currently burned his tongue like the bile twisting in his stomach and climbing up his throat.

"Sal, I said not to answer them back," Michel snapped.

The man waved a hand. "Least we could do, Michel."

"*No*, it's not. I said I made a deal."

"It'll be fine. Tonight, they'll know the Vannozzos aren't fucking around with their shit anymore. We're just as strong in this city as they are now—or we're damn close to it. They can't be fucking with us like they did with you. The boss gave his okay. It's done."

No, it wasn't fucking *done*.

Michel didn't understand how Sal could be so flippant about this. Maybe it was his raising under a man who made it his first priority to *never* get into a street war with another family, but Michel's first instinct was to fix an issue.

And *not* with violence.

His father didn't work that way.

A war between criminal organizations was nothing to scoff at, honestly. And it could happen *fast*. A few words tossed, and a punch thrown in the middle, and there they would be. *Fucked*. The entire city would be caught up in a chaotic, violent mess. No one would be safe—not innocents, made men, or anyone in between.

Someone like Michel?

Or Gabbie, even?

They were just fodder to this kind of shit.

So, no, he couldn't be flippant.

Not like Sal was.

"I made a deal," Michel repeated to a man he *thought* was his friend. He was seriously reconsidering that now. This never would have happened between his cousins and him back home. That was a fucking guarantee. "Sal, I gave my goddamn word to them."

Sal passed him a look, his gaze cold as the man arched a brow. "That's the thing, Michel … you don't have a word to give. Your word? It doesn't count here. You should keep that in mind the next time you want to speak for one of us. Now, be grateful we even give enough of a shit to answer them back for you."

Jesus Christ.

Was it even for him, though?

Because he didn't think so.

Michel's jaw ached from how hard he was clenching his teeth. "You know, it's getting tiring, Sal."

"What is?"

"The way you talk down to me."

Sal tipped his head in Michel's direction, saying, "You're not a made man, Michel. Something I was told you chose because you wanted to be a doctor. I guess being made wasn't good enough for you, huh? Oh, and you're not in New York anymore, in case you also forgot about that. You don't want me to talk down to you? Then, I suggest you remember your place. Let's be fucking honest, you're lucky to even be in the *conversation*."

Good to know.

Michel would remember that.

Absolutely.

• • •

What did Michel do when he needed to relax?

Billiards.

Pool.

The first time he ever played a game of pool, he'd been thirteen and his cousin John whooped his ass *horribly*. So much so that Michel almost didn't want to pick up a pool cue, and try again. Anything that didn't come easily to him was far too easy for him to give up. Except he did play again, and with each game, he got a little better.

Now, he could shark someone out of a thousand dollars like it was fucking nothing. Although, he tried not to do that often unless someone needed a lesson about not underestimating him. Funny how that worked ... he felt like there were a lot of people in Detroit lately that needed a reminder about Michel.

Despite the fact he wasn't a made man, and he didn't get a seat at *their* table, he still came from the biggest North American crime family. An organization his father had headed for decades. Did they think he knew nothing? That he wasn't capable of doing serious damage to them if he had enough inspiration?

Because he could.

Michel wasn't like them.

He wasn't *obvious*.

A silent sort of vicious.

That was a better description of him, but not one he wanted to focus on right now. As much as he wanted to show Sal and the rest of the Capo's men exactly what Michel was capable of doing, he knew it wasn't the *smart* thing.

And he tried to be smart.

Usually.

Instead, he resigned to keeping to himself for the past week. He didn't purposely seek Sal out after the conversation the weekend before at the club. There were lots of other things for him to use to keep himself entertained, and he *did* give the man his word, too. For the summer, he was working for the Capo, and he planned on seeing that through as much as he could.

After, though?

Well, his ties to the Vannozzos would be over. They were more trouble than they were worth, and Michel wasn't a fucking idiot. He could see a problem from a mile away, and he wasn't foolish enough to get closer to it.

Like this Irish thing.

He didn't ask what the Italians did.

He didn't want to know.

Were the streets tense?

Michel wouldn't know.

He went to the clubs, dealt to anyone who came up with the right word to get their drugs, and then he went *home*. He didn't seek out Sal, or the guy's men. A part of him was hoping that if he kept a respectable distance from the rest of the Italians, then *maybe* the Irish would realize he wasn't trying to antagonize them like the others were doing.

Simple, right?

Probably not.

Nothing ever was.

Michel sighed, and leaned on the pool cue as he stared at the clock across the bar telling him it was edging closer to ten at night. He liked this bar close to his place because they never asked for ID, and it was always quiet.

"It's been your turn for two minutes, man."

He glanced at the guy who decided to take him up on a game for a bet of fifty dollars. Change to Michel, really, but he was never one to turn down the opportunity to best someone at a game of pool.

A quick survey of the table told him he was about to win that fifty dollars, too. It wasn't that the guy was bad at the game—pretty decent, all things considered. Michel was simply *better*.

He liked that.

Being better.

Michel set himself up at the far end of the table near the left pocket. Bending down over the edge, he rested his stick on the wooden side, and measured how far the last striped ball on the table was from the cue ball, and which pocket he wanted to choose for it. His bigger problem was the fact that the eight ball was in the way, and if he sunk that fucker on accident *first* before the striped nine ball, then he was going to lose.

Not a problem.

He settled on a trick shot that would have the cue ball spinning back around to crack the eight ball into a pocket *after* sinking the nine ball into the right side pocket.

Michel pointed his cue ball at the far left pocket he planned to sink the nine ball into, saying, "Game with this shot—left pocket for the nine."

"No way you're going to hit that."

"All right," Michel replied dryly.

He bent down again, aimed his pool cue, and took the shot without overthinking it. That's when he always missed his shots, so he'd learned to just trust his instincts, and go with it. A lot like the rest of his life, honestly.

He wondered if Detroit was going to be the same.

Were his instincts about this place right?

Sure enough, the nine ball sunk into the far left pocket before the cue ball hit the corner, causing it to spin back around and crack right into the eight ball. He *almost* thought the eight wouldn't sink into a pocket when it slowed near the middle, but it crawled its way home.

Michel stood from the pool table, turning to face his opponent. The guy wasn't looking at him, though, but rather … at the woman coming their way.

Damn.

Michel's mouth went dry.

She looked good in tight skinny jeans that seemed to be painted onto her legs, showing off the shape of her thighs and hips. Not to mention *legs for days*. God, yeah, he was such a fucking leg man. She'd let her loose, red curls down around her shoulders, and while she didn't have a lot of makeup on, the red lipstick was more than enough to *pop*.

And that crop top?

Showing off her bare tummy?

A navel he'd like to *lick*?

"What are you doing here?" he asked her.

Gabbie came up alongside the table, and shrugged one shoulder. "They talk a lot—my da's people, I mean. I guess they're watching you. You frequent this place, huh? They mentioned it when I was around the other night, and I figured … if I had time, I wanted to come and say hello."

Michel blinked.

They were watching him?

Still?

Fuck.

"And what, you thought it'd be smart to come find me?"

Gabbie smiled. "Why not?"

"Because it's not *smart*."

Nothing was, lately.

He liked seeing her there, though. She reminded him of sweetness and sex. All rolled in one fantastic package that was probably going to get him killed.

Yeah, Michel was the smart one. Except when it came to this woman, apparently.

"You want to play a game?" he asked.

Gabbie's eyes brightened. "Absolutely."

EIGHT

"Do you want to rack?" Michel asked.

Gabbie took the pool cue he offered, acutely aware that the man who he'd been playing before had slipped away from the table without a word. Michel didn't seem like he was missing the man's presence, either. Likely not a friend, then.

"You can," she replied.

Michel shrugged those broad shoulders of his, and beneath the silk dress shirt, the action made his back muscles move in the *best* way. In a breath, Gabbie was reminded of what it felt like to have her fingernails digging into that back of his as he was working to make her see God as she came.

Yep.

She went there fast.

"Lady's choice," Michel said, tossing her a wink.

It was to her benefit, anyway. She got a nice view of his arse, and the back of his shoulders flexed as he leaned over the table to set the triangle up. Those jeans hugging his backside drew in her gaze, and she didn't even try to hide the fact that she'd been staring when Michel stood straight and turned around to glance at her.

In fact, she winked.

Michel chuckled, and pointed his pool cue in her direction. "Ladies go first."

"You racked the balls."

"I didn't play you last game and win, though. It's a new score card."

Gabbie nodded, happy that he knew the rules of the game. "I'll break, then."

"Let's see what you can do, *donna*."

That was fine by her.

She rounded the table, hyperaware of just how close Michel was standing to her side as she leaned over the edge with her pool cue ready. "Have you heard what's happening out there on the streets lately?"

"I'm purposely staying out of it."

Gabbie took the shot, and once the balls broke, scattering across the table, she watched as a striped ball fell into the far-left pocket. "Stripes for me. And on the other thing ... do you think that's smart to just close your eyes and pretend like they might not come for you, too?"

Michel cleared his throat, but didn't answer. Gabbie was fine with that. She hadn't exactly been expecting a response in the first place. Rounding the table, she eyed the balls and the possible shots she could take. Her next three sunk the balls in each pocket she called. Unfortunately, that left her without a shot that was *safe*. And by that, it meant the eight ball was in the way for every feckin' shot.

Damn.

She took what she would consider a *fake* shot ... something that would switch the table to Michel, but that was a risk, too. If he was as good as she assumed, given she watched him play for a bit with the other man before approaching the table, then he could very well take her for a ride in a few shots.

She liked risks, though.

That's why she was *here*.

Michel whistled when the shot she took missed entirely. "You had a good run there."

"You think?"

Gabbie passed him a sly grin.

Michel winked right back. "My turn, though."

"Go for it, pretty boy."

"That's offensive."

Michel leaned over the table.

She stared at his arse again.

"Yeah, you're right," she replied, "all I see is a very good-looking lad with a cock he knows how to *use*."

As she said that, Michel took his shot and missed entirely. She'd done that purposely just to see if it might work. A bit of a cheap shot, sure, but Gabbie couldn't help it. She might blame it on her raising any other day, but the truth was simpler ...

She liked to *win*.

What she wanted, she got.

Easy.

"That was dirty fucking pool," he said, laughing as he stood up from his crappy shot. His dark eyes met hers, and she swore despite his annoyance at her trick, she still saw appreciation shining back in his gaze. And lust, too. Just like that, her body was entirely too hot and the last thing she wanted to focus on was a game of pool. "You won't get that one over on me a second time—I promise it."

Gabbie wet her lips, whispering, "Shame, then. I was just getting started."

"Good to know." Michel's jaw tightened, and she didn't miss the way he looked her up and down as he rounded the table to put just a wee bit of distance between the two of them. "Take your shot, *bella*."

She surveyed the table as she walked from one end to the other, deciding which plan of action she wanted to take to—*hopefully*—sink as many balls as she could, and perhaps even win the game. All the while, she talked.

"There's been fights," she said to Michel, "where there used to be peace. Places where my father's men could work without the Italians stepping in, or vice versa ... now it's all up in the air. Someone tried to set a warehouse on fire last Wednesday, too."

Michel made a noise under his breath. "Irish or Italian warehouse?"

"Yours."

She didn't miss his scowl.

"What?" she asked.

"It's not *mine*. They're not mine, Gabbie. If those people were mine, they wouldn't have done things this way. Where I'm from, we don't start petty feuds with just anybody because we purposely try to *avoid* war."

She sucked in a burning breath, exhaling just as sharply as her gaze met his. "I think that's the problem with my da and his men—he doesn't care that you're not one of them. You look like them, talk like them, and you come from the same kind of people as them. You're basically the same, simply a different breed, Michel."

Michel arched a brow. "Has anyone ever told you that you know too much about the business of men?"

Gabbie considered that statement as she leaned over the table, and readied her shot. She took it as she replied, "Striped nine in the far left pocket."

The ball sunk in.

She stood up again.

"I have been told that before," she said, giving him a simpering smile, "but that doesn't stop me from listening. How can anyone be expected to survive when they don't even know what's going on around them?"

"Fair point."

"It's a risk for me to be here … seeing you." She sighed, knowing she would probably be in for a world of trouble when she did finally go home, and her father got word about where she had been. Still, she took that risk because she *wanted* to be here. "They follow me, too, and report back."

"Then why come?"

"I like you, Michel."

"Hmm."

She gave him a look. "And you like me, too."

A sexy, lazy smile graced his lips. "Another fair point."

"They're planning an attack."

That wiped the smile off his face, unfortunately.

"Your father's people?"

"Against the Italians," she confirmed.

"And what do you expect me to do with that information, Gabbie?"

Well …

"Whatever you have to, Michel."

Whatever he needed to survive.

"Even if it means playing a game of dirty pool to do it," she added.

Just like her.

Gabbie went back to the game.

And quickly sunk each and every shot she took. Once she was left with the eight ball, she grinned at the table, pleased with her skills, as she leaned against the pool cue. Michel, on the other hand, was staring at her from the other side of the table like he was just now seeing her for the first time.

"Something on your mind?" she asked him.

"I have not lost a game of pool in five years or more."

Gabbie nodded, appreciative. "You haven't lost it yet, though."

But he would.

She readied her final shot, took it, and sunk the eight ball in the pocket she called. Exactly as she expected to do, and probably the way he assumed she would, too. She hadn't even straightened fully from the table before Michel had crossed around to stand in front of her so that she was facing him.

Then, he was kissing her.

Hard, fast, and *bruising.*

It took her breath away.

Her lips felt numb.

She tasted a hint of vodka on his tongue when it slipped into her mouth to war with hers. His lips worked against hers so fierce, and hungry. There was no question what he wanted, and she was more than happy to oblige.

Her body begged for it.

• • •

Sex was better when one was in a state of desperation. Or, that's what Gabbie found. It's why she didn't even think twice about climbing into the backseat of Michel's car because *no*, she did not want to waste time going home, or to his place … she just wanted *him*.

Desperation was the reason she found herself naked in his lap. The car was hotter than it should have been, but not because it was idling in the dark parking lot. No, it was hot because of *them*. Because of their bodies moving against each other in their need to get off, but to use each other to do it.

His fingers dug painfully good into her hips, pulling her body down harder into his cock as his teeth found her throat again. Pain sluiced across her skin as the pleasure continued to build in her stomach, twisting and curling together until she didn't know where the pain began, and the pleasure ended.

"Fuck, fuck, *fuck*," Michel grunted against her neck, his breath hot as she rode him harder. "You love that cock, don't you?"

Gabbie would have responded, but she was just flying *too high*. Like her nervous system was being washed with pleasure, and her tongue was too thick in her mouth. The only sound she could make came out high, and broken.

She couldn't get enough.

She wanted *more*.

"Are you gonna come for me?" he demanded.

Gabbie whined. "*More, more, more.*"

Next to his name, it became the only thing she could really say. And even that mantra melted together the faster she spoke, and the more her need grew. *Yes*, she was going to come. And *yes*, she wanted more so it would be so much feckin' better when she finally did. His hands gripped tight to her backside, his fingers digging in hard enough to her arse that she was sure there'd be fingerprints left behind tomorrow.

That was fine.

She wanted his marks.

She wanted to feel him on her arse, and between her thighs every time she sat down or took a step. A beautiful ache, really. She'd use that feeling and this memory when she was in bed alone, and the desperation came again. It wouldn't feel as good, but she'd still *need* it. Just like he made her need this with him.

Michel's hand curved lower along her backside, his grip tightening to stretch her open as his other hand came down, too. She felt the slight pressure of two of his fingers against the tight hole of her arse before he was circling the ring of muscles.

Every part of her tensed.

Her sex *flexed*.

"*Here?*"

Gabbie's breath rushed out of her violently, but he caught the sound she made with a burning kiss that had her nodding to his request. "*Please*, Michel."

Her fingernails raked red scores down his pecs as one of those fingers at her arse pushed in. The pain was back again, but it was numbed because something else was there, too. Something thicker, and *teasing*. She swore everything became slower to her senses—she felt every single thing. His fingers working her arse as his cock stretched her open with every lift and lower of her hips.

There was something freeing about that.

Something wild.

And *raw*.

"Oh, my God," she choked out.

The second finger being fitted into her arse was what *really* did it. Her body wasn't slowly coaxed over the edge of bliss, but rather, he fucking *threw* her over it. The sensation was almost violent, but she found a part of her that had been craving that.

She burned *everywhere*.

And it never felt better.

Michel didn't let up on her for a second, either. His hand on her arse tightened to a painful point, and he dragged her harder against his own body. Working himself higher and higher until he released a low, guttural sound along the seam of her lips, and she felt him jerk inside of her tender sex.

That's when he slowed.

That's when she could breathe again.

His words whispered in her ear, making her smile and her heart beat crazy fast in her chest. "This is crazy. This is fucking crazy."

"But good," she returned.

Michel laughed against where the junction of her neck met her shoulder, his teeth dragging deliciously to her skin. "Where have you been all my life?"

She didn't have an answer.

"I don't know," she mumbled.

He pressed a soft kiss to her lips, a moment of tenderness in the roughness that had been their sex. It made her smile as she met his gaze. "I want you to take me on a date. A *real* date."

Michel blinked. "Right now?"

It was dark.

Way too late.

Nothing would be open.

Gabbie still nodded because she was *not* ready to let him go anywhere but with her for the moment. "Right now, Michel."

• • •

"Here, duckies!"

Michel's dark chuckles came close to her ear as his nose grazed the back of her neck. Gabbie had all she could do *not* to shiver from the feeling of his lips pressing to her skin with featherlight kisses.

"I don't think they recognize being called *duckies*," he murmured.

"Shut up."

"I'm just saying they don't speak human, Gabbie."

She didn't mind his teasing.

Much.

"Says the man who had a small bag of birdseed in his car because *bread is bad for the ducks.*"

His hands landed on her waist, and she *loved* the way his fingers dug into her sides. He squeezed, a silent warning for her to stop the teasing. She heard it loud and clear, not that it made much of a difference. If he could dish it, then the man would learn to take it. That was Gabbie's way.

"I told you, I jog here."

"Yes, with birdseed for the duckies, apparently."

"Because they quack at me when I pass, and I feel bad for them."

"Mmhmm. Of course, you do."

Michel let out a laugh. "You're impossible."

Gabbie winked at him over her shoulder as she pulled out a handful of birdseed. Michel wasn't wrong—bread was *terrible* for ducks. It got stuck to the roof of their mouths, and if it did get in their bellies, it would swell up to make them think they were full when they weren't. It was harder for them to digest, too.

She adored he had birdseed in his car to toss to the ducks when he jogged at the park. He wasn't *all* bad, despite what people in her family liked to say about the Italians. How could someone be bad if they remembered to feed the ducks when they went jogging? It was sweet, really.

"You must be getting hungry," he said.

"A little."

"You want to go—"

"Not yet."

She was enjoying this.

The park, peaceful at almost midnight, was dark and quiet. There wasn't a soul around, and the small pond was rarely ever this empty when she came to see it in the daytime.

"I like that you chose *here* for a date," she said.

Michel rested his chin on her shoulder, and wrapped an arm tightly around her middle. "Oh, why is that?"

"Most guys would pick a club, or something. Dinner, and a show. The *usual.* I like this better. It's just us, and we can talk."

"I would have taken you for all that other shit, too, but it's late."

It was.

Most restaurants were closed, although she was sure they could find a hole-in-the-wall diner to eat at, if they really wanted to. Not that any of the food would be the kind of stuff she was supposed to eat. Michel probably knew that, too, and took it into consideration without telling her he was doing it.

She appreciated it.

Gabbie grinned. "*All* of that for a date, too?"

"Yeah, probably not. I wanted to be alone with you … can't exactly do that when there's other people around, can I?"

Just like she thought, then.

"I come here a lot, but never this late."

"No?"

Gabbie shook her head. "Only on weekends when I don't have classes. And I haven't had the chance to come here since the summer break started."

"What are you studying, anyway?"

"Law."

Michel made a noise under his breath. "*Law*, hmm?"

"Don't sound so disgusted."

Michel laughed. "In my experience, lawyers have never done anything but try to put my father away for years."

"And what about the lawyers who *defended* him?"

He stiffened behind her. "It was usually my uncle—Giovanni. I just never thought to put him on the same playing field as the rest of them."

Gabbie shrugged. "You should. That's my goal, by the way. A defense lawyer."

"If you're as dirty in the courtroom as you are playing a game of pool, then I have no doubt you'll be amazing."

She elbowed him lightly for more of his teasing, but this time, he answered her back by sinking his teeth right into the side of her neck. A shot of heat pooled in her gut, especially when his lips pressed to the same spot, *hot and soft*. His arm tightened around her waist, pulling her in closer to his body.

"Why a doctor?" she asked.

Michel hummed under his breath. "Do you want me to use the same tired line everyone else uses when asked that question?"

"What line is that?"

"They want to help people."

Gabbie gave him a look over her shoulder, but he just smirked at her. "Don't you want to help people, too?"

"I do, but I won't lie and say that's the *only* reason."

"What else is there?"

"I had a romanticized idea of what being a trauma surgeon would be like, and in a way, I still do." Michel used his free hand to run his fingers through her loose curls. She probably could have sunk into his touch, the sensation of his fingers drifting through her hair was enough to make sparks dance in her nervous system. "And then there's the *pressure*. That's a big part of it, too, I won't lie."

"The pressure?"

"I work best under pressure. Someone pushes me to the limit, and great things happen. That's been my whole life, basically. I wanted to do something for work that was going to take me to the breaking point every day so that I was constantly at my best. I don't think I would be satisfied or happy, otherwise."

"Ah."

That made sense.

Michel let out a rumbling chuckle behind her. "I can't think of another job that's as high in intensity as a trauma surgeon, you know?"

"There are *some*."

"But none that interested me like that did."

"I get it." Gabbie scrunched her nose up as the ducks realized she was out of birdseed and started to float away from the edge of the pond. "What about ..."

"What, babe?"

"The family business. You never considered *that*? It seems like every man in my life, well, that was the first thing they gravitated to."

"I still dabble."

"From the sidelines, maybe," she replied, referring to his dealing.

"If you knew my mother, you wouldn't think it was just dabbling."

"Oh, do tell?"

Michel laughed, but tipped his head into her hair to muffle the sound. "Ah, I shouldn't be telling a little Irish girl *anything* about my family, Gabbie."

"First, I am *not* a wee lass, you feckin' eejit."

His arm squeezed her again. "Be nice."

"That was nice!"

"Insulting me is—"

"How we Irish people show our *affection*."

Michel let out a heavy sigh. "Guess I'll take your word for that."

Well, it was the truth.

"All right," he muttered, "my ma is ... well, if you were someone with a *big* name—"

"Like a celebrity?"

"Okay, that. Or ... politicians, someone rich, and so on."

"Mmhmm, go on."

Michel nipped her neck again. "She'd be someone on your speed dial to make sure you were supplied with whatever you needed to keep you happy."

Gabbie froze. "Like a drug dealer for the stars?"

"She'd be offended if you called her that. It's a whole organization. She controls dozens of girls who are constantly on call. It's what she's done since she was a lot younger."

"*Wow.*"

"Yeah."

"Your mam is a Queen Pin?"

Michel nodded. "Pretty much."

"And your da is a mob boss."

"Italians prefer the *Don*, but yeah."

"And you never considered the family business?"

Michel laughed again, and that sound soaked into Gabbie like nothing else ever had. She peeked over her shoulder just to see the way he looked when he was free, and happy. It was quite a sight—all those hard lines of his face softening just enough to make him look slightly younger, and joyful.

He held her tighter as his chuckles faded away. His lips were back on her skin again, his words whispering into her ear. His tone turned serious, and yet, his voice alone was enough to make her warm to the touch, and shivering all over.

"I love them, and I respect my family for what they've done in the criminal world ... never be confused about that, but it isn't me. Not entirely. I wanted to be *more*," he told her, "I needed to be more than what was just *expected*, Gabbie."

He would be.

She had no doubt.

"Never pretend to be average for the comfort or approval of others," she said. "It's the exceptional who change the world—not the status quo."

Michel's hand found hers, and their fingers wove together tightly. "Exactly."

NINE

"Don't take offense," Michel said as he came to stand in the entryway of the restaurant's private dining room, "but this is starting to get tiring."

Sal didn't even glance up from the paperwork he had spread out on the table, but he did nod to say he'd heard Michel's statement. That was it, though, nothing else came after. Michel shifted on his feet and shoved his hands into the pockets of his slacks. *Waiting.* Because clearly Sal didn't expect him to do anything else.

The man hadn't invited him in, and he didn't look like he was going to, either. The table Sal sat at to do his work—and pick at a plate of nachos to his left—had only *one* chair. The one he was sitting in, currently. He clearly knew Michel was standing in the entryway when he hadn't been quiet about his arrival, and Sal had gone as far as at least *nodding* to him.

Michel tried not to get irritated about the man's obvious disregard for his presence. Like it didn't matter that he was standing right there, at a time too early for it to be acceptable, waiting on the asshole across the room to pretend like he gave a fuck someone was there for him. He wasn't stupid—he knew how this went and being around men just like Sal for his entire life made this all the more clear to him.

Painfully so, even.

Sal was like any other man in the mafia who felt comfortable in his position and knew he had earned it. Anyone else who hadn't—people like Michel, or those actively trying to get their in—were beneath him, and he didn't mind making sure they knew it, too. Usually, Michel would brush this shit off because he didn't care what anyone thought of him, but today it rubbed him in all the wrong ways.

Hell, it had been Sal who called him in that morning. He hadn't even had the chance to crack open his goddamn eyes before Sal's voice was the one barking at him to *make a trip to the restaurant* that morning. He wasn't given any reason, or other orders, either. Just what Sal wanted, and that was that.

Like everything else lately.

It was what *someone else* wanted.

Michel didn't get a say.

This was one of the entire reasons why Michel didn't want to become a made man. He'd watched from the sidelines as his father's and uncles' lives had been dominated and controlled by the ways of Cosa Nostra. The mafia came first— *always. La famiglia* had to take precedence over anything else that someone on the outside looking in might consider more important.

And then as an older teenager, he watched as his cousins, Andino and John, decided to take their first steps into the family business, too. Suddenly, his best friends went from having the freedom to do whatever they wanted with him to having their days and nights controlled by men who would eventually determine if they were good enough to get their button—the *in* to the family.

Michel never faulted the men of his family for their dreams. He understood that the mafia was what they wanted—being made men was the only thing they had ever really considered for their future. On the other side of that coin, Michel chose *not* to pursue the business because he knew once he was in, there was no way out.

There was no way in hell he would ever allow someone else to dictate what he could or would do with his time, life, and future.

It was as simple as that.

Still, despite how irritated it made Michel to sit there like a dog waiting to be called on to get his scraps for the day, he did it. Not because he had to take that shit, but because he grew up learning one thing first—*respect*.

His father would have been sorely disappointed in Michel for not at least attempting to be respectful first and foremost before anything else. It was only the thought of Dante in the back of Michel's mind that kept him standing in that entryway until Sal decided he was finally ready to speak to the other man.

"We have a problem," Sal said quietly.

Even then, the man didn't look up from his paperwork or meal. Michel's brow knotted, and his gaze narrowed as he took in the space with new eyes again. He was just now realizing how *empty* the private dining room was when usually a handful of men would be scattered about the room.

An enforcer or two, and a foot soldier who was lucky enough to follow around one of Sal's men. Not to mention, the bookie—David—who almost always could be found at Sal's side. Friends since they were kids, or that's what Sal once told Michel. Nonetheless, there was never *no one* around whenever Michel was called in to see Sal for something.

The emptiness was concerning.

Michel wondered if he'd stepped into a trap.

"Did you hear me?" Sal asked.

He stayed still in the doorway, now *refusing* to take another step inside the dining room just in case. Safety first, and all that shit. It was becoming painfully obvious to Michel that there wasn't a single thing about Detroit, or the people in it, that he could trust.

Gabbie, his mind whispered.

It wasn't wrong.

She did try to help him—repeatedly.

"A problem, yeah," Michel returned. "I heard you. What kind of problem are we talking about here?"

Sighing, Sal took his sweet time packing up the papers on the table, and shuffling them into a waiting folder. It was only once the table was cleared but for his plate of nachos and glass of water that the man finally looked up at Michel. The first time he'd looked at him in the face since Michel arrived.

One couldn't miss the coldness in Sal's eyes. He let out a thick sigh, one loaded with tension and it easily filled the room, too. His thin lips, set into a hard, grim line, twitched. Another sign of his frustration—with Michel, likely.

"*You*, apparently," Sal replied.

Michel still didn't move, and in fact, he didn't even react to that statement. Although, if he were being an honest man, he would admit it was damn hard not to laugh at that. Only because what was he doing that could cause problems? He was purposely keeping his head down, doing his work because he gave Sal his word, and very little else.

Nothing to make issues, anyhow.

"Gabbie Casey, ring any bells?" Sal asked.

Michel stiffened.

Yeah, *okay*.

That could be considered an issue.

"Of course, it does," Michel replied carefully.

"Oh, good." Sal smiled, but it wasn't at all true, and his tone held a touch too much sarcasm. "So, I suspect you won't mind at all to explain *why* you were seen leaving a bar last week with the Irishwoman?"

Michel's teeth ached from clenching his jaw so hard. It was the only way he could keep his mouth shut, and say nothing. He really didn't think words were going to help his case here, all things considered.

Sal nodded when Michel stayed quiet. "If you thought the Irish are the only people following you on a regular basis, then you are *highly* mistaken, Michel."

Good to know.

He still didn't reply.

"This … thing we have with the Irish right now is a loaded gun waiting to blow. What we don't need, however, is more distractions because of *you* and that fucking woman. Do you hear me?"

"I hear you, but—"

"No, I didn't ask for a *but*, Michel."

"I could possibly help you to … smooth out the issues with the Irish." He wasn't exactly sure how, but he thought *anything* was possible. As long as someone wanted it badly enough, and in this life, no one wanted blood to spill enough that they were willing to let a war rage on within city limits. "If that's something you're looking at, Sal."

The man at the table scoffed. "Not at all."

Well, then.

Okay.

"Your closeness to the Irish is concerning," Sal added.

Michel did laugh at that one, although it was quick to die in his throat when Sal turned his gaze on him. "My *closeness* to them? They beat the fucking hell out of me after they kidnapped me!"

Sal raised a single brow high. "Yes, and you're the first Italian I know of in this city to have made it away from the Irish *alive*, Michel. Add that onto your clear interest in the Irishwoman, and it spells bad things for you."

"Excuse me?"

He didn't like what Sal was suggesting.

Not at all.

There were a handful of things that were *never* negotiable in the life, whether one was directly in it by being a made man, or they were simply an associate, like Michel. And one of those things was a person's *loyalty*. To the life, and the family. To the person allowing them a place in the business.

No excuses.

Loyalty was everything.

"Do I have to be concerned that the Irish could entice you to their side of things?" Sal asked quietly, folding his hands on the table as his gaze met Michel's from across the room. "Or is a simple order for you to stay away from the Irish, which means her, too, going to be enough for you to listen?"

No, it wouldn't be.

Michel wasn't going to pretend, either.

If he wanted to see Gabbie Casey, then he was going to do exactly that. Like fuck was this man, or any other man, going to make those rules for him. Besides, it also wasn't that simple for Michel where Gabbie was concerned. Nothing about the two of them could be easily summed up with a few words—he wasn't about to deny himself something he didn't even know well enough to explain to someone else.

He adored that woman, and the more time he spent with her, the greater that feeling became. It was addicting, in a way. There was a part of him that wanted to know where this was going to take him with her—somewhere amazing, maybe ... who knew?

He wanted to find out. He'd never connected with someone like he did with Gabbie. And someone wanted to tell him to, essentially, fuck off where she was concerned? Someone thought *they* got an opinion on his choices?

Not likely.

These Detroit *fucks* didn't know him that well.

"Since you didn't want to say it outright," Michel said, refusing to answer the man's question, "I will *tell you*. It's not my loyalty you ever have to wonder about."

As long as they looked out for him, he'd look out for them.

That's how Michel worked.

That was life.

It wasn't about the mafia.

Sal's jaw tightened as he muttered, "Don't make me call on you again, Michel."

Yeah, whatever.

• • •

Michel stepped into the club, letting his gaze drift over the people lingering near the entrance where they could drop off their bags and coats. Handing over his bag to the woman taking items from patrons, he kept his phone and wallet just in case.

He wouldn't say he was a truly familiar face at the joint, but he had been there enough to do business—make a sale—that the bouncer at the front didn't mind letting Michel pass for an extra hundred tucked in alongside his fake ID when the man asked to check it.

This particular club wasn't *mob-owned*. Not by the Italians, or the Irish. That was one of the many reasons why Michel liked the place when he had to drop in to make an exchange with a customer. And yet, it was still quite popular, and the mob had managed not to encroach on the place.

So far.

Anything with too much success was always a threat to the mafia. If they couldn't weasel their way in through bribery or blackmail, then they would simply turn to threats and violence to get what they wanted from the owners of the joint. It was only a matter of time.

That was background noise to Michel.

For now, anyway.

Another reason Michel liked this club? He considered it *safe*. At least, for the time being. If he was being followed, as Sal suggested the week before, then it wouldn't look at all concerning for Michel to slip into a club during the weekend to do a drop off.

He was pretty sure he didn't have someone on him twenty-four-seven from the Italian side, but more like some stupid fuck who kept Sal updated on Michel's whereabouts. He couldn't say anything about the Irish, but he wasn't really the person who needed to worry about them. He had his attention on his side of things with the Italians.

Which meant when he went into a club to work, he suspected the guy probably went off to do his own thing, believing his job was done. That was his mistake, and totally fine with Michel. He had other things to attend to now.

Checking his phone as he drifted in and out of the people hanging around the entrance and closer to the bar, Michel read over the last text that he had been sent. It was the only thing that was going to tell him where he had to go inside the club, so he didn't look like a fool staring around with no particular direction.

Middle of the dance floor.

That's all the text read.

He grinned.

Michel headed for the dance floor, weaving through the crowd of sweaty, drunk people. It wasn't hard at all to find the woman he was looking for once he knew where to search for her. She was the only one with that penny-colored hair, her mess of curls wild under the lights flashing up above, and her green eyes sparkling when they finally landed on him.

Gabbie.

Yeah, fucking no one was keeping him away from her. Not if he wanted to be near her, and he did. *Often.* Lately, she was the first thing on his mind in the morning, and the last thing at night. He reached for thoughts of her because he found comfort in them—she was the one thing he was most sure of here when everything else seemed like it was up in the air.

And he didn't even know her that well.

Did it make sense?

Hell no.

He still liked it.

A lot.

Michel said nothing as he came to join Gabbie in the swell of people. Here, it was a safe meeting place. They could leave with a crowd of people, and drift away out of sight without anyone knowing they were even together later.

Easy.

Like cake.

Still dancing, her hips moving to the beat of the music in a way that made Michel wish he had her tight ass pressed up against his groin while she did it, Gabbie reached for him. He was already going in to grab her, too.

Her sweet lips pressed against his—her taste was still the same, too. Sweetness, and sin. He couldn't get enough. Her tongue warred with his, and she never shied away from the forcefulness of his kiss.

Just a few days …

They'd met up earlier in the week, too.

But just a few days was too much time away from this woman. He didn't like that at all; he didn't want to have to *plan* when he could see her. That didn't seem fair when frankly, he'd just found her.

But he would take these moments. Stolen as they were, he would still take every single one of them that he was given. Under club lights, with people shouting all around them, *this* was what he'd waited all week for.

Gabbie's fingers tightened into his shirt, and her eyes danced with happiness as she peered up at him. "I thought you weren't going to get here tonight."

Michel chuckled, the sound muted from the level of the music. "I didn't mean to take so long."

She shrugged, still pleased.

That's all he wanted.

Her *pleased*.

Because *he* did it to her.

What was happening to him?

"But the better question," she said, grinning in that sly way of hers that he adored so much, "is when are we going to *leave*?"

Michel smirked right back. "Whenever you want, babe."

Then, their fun could *really* get started.

• • •

The best way to start a morning?

With a woman *sitting* on your face.

Michel decided next to fucking Gabbie, getting her taste coating his tongue as she rocked against his mouth and begged for more was probably the best thing in the world. The more turned on this woman was, the hotter she became. Her skin, her pussy, her *cum*. All of it.

And he couldn't fucking get enough.

Michel wrapped his palms around her ass to hold her steady as her movements became more frantic the closer she came to her orgasm. Her thighs tightened around his head, and he looked up to see her fingers digging into the leather-covered headboard as her head tipped back, and the sexiest moan fell from her lips.

"Oh, my God ... *Michel.*"

Yeah, nothing better.

She shuddered when he drew her clit between his lips, and sucked hard on the bud. Her thighs clenched as she broke all apart above him, those cries becoming breathless with every spasm of her body. He decided, too, that nothing was better than watching Gabbie get off because he was the one making her do it.

It was primal, really. That tightening in his chest, and the male pride that coursed through his system. His fucking cock ached like nothing else, which wasn't something he bothered to hide when she slid down his body like a cat who had just gotten her cream. That sexy smile curving her pink lips teased him as she drifted lower on the bed until her hands were stroking him awake, too.

Her fingers flexed around his cock—stroking him harder at the tip, and then looser at the base. And when she added her mouth to the mix, too? Sucking him as she jerked him off?

Michel had no fucking control. His hands fisted into those red curls of hers, and his hips lifted to get just a little bit more of his dick into the wet, warm heat of her mouth. That tongue of hers flicked and flattered against the head of his cock every time she came up again, making him see stars whenever he closed his eyes.

"Holy fuck," Michel grunted out. "You're going to make me blow my load if you don't slow down."

She didn't seem to care.

He was fine with that.

Michel lost himself in the feeling of her mouth and hands working his dick while he reveled in the silkiness of her hair tangling with his fingers, not to mention the curve of her back, and the peak of her ass as she lifted it higher.

Yeah.

He came harder than he expected.

Gabbie took every fucking drop, too.

Was it supposed to be this hard to breathe?

Michel released Gabbie's hair from his grip, so that he could scrub his hands down his face and try to see straight again. As he blinked, and peeked through his fingers, he watched her rest along the curves of his body, her softer form melding perfectly with his hard lines.

God.

She was a sight.

"That was a *great* way to wake up," she told him, grinning.

Michel chuckled. "Tell me about it, although that's not what I meant to do."

Her eyebrow arched. "Why?"

"It's five—nobody is going to see you leave my house because I doubt any of them are watching me right now. It's a *Sunday.* Everybody will be trying to get as much sleep as they can before they have to show up and make face at church."

That was just how it worked for made men.

Michel lived his whole life watching it.

"So, you woke me up, and then decided to eat my pussy just so you could tell me I had to leave?"

He eyed her, and shrugged. "Kind of, yeah."

She smacked his side lightly with her palm. "*Arsehole.*"

"I'll make it up to you."

And he would.

"Let's get up," he added.

Gabbie made a disgusted noise. "*Fine.*"

It took them no time at all to get dressed, and head downstairs.

"I can't believe you're kicking me out of your place first thing in the morning," Gabbie joked

She tossed him a sexy little wink over her shoulder. At the same time, she pulled on her shoes and jacket. Michel lingered a few steps down the hall, leaning with his shoulder to the wall to keep himself from grabbing a hold of her. If he did that, then he was going to pull her back to bed. The two of them would never leave it.

"Do you do this to *all* the women you bring home?"

She still had that joking tone, sure, but Michel's reaction didn't factor that in at all. He pushed away from the wall in a blink, and crossed the small bit of space between them before she had even looked up from the zipper of her jacket.

He caught her around the waist with one arm, and his lips came down on hers with bruising intent. He only had *one* thing in mind, and he needed to make sure it was absolutely clear to this woman, so she never had to wonder about it. Even if she *wasn't* wondering at all, or she didn't care, he still wanted his position to be understood between the two of them.

Gabbie's sweet little gasp was swallowed up by his kiss. She still tasted like *him*—like their sex, and his bed. Her warm mouth only urged him on, and he couldn't stop himself from letting his hands travel over her body as he pushed her into the wall.

She squirmed under his hold, the same way she did in bed when he pinned her down, and fucked her harder. And yet, never once did she break their kiss, even as her nails slipped under his T-shirt to score lines down his back.

Fuck.

He loved that sting.

But he was reminded of the time.

Their situation.

And what he wanted her to know.

Michel pulled away from the kiss before he could get too carried away. He didn't miss the way Gabbie pouted, but really, it only made his dick twitch. Like he might enjoy showing her just what he could do with that pout of hers.

Back on task, Michel.

Right, right.

"There's no other women coming in here," he said.

Gabbie blinked. "What?"

"No women. Not here. Just you."

"I was—"

Michel nodded, stopping her from saying more. "You were joking, babe, I know. But I wanted that to be clear here. There's no one else I'm seeing in *any* kind of way. It's just you, that's all."

A sweet, sexy smile curved her lips.

"*Just* me, huh?"

"Just you," he echoed.

Gabbie's tongue peeked out to swipe across her bottom lip, and he had the strangest urge to press his thumb against the seam of her mouth just to feel the warmth and wetness she left behind. Everything about this girl did that for him—drove him crazy, and made him want to do things he'd never gave a single shit about before.

Why?

He didn't know.

It didn't matter.

It just *was*.

"That's good to know," she told him.

Michel winked, and dropped one more quick kiss to her lips. He couldn't afford much more because if he did drag her back to bed, the risk was too high that someone might see her leave later in the day. *God.* He wanted to keep her here, though. So badly it made his fucking heart ache like nothing else ever had.

Gabbie didn't miss the shift in his mood if her lowering gaze was any indication. That soft smile slipped from her lips, and she patted his cheek with a gentle palm. "Next time, right?"

"Yeah, babe, next time."

"We'll figure something out."

"You know it."

Her smile was back.

He liked that better.

"I better get going," she said, slipping out from under his embrace. "But call me later, aye?"

Michel nodded. "I will."

He was fine with turning to watch her open the front door of his house, and step out on the stoop. He only started to turn away when the door began to close behind her, and she was almost out of his view.

Then, the shooting started. Bullets peppered the side of his house as tires screeched somewhere outside. Glass shattered.

She screamed.

The first thing Michel ran for was *her.*

TEN

All Gabbie had to do was close her eyes, and she could hear the bullets again. She could smell the crisp air that suddenly tasted *bad*, *dirty*, and *wrong* as she dropped to the ground to get out of the way. She could feel the panic swelling in her heart again, squeezing so feckin' tight that she couldn't breathe.

Behind her eyes, she saw it all.

Clear.

Painful.

So real.

Because it was real.

It did happen.

"Get out of me feckin' way before I *nail* my goddamn fist to your mouth permanently, you absolute *gobshite*."

Gabbie knew her father was in the hospital before he ever even stepped a single foot inside her room. She could hear his bellowing all the way down the hallway. She wasn't exactly sure where Michel was now, but she was hoping he managed to get out of sight. He'd slipped out of her room when people from her family started showing up, and things got a little tense in the waiting room because he was simply there, sitting in a chair.

It pissed her off.

She wanted *him*.

No one would understand. He wasn't like *them*. He wasn't *their* people. He was the other—the outsider, and the enemy. They wouldn't care that all she wanted was for him to crawl in her hospital bed, wrap her in his arms, and hide her away from the rest of the world while she waited for her father to arrive.

She closed her eyes, pain slicing through her heart because she was quite aware of just how alone she was in her hospital room despite the nurse that tittered around. She hadn't been injured—not *really*. A few scrapes from falling to the wood of the front porch to avoid the spray of bullets. A bruise on her knee from Michel dragging her back inside the safety of the house as he shouted for her to keep her head down.

Still, the few injuries and stress of the day were enough for the hospital to decide to keep her overnight given it had her glucose levels rising dangerously. Police came in, too. They took her statement—not that she had anything to say because she was well aware of how this life and world worked. She couldn't speak at all, so she mostly lied when asked for details. They took her clothes; the hospital gave her a gown to wear, and strapped a paper bracelet to her arm that designated her as a patient.

She didn't want to be here at all.

Anywhere but *here*.

Gabbie didn't know …

Would she have survived if he hadn't came out to help her?

Would she still be here?

She couldn't think on it for very long. It took no time at all before her father had made his way down the hallway, and darkened her doorway. The nurse in the corner, refilling her water jug and cup of ice, didn't even notice his presence until she turned to leave and *there he was*. All towering six-feet-five-inches of an angry Irishman who looked like he was about to kill her if she didn't get the feck out of his way.

"*Move*, lass," he uttered through clenched teeth.

The nurse blinked. "Excuse me?"

"*Get out.*"

That time, his words echoed back to them as it bounced off the walls from the level his tone took in his anger. The nurse didn't waste time getting the hell out of the room, and honestly, Gabbie didn't blame the girl.

She was ready to shrink away when her father's gaze landed on her, too. Funny how that worked … except it wasn't funny at all.

"*Gabbie*," he said, voice thick with emotion she couldn't place.

Gabbie stared at her hands. "I … I'm so—"

The apology was the first thing she thought to say. Not because she blamed herself for being at the wrong place at the wrong time, but simply because whenever her father was mad, the first thing she did was apologize for angering him.

"Don't … *Christ*, lass, don't you *dare*."

She looked up, then, finding her father just beyond the doorway of the hospital room. At his sides, his fists clenched into tight, shaking balls. In fact, his entire body vibrated the same way, shudders wracking his shoulders as his jaw tightened almost rhythmically.

Charles let out a hard breath, his gaze taking her in on the bed like he was trying to imprint every inch of her to his memory. Or maybe, he was finally taking her in and making sure she was, in fact, fine. She didn't know what he had been told when he got the call that she'd been involved in a drive-by, and was now at the hospital.

Knowing him, he had not taken it well.

At all.

She could tell just by looking at him that he hadn't taken it well. She didn't need her father or someone else to confirm it.

All of his fears for her … he was staring at.

Wordlessly, her father closed the door to the hospital room so that their conversation could not be overheard. Or maybe it was that he didn't want anyone else to see his very obvious fear and pain as he regarded his daughter again. She sat still on the edge of the bed as he closed the space between them—she was back to *that* again, back to not being able to look him in the eyes.

He had to know.

Where she *was* when it happened.

With Michel.

"Last night," he said quietly, directly in front of her, "what did you tell me?"

The lump in her throat grew thicker.

She couldn't talk.

"*Gabbie*, speak to me," Charles ordered.

"I said I was going to bed early," she whispered.

"*But?*"

"I snuck out the back, and met up with Michel."

Peeking up, she saw her father nod. "Where you were with him *this morning*, aye."

Oh, *God*.

"Yeah."

People were wrong.

The truth was *not* easier than a lie.

"I knew," her father said, dragging in a heavy breath as he spoke, "that you were seeing the young Italian man for a while now. I hoped you might come to me with it, but when you didn't … I knew that I had to make a choice. I had to send a message to them—to *him*—that this was unacceptable to me."

Gabbie's brow furrowed. "But *why*? Why can't I—"

Her father grabbed her arms, then, both of his hands circling around her hard enough to *hurt*. His fingers dug into her skin until her muscles wanted to protest from the ache. He shook her hard, forcing her to glance up at him so she could see the sheer *terror* staring back at her.

"I *made a choice*," he said, "because I believed you even though you'd lied to me again and *again*. Do you understand me? I made a choice this morning that would make it clear to that young man where I stood about what was happening when my back was turned. And because you lied to me—"

Gabbie blinked. "You ordered the drive-by?"

Charles let her go, and took a step back, his hands shaking again. She understood, then, why her father was so entirely set off balance. She got it—*really* feckin' felt it in her bones like nothing else in her life before this moment. Her own father had almost killed her. Oh, sure, she understood that her lies and his trust in her had caused it, but his choice was still made.

He could have been burying her.

He understood it, too.

More than anyone.

It hurt her in a visceral way to stare at her father in those seconds. For more reasons than just the obvious. She wanted to be *mad* at him because didn't she have every right to feel that way over his mistake? And yet, she felt most mad at herself because she, too, was at fault here for this mess.

In a way …

There were parts of her that still didn't want to feel the hints of emotions teasing at the very fringes of her senses. The betrayal that clung to the echoing beats of her heart, and the disappointment that ached in her bones with every breath she took. If she *truly* felt those things, then she would be bitter.

She loved her father.

Loved him so much.

Gabbie never said he was perfect, and she was the first to point out his flaws. Yet, he was still her father first before anything else, and she was not willing to let something like bitterness or contempt stain that love she felt for him.

But it was still there.

Taunting her.

She was disgusted that *this* was where it had finally brought them. To this moment of her almost dying. And for what? Because of a feud she had never really understood? Because her father and his men couldn't play nice with others, and didn't care to try? She was well aware that she didn't have a great understanding of the mafia and the world her father lived in every day of his life, but was it worth this?

Was she worth *that?*

Gabbie didn't know.

She didn't think her father did, either.

"It was *you* that ordered the drive-by this morning," she said again.

It needed to be said again.

It had to be heard again.

"I'm sorry," Charles mumbled. "I'm so sorry, Gabbie."

"*This has to stop, Daddy,*" she told him. "Don't you understand? It has to stop now."

He nodded fast. "And it will. It *will.*"

She wanted to believe him.

But could she?

• • •

Gabbie was almost drifting to sleep in the hospital bed when the jiggling of the doorknob had her blinking back awake instantly. The hospital had long since quieted—visiting hours were over, and despite her father's complaints, he wasn't allowed to stay.

She ate a snack that the sweet nurse brought in, and realized all at once just how knackered she was. Sure, she kept asking for her phone so that she could call Michel, but no one seemed to know where in the hell it went. She resigned herself to falling asleep when nothing on the small TV seemed interesting, and she really didn't have anything else to do.

Peeking over the pile of blankets, and expecting the same nurse to check in like she had done an hour earlier, Gabbie froze in the bed. It wasn't the nurse at all.

"*Michel.*"

He winked, gave her a smile, and slipped in the room without ever saying a word. He closed the door behind him, and she swore it didn't even click when it latched shut. His footsteps couldn't even be heard as he quickly crossed the room, and came to the side of her bed.

"Did they make you leave?" she asked.

He shrugged, his hand coming up to stroke her cheek and move some of the wild curls out of her face. The graze of his fingertips along her cheekbone was enough to make her eyes flutter shut, and she reveled in warm, soft skin against her own.

"No one *made* me do anything," he said, making her open her eyes again to look at him above her. "But it wasn't exactly comfortable out there. Someone was kind enough to say I probably didn't want to be here when your father finally came around, so I slipped out and walked around until visiting hours were over. I snatched an ID someone had left sitting around in the cafeteria to get back in your ward once everyone was already gone."

He flashed the badge in question, chuckling. "I'll drop it off at the nurses' station before I head out again."

She blinked. "You didn't actually leave?"

Michel smiled. "Why would I leave, Gabbie?"

"I just ... never mind."

In the next breath, he bent down so that he could drop a sweet kiss to the very tip of her nose. Gabbie couldn't help but grin under her pile of blankets, suddenly a hell of a lot warmer than she had been before. His hands slipped in to cup her face, so he could tilt her head up a bit, and get *another* kiss.

That one wasn't as innocent.

Still sweet, sure.

But it burned her from the inside out, too.

"Scared me to *death*," he whispered against her lips.

"Me, too."

"I bet."

"Thanks for staying."

Michel laughed darkly. "Oh, I wasn't going anywhere. Fucking *nobody* was keeping me out of here, no matter what I had to do to get back to you."

God, she loved that.

And him.

She was starting to think she loved him, too. No, that was a lie. She didn't *think* it at all. She knew it, deep down in her heart that raced whenever he was near, and the way he made her feel just by looking at her. She knew he was in a room simply by the way her skin prickled in the best of ways. It was crazy—she would never deny that.

But love didn't make sense, right?

Love was supposed to be insane.

Nonsensical, even.

People started wars over love. They *died* for it. To keep something they cherished so very much, they would do anything for it.

So would she.

The lump in her throat was back again. It had disappeared for a time, but now that her mind was running *crazy* ... it was back to keep her silent again.

"You okay?" Michel asked.

Gabbie smiled. "As long as you're here, I'm grand."

She could tell him another time.

They would have more days.

Her father said it, right? He was going to make sure this didn't happen again. Charles would stop this stupid feud so that it didn't get any worse. Surely, that meant she would have a lot more time with Michel, so this could wait.

"I'm here for as long as you want me," he said.

"I like that."

Michel sighed, adding quieter, "Well, at least until early in the morning, and then I'll slip out again. Don't want anyone having a fit seeing me here, right?"

Gabbie scowled. "*Yeah.*"

"Don't do that. Only smiles with me, babe."

Her laughter colored up the room. "Get in this bed with me, then."

"Whatever you want."

Michel wasted no time crawling into the bed, and while there wasn't nearly enough room for them both, somehow, they made due. Both ended up on their sides with Gabbie tucked into Michel's chest, and his arms locked around her form like bars keeping her away from the rest of the world.

Exactly like she wanted.

He pressed a kiss to her forehead.

All the exhaustion that had been teasing her right before Michel came into the room was back in a blink. Her eyes drifted closed, but she didn't mind now that he was here. No doubt, he would wake her up in the morning to say goodbye, too.

That was all that mattered to her.

In her dreams, she swore he whispered, "*Ti amo, cara bella mia. Sempre.*"

She didn't know what that meant.

It still sounded *lovely*.

• • •

"All right, into the car you go, lass." Charles bent down just enough that he could stare at the man driving. "And you, you feckin' wagon, you best make sure you drive like you know how to. You understand me?"

"Yeah, boss. I got you."

Charles smiled, and straightened. "As I thought."

He held opened the back passenger door for Gabbie, and she just shook her head before slipping into the car. The heater had been turned on which was enough to make her feel slightly better—at least she wasn't standing in the wind, anymore. Her father had thought far enough ahead to make sure that he brought her a new coat, and a change of clothes to wear after her discharge from the hospital.

She was *not* walking out of there in a feckin' gown.

Charles had been the first person, after Michel left, to enter her hospital room that morning. Visiting hours hadn't even started when he showed up, but there he was. Apparently, he had gotten on the phone with the doctor to have her discharged as early as possible.

She was grateful.

It was only once her father was in the car, too, next to her in the back seat that the driver pulled away from the curb. She passed the hospital a look over her shoulder, watching it and the bad memory of being brought there fading the further away they drove.

Another silver lining.

"How're your glucose levels today?" her father asked.

She shrugged. "Better."

It wasn't a lie.

Her body still ached, and mostly, she was knackered. Yes, she had gotten a restful sleep, but trauma was exhausting in general. The bed was going to be her favorite place for the next several hours, simple as that.

"I just can't wait to get into my bed," she said, sighing.

Charles stiffened.

Gabbie didn't miss it. "What?"

"Nothing," he said carefully, "I just thought you might like to stay with me for a wee bit ... this was a lot to take in, that's all."

She blinked at the passing buildings. "But I want to go home."

"And I would like to see you with me for a bit."

"Daddy—"

"Gabbie, don't argue. We'll discuss this another time."

She *would* have argued.

But she was so feckin' done.

"Fine," she grumbled.

Not that this was a surprise. Charles had never changed in all her years, and the first thing she thought about when it came to her father was just how overprotective he could be when it came to her. She should have expected this to happen, honestly.

"Things are about to get better," her father said quietly.

She glanced back at him. "Will they?"

"*Much* better, sweetheart."

She had a feeling he meant the Italians.

She *hoped* that was it.

For more reasons than he knew.

ELEVEN

Maybe it was because Michel had grown up around the kind of wealth that was both stunning and surreal, but the sight of money never did very much for him. Not like some people who practically salivated at the sight of stacked bills on the table.

He'd once watched his grandfather buy his grandmother a thirty-carat gold chandelier the size of a small car to hang in her library just because he thought it would go with the *theme*. His mother bought herself a private jet for her fortieth birthday and didn't even ask for the price tag before handing over a card to pay for it. The watch on his wrist, currently, cost an easy five grand and that was before the case he used to store it and keep it constantly spinning to maintain time.

Money wasn't a new concept to Michel. There was nothing about it that he found particularly miraculous because he'd been desensitized to it. No doubt, that was his incredible privilege staring back at him—someone might find it disgusting that they assumed he didn't truly appreciate the value of money, even if that wasn't the case.

It simply didn't make any difference to him when money was around. Which was a topic for another day, but he found it also did him a lot of good at times where money was on the table.

Everyone else in the room?

Watching that money.

Michel?

Unimpressed.

His father liked to say that nothing good came from men who were entranced by a small stack of bills. They couldn't be trusted not to *touch it*. Seemed simple, right? Dante had a point, a *good* one.

Michel never had any desire to reach out and put his hands on something that didn't belong to him just because it looked pretty and seemed foreign to him. Someone else, though? It became a constant urge they had to fight.

Nothing good in this business.

"Michel, you're up next," Sal said.

Tribute was another concept that wasn't anything new to Michel. Growing up, he'd watched more than one tribute meeting from afar as his father sat at the head of a table, accepting his payments from every Capo in *la famiglia*. He'd also partook in the Cosa Nostra tradition more than once during his high school years when he was dealing drugs, and had to pay a portion of his earnings to one of his cousins making their way up in the ranks of the mafia.

Once a month, people gathered to meet whomever they owed their portion to, and handed it over. It wasn't the *actual* tribute—that happened when the made man took *his* portion from the earnings he made through several venues, including people like Michel, to the man heading the family. *The boss.* Like Michel's father.

He'd been lucky enough, or that's what people would tell him, to be on both ends of the spectrum. The person on the front lines making money for the Capo, and the person in the room when that Capo brought his earnings into his boss to pay the tribute. He understood what happened now when he paid this money to the Capo, and he knew *very well* what would happen when Sal took his portion higher up, too.

Some details of tribute might vary between families. Things like how much of a percentage one might pay from their earnings, or how they might pay it to the boss be it through an envelope filled with cash, illegal transfers through offshore banks, or even safety deposit box pickups. Those were the minor details.

But the tradition itself?

Tribute?

Never changed.

One always had to pay the boss.

Michel stepped up to the table in the restaurant as the other man moved back, already done with his time there. The stack of bills on the table filled over half of it, though, all separated in different denominations. It was enough to make the man— a new bookie, Michel thought—glance back to look at the cash one more time.

In front of Sal sat a black notebook which he used to write down each person's initials, and the money they brought in. It was how the man made sure no one was stiffing him when he could look back *months* for trends in payments, and more. There was always a bit of variance month to month, but nothing major. And if someone had constant variances that were concerning, then Sal had the proof staring back at him to deal with the issue.

Nobody wanted that.

To someone else, they might open that book and wouldn't have a clue what they were looking at. Sal didn't seem to have that problem at all because he knew exactly what he was doing to keep track of his money and people.

Sal was already scratching Michel's initials down on the paper before he even spoke to him—*M.M.* "Put it in, and pay it down."

Michel, unconcerned about the rest of the money on the table, and the other people in the room who were currently waiting their turn to pay or leave, pulled out a three-inch stack of bills that he'd made over the last month. *Another* month working for Sal as a dealer. Almost three altogether. A big part of him was ready to just focus on what he came to Detroit for.

Med school.

Before Sal could tell him to do it, Michel slipped half of the bills into the machine that would easily count the money, and spit it out on the other side. Once that half a stack had gone through, the machine beeped loudly, and a number came up on the screen in digital, red numerals. Sal nodded, and pointed his pen at the machine before plucking up the neat stack on the other side to begin separating it out by denomination.

And also, *recount.*

Because despite having the machine to do the counting for him, Sal was particular. Like all made men were. Every man Michel knew in this life liked to say the mafia was a nickel and dime business. Every single cent had to be counted, recounted, and possibly checked again.

"Again," Sal said.

Michel put the second stack in as the Capo worked on the bills in his hand. "I started classes at the beginning of the month, so this is my last one."

Here it was the end of September, and he barely blinked.

Sal nodded. "If you want to keep this up while you're there—"

"I would rather not, actually."

A chuckle left the Capo.

"Keeps you busy, huh?"

Not *that* busy.

Michel was simply done, at least for here in Detroit. He wasn't so stupid that he didn't recognize some of his problems for what they were in the grand scheme. At home, he never would have put up with some of the shit he did here simply because he was *Dante Marcello's* son. A boss's child dabbling in the family business, and nothing more. That afforded him respect he didn't get here.

Was it petty of him?

A little.

Didn't change the fact it was true.

"I need to focus," Michel said, "so this is my last one."

Which also wasn't a lie. He tried to keep up the dealing for the month as he started back with classes for his second year of pre-med, but it was a fine line. And not one he wanted to walk.

"Sounds fine."

The machine beeped, and a number only a few dollars off from the first half of Michel's payment popped up on the screen. Sal made a noise under his breath— appreciative and approving because that was the only way he said anything to let his people know that he thought they had done a good job over the month to bring in money.

Michel never did this for the money, though.

That sound meant nothing to him.

"You're good to go," Sal said, scratching Michel's total into the notebook beside his initials. "And remember to keep your head down, huh?"

Michel nodded. "You got it."

Turning around, he was ready to make a beeline for the door, and head the hell out of there. He had plans that afternoon, and he wanted to get to them sooner rather than later. Especially as those plans included a sexy redhead with green eyes that he swore was the whole world staring back at him when she looked his way.

"Oh, one more thing, before I forget," Sal called at his back.

Michel's steps slowed to a halt as he tossed a look over his shoulder. "What's that?"

"At the end of October, we've got a meeting. You were requested to be there."

"What kind of meeting?"

"One you're to attend."

Except he was only one month into his second year of pre-med, and he really didn't have time to be running around because *Sal* told him to. "Yeah, but—"

Sal glanced up, and his gaze narrowed in on Michel. "It's not a request, and it wasn't permission for you to ask questions, either."

Well, then …

"All right," Michel muttered.

It did leave him unsettled.

"Don't fuck this up, Marcello."

That was when he knew …

The lack of a nickname did it.

He and Sal weren't friends anymore.

Michel was okay with that.

• • •

"Your father was considering taking a trip to California with me soon," his mother said on the phone as Michel walked up the steps to the small house he rented. It was better than some of the shitty apartment setups closer to the college, and far better than *dorms*. It meant farther to travel when he was attending classes, but he didn't care. "And I thought, I *may* be able to convince him to make a stop in Michigan, too."

Michel smiled, the idea of his parents stopping in for a visit making him happier than he thought it would. After the summer he had running from one end of Detroit to the other, getting the shit kicked out of him, and *more* … well, that reprieve of his parents would be nice. Now that the end of September was here, and October was looming, he was ready to put the summer behind him as much as he could.

"I might even be able to convince Catherine to come along," his mother said.

Michel laughed at that. "So, she could complain about the city like she does when she's in New York City?"

"She doesn't—"

"A little, Ma."

"Yeah, well, that's your sister."

And he loved her.

Mostly.

"When were you thinking of coming?" he asked.

"The New Year likely, since you've said you're not coming home for the holidays. But also for Dante. You know how your father is when I want him to take a trip with me. He needs to plan *all the things*. Such a fickle man. He needs to make everything far more difficult than it actually *is*."

Michel could imagine his mother saying that while rolling her eyes *and* making air quotes just because. Sometimes, his parents seemed like two entirely different people, and one might wonder how they had come to be married and in love at all. He was not one of those people because he had a private look at his mother and father—they were far more alike than they were different in more aspects than people were privy to.

"Well, just let me know when you're coming and I will make sure to set some time aside for it, okay?" he asked.

"Oh, you need to *make time* for your mother, do you?"

Michel grinned. "Never, Ma. All my time is for you."

"Better be."

Italian mothers and their boys.

It never changed.

"I know I don't tell you this a lot … but that's mostly because you've never asked, Michel," she said, her tone growing soft like it only did when she was speaking to her children, "but Catherine—your *mother*, not your sister—would be very proud of you much like we are. I hope you know that."

"I don't really think about it, Ma."

Catrina quieted before saying, "Well, if you ever do, I'm sure she is."

Michel stopped on the stoop just a foot away from the front door. Glancing to the side, he couldn't quite shrug off the heaviness that had come to rest on his shoulders in that moment. There were a lot of things about his biological mother that he didn't know but that wasn't because Catrina held back. It was because he never thought to *ask*.

"Do you think she loved me, Ma? I know you said I was born because of bad circumstances, and not because she chose the situation, but—"

"She died loving you. She loved you so much she died *for* you."

"Yeah, okay."

"Now, back to *you*."

Michel rolled his eyes as he stepped up to the front door of his home, pulling out a set of keys to unlock the front door. "There's nothing interesting about me, Ma."

"You're staying out of trouble?"

"Sure."

Mostly.

He knew better than to tell his Ma otherwise. Sure, his parents never said much about his choice to dabble in the family business throughout his high school years, but he didn't know if it would be the same when he was in a whole other state than them, and his father couldn't control the men *around* him.

So …

He kept quiet.

Catrina was saying something else, but Michel wasn't listening. He was more confused by the fact someone opened his door before he could even turn the key in the lock. He laughed at the grinning woman on the other side of the threshold, forgetting all about the fact his mother was still on the phone with him.

"You weren't supposed to get here until *later*, Gabbie," Michel said.

His girl winked. "Are we going to complain, though?"

"Gabbie?"

Michel heard his mother's voice on the phone. It brought him back down to reality *fast*. He put one finger up to ask Gabbie for a second after he stepped inside the house, and closed the door behind him. "Sorry, Ma, I just … have a friend here at my place. I will call you back, okay?"

"A *friend?*"

He sucked air through his teeth, eyeing Gabbie from the side as she waved her fingers over her shoulder before disappearing down the entry hall. Did he mention she wasn't wearing anything but one of *his* T-shirts? Because *yeah*, fuck. She even answered the door like that, goddammit. A peek of her ass flashed him before she turned the corner to head toward his bedroom.

She didn't have panties on, either.

Yeah, good God.

Because God was so good to him.

Okay, he could see how this was going to end.

Well.

It was going to end very well.

"Michel, a *friend?*" his mother asked.

Nothing like his ma to remind him why he couldn't have an erection right at this moment, or a reason to be ashamed of the one that was growing in his jeans. "Yeah, Ma, a friend. One I think you would love. So, I'm going to get back to her, and—"

"Call me later," Catrina said, a sly smile in her tone. "Because you *will* call me back about this."

"I'll try."

"Michel—"

"Love you, Ma."

He hung up the phone quicker than ever before, and dropped all his shit right there in the hallway. He discarded his clothes as he walked through the house, too, and was mostly naked by the time he got to the bedroom to find Gabbie sitting on her knees in the middle of the bed. Her fingers curled into the hem and neckline of his shirt, twisting and pulling the fabric to flash her bare stomach and a sliver of her pussy at him.

"*Goddamn.* You're killing me here," he said.

Gabbie laughed. "But that's the fun part."

She wasn't wrong.

Flashing a foil packet at him, Gabbie flashed her teeth in a wicked smile before she tossed it to the end of the bed. Michel couldn't shed the rest of his clothes or get that condom rolled down his length fast enough. His fingers felt like they were fumbling *way* too much. She was already on her back, red curls splaying out over the pillows as he climbed between her thighs, his hands curving around her thighs to widen them even more.

"*God*, yeah," she mumbled.

He reveled in the sting of her fingernails dragging down his back as he buried himself as deep as he could get inside the heaven that was Gabbie's pussy. There was something about the way she took him every time, stretching open for him and coating him with her arousal, that drove him *crazy*.

Her legs wrapped around his waist when he let them go. He only did that, so he could get his hands wrapped into her hair. Or one of them, anyway. His other found her throat as he started to *really* pound into her. He felt the thrum of her heartbeat pulsing hard against his touch, and every noise she made vibrated to his palm.

"*Harder,*" he heard her whisper.

His hand slipped up higher on her throat, pushing her head back as he cupped the spot just beneath her jaw. Those green eyes of hers blew wide to watch him hover above her as their bodies moved together in a rhythm he now found familiar. The way her lips trembled, the way she withered under him the closer she came to her orgasm, and how her nails dug in deeper when he was getting her *just right.*

Fuck, yeah.

"Come on, come on," he urged. "Give it to me."

She did.

And it was *amazing.*

Crying his name, a pink flush rushing down her throat and breasts, and so fucking perfect. He tipped his head down to capture her nipple between his teeth as his back tensed with his own oncoming orgasm. It took nothing at all for him to fall over the edge, too, emptying into latex while pinning her to the bed at the same time.

"Mmm."

Gabbie's happy little sound made him laugh against her breast. She went from wild to *sweet* in an instant, and he loved that.

Out of breath, but feeling better than he had in *days*, Michel asked, "Did you hear about a meeting around the end of October?"

"A month from now?"

"Yeah, babe."

He didn't know if the one Sal mentioned was going to involve the Irish, but he figured he should at least ask Gabbie. Her father had kept her at his place for a week after the shooting, but then she threw a fit that apparently convinced him it was time to send her home. That was two weeks ago—so it was a toss-up if she knew anything or not about a possible meeting.

Plus, Sal hadn't given details.

It might not even *be* the Irish.

Except ... who else would it be?

Gabbie's head popped up a little more, so she could see him as she spoke. "No, I haven't heard anything. But if there is one, I'll find out."

Michel grinned, and rolled them both over so that she was sitting on top of him. He pressed a fast, hard kiss to her lips, taking both of their breaths away again in the process. He'd just got finished fucking her, but already, with her shifting on top of his still semi-hard cock, he was ready again.

"That's what I fucking love about you," he said against her lips.

She got shit done.

Gabbie stilled. "Do you?"

Michel blinked, pulling away slightly. "What?"

"Love me?"

He didn't even have to think about it.

Not really.

Nobody ever said love had to make sense.

Or even ... *be sane.*

"Entirely too much," he admitted.

Gabbie's bottom lip caught under her teeth as she whispered, "Good to know, Michel."

"Why is that?"

"It's only fair that if I love you, then you should love me, too."

Ah.

She was right.

That was good to know.

Gabbie smiled up at him, her grin turning a little shy at the same time. "I know you're busy with school and so am I but—"

"I'm going to make time for *you*. I will figure it out."

That much was a promise.

Maybe it would only be once a week, or even an hour every couple of weeks. That didn't matter to Michel as long as he got that time with her.

"You better," she said.

He just kissed her again.

• • •

Thanks to Gabbie, Michel learned the meeting was, in fact, something between the Italian Vannozzo Cosa Nostra and the Irish Casey family a couple of weeks before it even happened. It was just enough time for him to think he was prepared for what might happen when it finally took place, but apparently, he was wrong.

They also ended up switching dates at the last minute, too, so instead of the meeting happening at the end of October, they set it up for the first Saturday of November. He was feeling the cold chill in the air because of it, too, but he didn't think it was just from the wind.

Michel still stiffened at the Irish flag hanging proudly over a pub's door as he stepped out of the back of a car. Sal was already waiting at the curb, his arms crossed over his chest as he gave Michel a once-over.

"You managed to throw on a blazer today," Sal said.

"I dress fine on regular days, too."

"Sure, sure. Cat's out of the bag, then?" Sal gestured at the flag in question, smirking a bit. "You know now what you're here for."

"Is the Vannozzo boss showing up today for this meeting, too?"

Sal made a noise under his breath. "No, I was told, *the New York fuck is your issue who caused a problem, so you deal with it.*"

"Interesting."

Michel wasn't sure if he believed that, or not. Any boss he knew dealing in Cosa Nostra would be quick to make sure he was at a meeting that would handle another family. Especially if said family was in the same city as him.

He didn't call Sal out on his lie, though.

Now was not the time.

Sal reached out, and clasped a hand tightly to Michel's shoulder as other Italians stepped out of their vehicles, too. "The Irish boss called this in, and I was nice enough to oblige on account of *you.* We don't need you causing any more issues, right?"

Why was it just him?

It hadn't been *just* him.

Weren't the Italians the ones who decided to go ahead and make asses out of themselves after Michel had already settled the issue with the Irish boss? He'd made a deal, and it was Sal and his men who decided to go against that without caring about what Michel thought.

He might have stirred the pot.

He did *not* make it boil over.

"So," Sal continued, moving forward toward the pub's entrance door with Michel close at his side, "we're going to have this meeting, you're going to sit beside me and keep quiet, and then we'll see where we go from there."

"And you're willing to talk *peace?*" Michel asked.

Sal chuckled. "There is no such thing as peace with the Irish."

Right.

Then what were they even doing here?

Michel was still trying to figure that out.

And Sal, too.

What was his fucking endgame?

TWELVE

"You can stop looking sour anytime, lass," Charles said, taking the glass of black stuff the pub's bartender offered with a nod. "Just because I ask you to sit back and be quiet doesn't mean I plan to do anything rash today."

He kept saying that.

Gabbie found it hard to believe.

Still, there she sat on a stool at the pub where her father decided they were going to hold this meeting with the Italians. She came because her father said that Gabbie being there was a show of his *faith*. He would not cause violence around his daughter when his entire life had been dedicated to keeping her safe.

Okay, that was fair.

And not a lie.

She still *worried*.

"It's time to put an end to this," her father said.

He turned his back to her so that he could survey the floor of the pub and the men inside. Scattered about at different positions, the men remained seated in the booths, waiting for the meeting to finally get started. Out the window, Gabbie could see the different cars that were beginning to pull up. It was just about time for them to start this thing, it seemed.

So, why did she feel so heavy?

Why was her chest tight?

Oh, aye.

Because history told them that nothing good came from Irish and Italians attempting to work together. It simply didn't work that way—they were too different, both culturally and within their respective organizations.

She was a realist.

Even if her father wanted to be an optimist.

A bell chimed overhead, and Gabbie's gaze shifted to the entrance of the pub. The first two people to step inside had her tensing on the stool even as her father offered the men what she considered to be a friendly smile.

Michel stood beside the man dressed in all black. She didn't recognize the other Italian's face, but from what she knew about Cosa Nostra through hearing people talk, he had to be important. Or at the very least, he held *some* title that allowed him to come into a meeting first with a rival family, or even, be there at all.

"Casey," the man greeted.

Gabbie didn't miss the way her father's lips threatened to pull into a scowl at the Italian man standing beside Michel greeting him by his *last name*. A wee bit rude, all things considered. Especially if they were all here to make nice, and calm any of the issues that had been left to fester too long between their two organizations.

Friends didn't spit out last names like it was dirt.

This man did exactly that.

Already, they were starting out in a bad way. Gabbie didn't need for her father to confirm that for her to know it was true. Still, Charles stepped forward with a hand outstretched to take the Italian's that was offered back. The two shook hands before her father gestured at the only table that had been left in the middle of the floor.

A single chair sat on one side.

Two were on the other.

"Sit," Charles said, "and we can begin this meeting."

Michel's gaze drifted to Gabbie, and for the first time, she really stopped to take note of him. She hadn't before only because he was the *one* thing in this pub that she currently felt comforted by, in a way. She didn't think Michel was going to do anything to purposely make this go sour. After spending an entire summer sneaking around with this man, she felt like she probably knew him better than anyone else in her life.

She trusted him.

Others, not so much.

He looked good in his black blazer with a silk shirt underneath that had the top two buttons undone at his throat. It gave her just a peek at the golden skin beneath, and reminded her what it felt like to have that skin pressing against hers in *all kinds of wonderful ways*.

Except this wasn't the time.

But that's what Michel did to her.

Michel passed her a quick smile, and she returned it just as fast. Then, the three men took their respective chairs at the table as the other Italians that had been brought along slowly began to trickle into the pub.

Only a handful.

Six, in total.

The same number of men her father had inside the pub, she noticed. Gabbie had to wonder if that was purposeful, or not. It wasn't the right time to ask, but she assumed yes. She also thought it was very likely that each side here today had a number of men posted outside somewhere to keep an eye on things just in case.

Everybody needed a backup.

"Are you willing to calm the violence on the streets between your family and ours?" the Italian man asked at the table.

Charles brow dipped, but other than that, he didn't give much away. "Are we pretending, then, that your lads didn't attack my family after an agreement had already been reached with your ... friend here? Michel, is it?"

Michel cleared his throat. "I explained the agreement—"

"He doesn't *speak* for us," the Italian man snapped.

"But I did tell you, Sal," Michel argued. "I made it clear what the Irish wanted."

Sal didn't even glance in Michel's direction. In fact, he didn't take his eyes off Gabbie's father. "You seem to be mistaken, Casey. You can't ... attack one of ours, and then expect us to let it go simply because you allowed him to live. That's not how it works."

Charles' back tensed as he leaned forward a bit. "And yet, in almost the same breath, you dared to tell me he doesn't *speak for you*, lad. Which tells me you're willing to play word games, but for what goal? What load of shite are you trying to feed me here because you Italian feckers always have something on the side, don't you?"

Sal stood fast from the table, the chair skidding out from behind him before it crashed to the floor. That sent several men sitting around the pub in booths flying to their feet, too. Someone racked a gun—Gabbie heard the sound echo, but no one was looking away from the three people at the table to really figure out who it was.

Charles stood from his seat, too. Although, he did so with a great deal more grace and care than the Italian man had done. His chair didn't topple over, and he took the time to fix his suit jacket as he eyed Sal with unbidden contempt.

"You *dare* to insult me with childish names?" Sal demanded, pointing a finger at Gabbie's father.

"Are you not accustomed to being told when you're acting like a feckin' eejit, lad?"

Sal's face reddened. "Irish *trash*. That's what all of you are."

"Sal—"

Michel's warning, though he hadn't stood from the table quite yet, was interrupted by the other man shooting him a glare. To his benefit, Michel didn't shrink away from the look, but he did shake his head.

Like he was over it.

Gabbie understood the feeling.

She almost wanted to hide.

She probably should.

This was getting bad, and fast. Her father would have been the first to tell her to slip out the back, and wait until the dust had cleared. On any other day, she might have listened. But at the same time, on any other day, she would not have been there.

She was only there because of Michel.

And her father's request for it.

Gabbie didn't move from her stool because Michel was still sitting at the table, and she worried what might happen when she wasn't there to see it. Men in this life were always far more likely to keep peace and not turn to violence when there was a woman around to check their behavior and inclinations.

Or, that's what her father liked to say.

"A *month*," Charles spat out, his calm façade cracking a bit. "An entire month wasted planning this meeting because I thought—*wrongly*, mind you—that you Italians had a serious need to quit this bollocks between us on the streets. But don't worry, I understand now what this was really about, lad."

"Oh, do tell?"

"You don't want peace. You want a real *war*," her father said, deadly calm again. "And if you continue, I promise that you will get it."

"Is that a threat?"

"Get out of my pub before I blow you out of it, Italian."

"Daddy—"

Michel's gaze flew to Gabbie when she finally decided to speak up. A part of her stupidly thought that *maybe* she could calm this situation back down, and remind her father of exactly why they had decided to do this in the first place. No one wanted a war in the streets of Detroit between two rival criminal families.

It wouldn't do them any good.

It would be *very* bad, though.

Charles lifted a hand, quieting her. "Not a word, lass."

Michel nodded at her. "It's okay."

"And *you*," her father snapped, his attention flying to Michel. "I wonder if your Italian friends here know that you continue to see my daughter when you believe they're not smart enough to be watching you, Michel. Do they know you bed an Irishwoman regularly enough that it's questionable whether you even know which side you're playing for anymore, lad?"

"Daddy!"

Sal's gaze cut to Michel again.

Michel said nothing.

Charles smiled coldly. "Now, get the feck out of my pub."

• • •

"Why would you do that, Da?"

Charles didn't bother to entertain Gabbie's question as they arrived back at his home. Instead, he walked right past her, not even bothering to remove his boots or coat. If that was the game he wanted to play, then she didn't mind going along with it.

"I asked you a question!"

"And I don't have to answer it," he replied dryly. "You're under some sort of impression that I owe you an explanation, Gabbie, and I do not. I am your father, not your friend or otherwise. You are the *child* in this relationship. And it does not matter that you are edging closer to twenty-one every day because at the end of it, that changes *nothing*. I am still the parent, and you are still my child."

Gabbie heard the door open behind her, and footsteps as men trickled into the house. She'd driven to the meeting with her father, and his driver. She came back to his place because this was where her vehicle happened to be.

She didn't plan to stay, though.

Not after today.

"Why would you put my relationship with Michel into the conversation like that?" Gabbie demanded, following her father deeper into the house. Men trailed behind her, too, but she refused to pay them any mind. She was going to get an answer from her father one way or another. He didn't have to *like* it. "If you have something to say about the fact I see Michel, then you should bring it to *me*."

"What good would that do?"

"What?"

In the doorway of his office, Charles spun around to face Gabbie with fire in his eyes. For the first time in as long as she could remember, a part of her wanted to shrink away from the way her father was looking at her right then. So mad, and *disappointed*. It was as though he was seeing her through new eyes, and this was not the person he wanted to see staring back at him.

She could say the same to him.

Still, she held firm.

She didn't move.

"What good would it do me to tell you to stay away from the lad, hmm?" her father demanded sharply. "I think I have said more than enough over the last several months since you've run around with the prick that it's clear I don't *approve*. But whatever it is, you're determined to see it through, so I might as well let you get it out of your system now before reality comes to wake you up."

"What does that even mean?"

Charles scrubbed a hand down his face. "You'll learn in time. As I intend."

"I—"

"And as for that Italian *fecker*," her father continued, "he needs to pick a side, Gabbie. If he wants to entertain the Italians in the daytime, and then shift with my daughter in the shadows when no one is looking, then the man can't be trusted, can he? A lad like that ... his mind is too *sharp*, lass. They had to know what he was doing, and then he can decide what he really wants to do. I know where he comes from, and you have to *watch* him like it, too. I need him to know that I am aware of his choices, and he has others to consider now."

"Are you giving him the ultimatum, then? Them, or *us*?"

Charles arched a brow. "It isn't that *complicated*, sweetheart. You don't have to understand when all I want you to do is follow along."

Wasn't it that complicated?

She thought so.

"Follow along with *what*?"

Charles waved a hand at her, and she knew what that meant without him telling her. A dismissal. He was done with their discussion, and she was quite aware how that worked with her father. Once he was done, he was *finished*. No amount of her prodding or pressing would get more from him.

"I have men to deal with," he told her. "And you haven't checked your sugars since this afternoon. Go do that now."

"My sugars are fine!"

"*Do it.*"

She wasn't a child.

She still felt like it sometimes.

Charles gestured at the group of lads that had attended the meeting, too, and were now waiting in the hallway just beyond Gabbie. Without waiting for her to really move out of their way, they pressed past her in the tight quarters, not even bothering to excuse themselves or pass her a second glance.

She wasn't important.

Dismissed.

"Da—"

"Go, but not too far because I expect to speak with you again later," her father ordered one last time. Then, to the men in the office, he added, "They never intended to settle, lads. That much is clear. We won't act ... *yet*. We'll wait and see what they do first, aye, and then we'll make the hard choices."

Charles shut the door in Gabbie's face, essentially leaving her alone in the hallway. It was amazing to her how she could feel *so many* things all at once. Anger warred with her disbelief and astonishment. Panic swelled in her heart, swirling with anxiety and sadness.

Did it really have to be like *this*?

What did that mean for her?

For Michel?

For *them*?

She didn't know, and she didn't like it.

The muffled voices continued on behind the office door, and she glared at it for a full minute before finally deciding to head out. A few things weren't lost on her, though. Like the way her father said they wouldn't act *yet*. She took that to mean good things. There was still a slight chance this newest problem could be settled … somehow.

Her faith was low.

Hope was still there, though.

Secondly … she heard her father loud and clear on Michel. He wasn't impressed, and he didn't approve, but he knew better than to tell her to stop. He was never going to lock her down, and force her hand where Michel was concerned. Perhaps Charles loved her too much to do that, or he simply knew it would be pointless.

Either way, Gabbie had options, too.

But what exactly were they?

The phone in Gabbie's pocket buzzed, and she knew before even pulling it out who it would be texting her.

Michel.

She wasn't wrong.

His text was simple.

Meet me at the pool tables tonight.

Was it safe?

Did it even matter?

Gabbie looked over her shoulder at her father's office well aware that he had told her to stick around. She wasn't supposed to leave, and he wouldn't be pleased to find out she did, not to mention, that she had gone for Michel.

Those were her options, though.

Him, or *them*.

Her father would always want her to pick the family.

She was always going to pick Michel.

Including now.

I'll be there, she texted back.

THIRTEEN

"I should kill you."

In the backseat of the town car flying through the downtown streets of Detroit, Michel's first thought was *that's nice*. Thankfully, his arrogance decided that probably wasn't the right thing to reply to Sal's statement, and he kept quiet. Turning the screen of his phone off as the Capo looked over at him from the other side of the vehicle, he wanted to keep his last text to Gabbie asking her to meet up with him later private from the man.

Especially after that statement.

"Pardon me?" Michel asked.

"*Yes*, exactly that," Sal snapped back at him. "Excuse *you*, Michel. You seem to forget what blood runs through your veins, and where your loyalties are in this city. Would you care to let me remind you?"

Michel's jaw clenched. "Not particularly."

He seriously doubted Sal gave a shit about Michel's opinion here. And he didn't particularly care to hear Sal spew his bullshit, either.

"I should kill you," the man repeated, shaking his head, the frustration clear in the lines on his brow. Tension drifted through the car, heavy and unpredictable. A lot like what Sal's intentions with Michel were, and what he might do next. "If you were *any other* man, I would fucking kill you for what you did here today."

Michel arched a brow. "And what did I do? Take off classes because *you* demanded I follow you to a meeting today. I'm not a made man—I don't have to follow *your* goddamn rules, Sal."

"I've never been more aware of your standing, Michel. Trust that."

"What in the—"

"The only thing that's keeping you alive right now is the fact your father is the boss of the largest North American crime family—that is *it*. Because if your father wasn't who he is, I would have you delivered to him in enough little pieces that they would never be able to put back together before they buried you."

Okay, that was quite a threat.

Michel respected it, even.

"All this because I chose to see Gabbie Casey," Michel stated.

It wasn't even a question.

Sal laughed a bitter sound, and swung his gaze to the window where he could watch the buildings and streets pass their vehicle by. "*See*, right? That's a funny way to explain how you've been regularly fucking the Irishwoman behind everyone's back, I suppose."

Was it behind their backs, though?

Because Michel didn't think so.

There was a difference between purposely doing something with the intent of hiding it from others, and simply thinking it wasn't anyone's business in the first place. He was more of the latter opinion than the former. This conversation was the perfect example of exactly why he felt like that, too.

They didn't care about him, or what he wanted. All they expected Michel to do was toe the line of what they thought was acceptable, and his opinions didn't matter at all to their endgame. Something he still hadn't figured out, and it was yet another reason why he didn't trust one of them anymore.

"I'm not a made man," Michel told Sal again. "You don't, and will *never*, get to dictate to me who I can date, or otherwise. And even if I *was* a made man, you can bet your ass that I would always defer to my father before I would ever remotely consider defaulting to your opinion or wants about my life."

Michel wanted it heard, no excuses.

It better be understood *now*.

He'd let the Detroit faction of the Marcello family control him a little too much since making friends with Sal, and some of the others in the man's crew. It was made worse when he agreed to work for the man, but that was over now. Sal didn't even have that way to control Michel, anymore, and good thing. Because he'd have told him to shove it right up his ass after today.

"I hope that's fucking clear," Michel said, his tone as sharp as a blade's edge. "Because I don't ever want to have to say it again. You have never—and will never—get a say about me, or my choices because I didn't take *your* oath. Remember that."

Sal chuckled, dark and edgy. "Oh, I can't forget it. Honor, respect, and loyalty, Michel. Three things the code of Cosa Nostra asks from us men. All things you don't seem to have the slightest grasp on in any way."

That was offensive.

Michel refused to show it.

He knew honor, respect, and loyalty better than *anyone*. Especially in this life, and in his own personal dealings. His father made sure he understood that even if he wasn't a made man, his word and being an honorable man who understood his standing against other men would be the only thing that allowed him any kind of respect or trust in their world. Because his last name wouldn't matter if they couldn't trust him. The people who raised him wouldn't make a single difference if a made man felt like Michel was a complication or a traitor to the family.

Like right now, his mind pointed out.

That's exactly what Sal was seeing him as *right now*. A man, who, despite not being made had still been given a place at the table although his voice had never been very loud in the grand scheme of things. Not that it mattered.

He'd still been given that privilege.

And he shit on it.

To Sal, anyway.

It was then that Michel realized exactly how much trouble he was in. It wasn't something Sal said that scared him, or made him think Detroit was no longer safe for him. Rather, his own mind reminding him that he wasn't playing in familiar streets anymore, but in a way, the rules still applied.

Fuck.

The only safe way to get himself out of this situation would be to leave Detroit. And while it would set Michel back a year, likely, for his pre-med … well, it would be worth it. Because it literally meant Michel would at least be able to continue to go to school. If he stayed in this city, there was no guarantee that he would continue to see the morning light.

He was in *danger* here.

And so was she.

It was that fleeting thought that quickly ripped away any idea that Michel might leave Detroit right now. There was no possible way he was going to head out of the city while Gabbie was still here, *alone*. No doubt, with a street war raging on around her that would only make her collateral damage to them in the end.

The Italians didn't care.

Not about her.

She could die—*so what?*

That would be their first and only opinion about it. Michel wasn't quite the fucking same, clearly. He also didn't know what in the hell he could do to either stop this shit from spiraling out of control, or to fix *everything*. Weren't they already beyond that point now? Because it sure as hell felt like it.

Sal glanced over at Michel, his nostrils flaring in his anger. "You're to stay away from the Irishwoman. It's not negotiable."

Right, right.

That was expected.

And impossible.

Michel loved Gabbie.

His heart was in that woman's hands, and his soul was now inexplicably tied with hers. There was no way these idiots were going to keep him from being near that woman if it was what he wanted to do. It might take him a while to see her safely, especially if Sal was going to be a prick about it, but that was the thing.

Michel was a patient fucker.

A silent sort of vicious.

This was not going to work the way Sal wanted it to, but Michel figured now wasn't the time to point it out to the man. He probably didn't care to hear it, anyway. Besides, for the time being, Michel had other things to focus on.

Like getting out of here.

Or stopping it all.

Something.

Gabbie drifted into his mind again—her worried face at the pub in the background of a meeting where she never should have been in the first place. Sal hadn't mentioned she was going to be there, and she'd not told him, either. That led Michel to believe it was probably a last minute decision on her father's part.

Which said something else, too.

Was Charles Casey trying to make a show with his daughter? Was bringing Gabbie today his personal way of showing *faith* to the Italians? Did he just extend his respect to them only to have it shit on by Sal?

Likely.

That had Michel wondering if the Irish boss was really as hard up for this war as Sal was trying to make him out to be. Why would he even attempt to make peace or show faith to the Italians at all if all he intended to do was cause a goddamn problem in the end?

It didn't make sense.

Michel couldn't think on it for too long because Sal decided he wasn't quite done bitching yet. It was hard to focus on one thing when a droning voice continued to mutter in your goddamn ear like a person was supposed to care.

He was beyond caring now.

"Do you know what those Irish bastards did while we were in that meeting today?" Sal asked.

Michel's tone was dry as he replied, "No, but I'm sure you plan to tell me."

Sal's gaze cut to him.

He stared right back, unfazed.

"They attempted attacks on several of our locations in the city," Sal said, not a hint of deception playing on his features. "Molotov cocktails thrown through a couple of windows, and a drive-by shooting at my father's barbershop. They never intended to make peace. This—today—was a ruse to get some of us away from areas they wanted to target. Nothing more, and nothing less."

But was it?

Michel didn't trust something someone told him *just* because they said it. Anyone could lie, and it all started by making their lips move to say the words. Sal wasn't any different or special just because he was a made man.

"But by all means, Michel," Sal continued, dragging him from his thoughts, "if you feel such a strong urge to dabble with the Irish, you should go ahead and do that. Just know what that means for you in this city."

Still, Michel remained silent.

Sal seemed to like that. "Good. I'm glad we understand each other now. Stay the fuck away from them. *All* of them, including the woman."

Right.

Sure.

But probably not.

"I'll have my driver drop you off at your home," Sal said, turning to deliver the order to the man in the driver's seat.

Michel was fast to speak up, then. "I'd rather relax for the night. If he could drop me off at the bar near my place, that'd be great."

The one where he played *pool*.

Where Gabbie was meeting him ...

Sal shook his head as though he didn't know what to do with Michel anymore. "Fine, the fucking bar—maybe a drink will make you less stupid."

Michel brushed off that insult, too.

Barely.

• • •

Michel knew the exact moment Gabbie walked into the bar. It was like every single one of his nerve endings sensed she was close and forced him to look up from the pool cue he was using to leaning against as he surveyed the table in front of him. Well, to anyone else it probably looked like that's what he was doing. Really, his mind was going over every single detail of each incident or meeting that he knew about between the Italian and Irish families here in Detroit.

Considering ...

Wondering ...

Plotting.

And then his body felt Gabbie's presence near, and he looked up to find her. At first, his attention went to the front entrance of the bar. He should have known better because nothing about his girl screamed *stupid*. She knew better than to walk into the place where anyone might see her.

Instead, Michel found Gabbie approaching him from the back of the bar. The hallway she'd come out of led to back rooms, bathrooms, and exit doors. There was usually someone in the back doing one thing or another, and would let someone in from the outside if they knocked on the door, and said they'd been out having a smoke or anything.

It wasn't mob-owned.

They weren't suspicious.

Michel said and did nothing until Gabbie was right in front of him. Close enough for him to *really* check her over and make sure she was okay, even if he had just left her not very long ago. And she was just close enough for him to reach out and grab her.

He did just that.

Once Gabbie was tucked in to his chest, and his arms were locked around her back, he felt slightly better. Like his world had finally tilted back on its proper axis, and everything was all right again. Strange how that worked.

She hid her face in his chest, and her hands fisted into his shirt. He wasn't sure how long the two of them stayed like that—a minute, but maybe two. Long enough that the sounds of the bar drifted into the background, and it felt like it was just the two of them doing their usual thing together once more.

Nothing was wrong.

Everything was fine.

For now.

He knew it was just a beautiful lie.

"Were you playing pool alone?" she asked, her voice muffled into his shirt.

Michel chuckled, and pressed a kiss to the top of her head. "I was—seems everyone who frequents the place knows they can't win against me, I guess."

"Don't be cocky."

He grinned as she leaned back just enough to look up at him. Her pretty lips had curved into a sly grin—one that told him she was joking. Always keeping him on his toes, this woman. How in the hell was he supposed to stay away from her?

If it keeps her safe, Michel ...

He ignored his inner voice.

It wasn't wrong, though.

They all had to make hard choices sometimes for the people they loved. That was yet another lesson this life had taught him. Sacrifice was ever-present, and more important than most men understood when it came to the mafia. To keep someone safe, a man needed to be willing to make the decisions that wouldn't be acceptable or appreciated to the person they loved.

They didn't *have* to like it.

They only had to understand.

Michel didn't want this to be one of those times, but he couldn't make that promise, either. There were a lot of variables around him and Gabbie, at the moment. A lot of *unknowns*, and he hated working on those.

That was a problem.

"Does your father know you're here with—"

"Absolutely not," she interjected sharply.

"Yeah, I figured."

"He wouldn't have let me come. I *was* coming ... I didn't want to fight."

Sure.

That, and she loved her father. Michel wasn't going to call her out on that little tidbit of information, but it factored into the decisions Gabbie made. Especially when those decisions revolved around the only other man in her life that played a big part in the things she would or would not do.

Her love for her father was the one thing that allowed her to overlook Charles' heavy control and influence in her daily life. He only needed to hear her talk about her dad to know that was the case, but he didn't think now was the right time to explain that to her, all things considered.

"What's going to happen now?" Gabbie asked.

Just like that, their moment was gone. They could no longer pretend this was simply another day to them where they were meeting up as usual, and things would go back to normal like it always did. He didn't blame her for asking because it was still on the back of his mind, too. Hell, it wouldn't leave him alone.

"I don't know, but it's going to be fine," he assured.

Gabbie didn't look like she believed that. "*How?* You were at the same meeting I was today, Michel! This is a complete feckin' *mess.*"

She wasn't wrong.

That wasn't really Michel's problem currently. The level her voice raised to, however, was a problem. He tightened his arm around her back, drawing Gabbie closer to his chest as he quickly scanned the bar.

A couple of people shot looks their way, but it wasn't anything that concerned him. The bartender behind the bar chatted on a phone with his back turned to them, but that wasn't anything unusual, either. And the man was laughing on his call, too, so Michel figured it wasn't as though the man was calling out to let someone know they were there.

It was always a possibility.

Michel couldn't help the paranoia right now.

"Calm down," he muttered into Gabbie's hair.

She stiffened. "You know that's the *worst* possible thing to tell a woman, right?"

Was it?

"I'll take your word for it," Michel replied. "But seriously, we *will* get this shit figured out. Everything is going to be *fine*, Gabbie. You and me? We don't even have anything to do with this, we're just the bystanders."

She swallowed hard, her green eyes wide with fear when she met his gaze again. "Bystanders die all the time, Michel."

Again—his girl wasn't wrong.

"I know," he said thickly. "I'll figure something out."

"*What?*"

He didn't have that answer yet. Things weren't clear enough for him to really make a choice about what might be their next move. The unknowns were still too many for him to be comfortable, really.

"The Italians want a war," Gabbie muttered.

Michel didn't doubt that.

But were they the only ones?

"Then, why was it the Irish attacking us today during the meeting?" he asked.

Gabbie stiffened in his hold. "We didn't ... my da made sure everyone was accounted for, and safe for the meeting today."

"Someone could have stepped out on their own to do it, Gabbie."

"They don't do that. *No one* steps out of line against my father."

"Are you sure—"

"How does that work with *your* dad, Michel? Do people often go against what he tells them to do, or does the first mistake by a man teach the rest how to stay in line?"

Her question was rhetorical, so Michel didn't answer because he already knew what it would be. *No,* people no longer deliberately went against his father's orders. It was a death wish, frankly. That was how the boss remained in control.

Sure, the Irish were a little different with their rules and ways. No doubt about that. It didn't change the fact that a criminal organization was still the same when it came to the person at the top.

They wanted to stay at the top.

"Something's not right," Michel said.

Gabbie frowned. "What do you mean?"

"With the Vannozzos. Something isn't right there."

He knew it.

But what was it?

FOURTEEN

All at once, Michel stiffened, his arms locking even tighter around Gabbie. So much so, that she swore her ribs protested from it.

"Shit," he hissed.

Gabbie didn't even have time to ask what made Michel upset because he quickly pushed her down with his back still turned to the rest of the bar. She didn't even question what he was doing, simply kneeled on the floor by his feet. There, the pool table kept her hidden where it was set up close to a wall.

Glancing up, she watched Michel turn to nod at something—or *someone*—she couldn't see on the other side of the pool table.

"David," he greeted.

David, *who?*

Gabbie had no idea.

"I didn't know you to frequent this place," Michel said.

A man chuckled, and she heard palms slap to the edge of the pool table. "I don't, man, but after today … well, we all have to look out for one another, don't we?"

"And how are you looking out for me, huh? Because I'm doing fine on my own."

"Right, right."

Gabbie tugged on Michel's pant leg—it was her silent way of letting him know she was okay down there, if he was fine doing what he was doing up there. She understood exactly what was happening now. Michel saw someone come into the bar that would recognize who she was with him, and did the only thing he thought would keep her hidden for a time.

She could deal with that.

For now.

Michel didn't even acknowledge she had pulled on his pant leg. He simply continued his conversation with the man like nothing was wrong. "Did Sal send you over?"

"Maybe he wanted me to check in, but also to deliver a message."

"For what?"

David chuckled. "Seems they're going in on some Irish places tonight. Things that'll *really* mess up their business—always gotta fuck with the money if you want to hit them where it hurts, right?"

"Put them on their knees, you mean."

"Exactly. They've got some construction rackets going on seeing as how the Casey's own a few different companies doing work in the city. They're planning to go in a few sites, and fuck some shit up to take away profit there first. They'll work outward from that. It wouldn't be wise for you to be out and about tonight. The Irish will be in an uproar, and likely willing to hit any Italian they see as punishment for what's about to happen. That's all. Sal thought you might like to know."

"Sal's moving fast, isn't he?" Michel asked.

"He has to—it's us or them, Michel. What do you expect him to do, wait around until the Irish decide to hit us *again?*"

Michel stayed quiet.

Gabbie thought about her father.

His men.

And Michel, too.

It was strange to her how all of her worries could swirl between the lines to merge it all together. It should have been clear—*simple*, even. Her loyalty should have only been with her family, and yet she loved someone outside of it, too. She couldn't *only* worry about one when there were more factors at play here.

God.

Why was this such a mess?

"It's not that I expect him to sit around and wait for more violence to happen," Michel returned, "but I assume the entire family might get together and have a discussion about what's going to happen next. That's all."

That's how it worked for Gabbie's father, too.

Michel had a point.

"You assume they haven't," David returned.

"It's been a few hours since the meeting, man."

"Who said it happened today?"

Michel's body tensed—Gabbie felt it in his *legs*, for feck's sake. "So like I said, then, he's moving *fast*."

"Everyone is."

"Thanks for the heads up."

"Care for a game of pool?" David asked. "Someone said you were pretty good, and you know how I like to make *bets*, huh?"

Michel's gaze did drift downward, then, and Gabbie looked up at the same time. It was just a split second—not very long at all, and she doubted the man on the other side of the table even noticed Michel's brief distraction.

Still, they looked at each other.

Her heart thumped so hard that she could feel it in her throat. It was enough to make her want to be sick. *No*, they couldn't play a feckin' game of pool. She couldn't stay hidden on the other side of the goddamn table when they would be walking *around* it.

"I think I'm going to head out, actually," Michel said. "Like you said, I wouldn't want to be caught out on the streets tonight, right?"

No, Gabbie wanted to say.

She didn't want him to leave at all. Who knew when the next time they could see each other again would be? Between his pre-med, her classes at college, this shite between their families ... and *more*, when would they get any time at all?

Never.

That's when.

"I'll walk you out, then," David said.

Michel tensed again.

Gabbie *flinched*.

"Yeah, man, sure," Michel replied tightly.

She had to physically stop herself from grabbing onto Michel's legs to keep him there with her. A part of her knew without a doubt it was going to be *weeks* before the two of them even got a chance to be near one another again.

Her heart felt like it was dying.

Still, she stayed hidden even as Michel moved away from her, and rounded the table. Just before he was gone from her sights entirely, he glanced back and caught her staring at him. It was quick—just a blink, and she would have missed it.

He winked.

Then, he mouthed, "*See you soon.*"

It made her smile.

He was always doing that.

And then he was gone.

Gabbie didn't know how long she stayed down there—another minute or two before she dared to at least poke her head up over the edge of the table, and scan the bar. No one seemed to notice the redhead at the pool table when she stood straight up, deciding it was safe enough for her to leave.

Michel was nowhere in sight.

Neither was his friend.

Gabbie waited by the pool table, staring at the front entrance where he would have left, just long enough to see if Michel might come back. There was a chance, right? Maybe his friend got in his vehicle first, and left before Michel did. Then, he could turn around and come right back in to see her.

He didn't come back.

Gabbie slipped out the back of the bar the same way she had come in. Each step she took made her heart grow heavier, but she pushed the feeling down. They would figure it out, right? They always did.

The phone in Gabbie's pocket rang, dragging her from the thoughts warring in her mind. She checked the screen just long enough to see Charles' name looking back at her. *Shite*. It seemed her father noticed her absence before she hoped he would.

Nothing ever went right.

"Da," she greeted, picking up the call.

"Where are you? I told you to stay close, didn't I? And you *left?*"

He didn't feck around.

Gabbie thought up a quick lie. "I needed a breather. It's been a long day. I decided to take a drive, okay?"

"That doesn't tell me where—"

"Coming home right now," she interrupted. "I'll be there in fifteen minutes."

… yeah, if she drove like a madwoman.

Maybe she would.

"*My* home," her father ordered.

Oh, were they going back to that?

Great.

"Of course, Da."

He hung up the phone.

Gabbie breathed a little easier.

• • •

A month.

A whole *month*.

That's how long it took before Gabbie and Michel were able to make time to attempt to meet again. Sure, they texted daily, and she called him when it was safe to do so. Their conversations were often far too short, and a wee bit … *careful*. Both of them were mindful not to say something that might upset the other. Neither wanted to give away too many details about what was happening around them.

Gabbie didn't think she was going to be able to get away from her father—he was still making her stay at his home—which he had men on *twenty-four seven* now. It was constant; she hated feeling like she was being babysat. A man drove her to classes at the college, and back home. If she needed to go to an appointment, or to the gym, he took her there, too.

She told Michel all of that. He needed to know if they were going to make this plan to see one another work, right?

By complete accident, Gabbie noticed the man who took her to school tended to disappear around eleven in the morning when she was in her second class of the day. No one told her that he left for a time, and came back before the class was even over. She only found out because three times the week before, with her sugars acting up, she stepped out to handle what she needed in the bathroom and realized … he wasn't in the hallway.

She let Michel know.

A plan was formed.

Gabbie's hands trembled a bit as she came up to the hotel room with a brass *9* hanging above the peephole. She was going to get in a lot of trouble for this—no doubt about it. Already, she bet the man watching her knew she had snuck out on him at the college. Her class ended a half hour ago, so they were probably on the hunt for her.

Her father would be in a panic …

Worth it.

Tomorrow, she would deal with the hell from her da. But this was her *one* chance to see Michel after an entire month of being away from him, and she wasn't passing it up. Everyone had to take risks, and this was hers.

Undoing the tie on her coat—the beginning of the month had brought with it even colder weather than ever—she knocked on the hotel door. Light footsteps echoed behind the door before it quieted, and then just as quickly, it was opened.

And there he was.

Michel stood behind the door, the dim lighting in the room shadowing him just enough to make him look like a dark angel standing there. She kind of loved it.

"It worked, then?" he asked.

"I guess so."

That was literally the only thing she was able to say before he yanked her into the room, and slammed the door behind her. Gabbie's back hit the door, and Michel's lips found hers. The kiss was brutal—making her high and spun all at the same time.

Yeah, a month was *way too long*.

Gabbie didn't care how rough Michel was as he tugged the clothes from her body. The only thing she could think about was just how close she could get to him in the least amount of time possible. His tongue lashed against hers, his teeth drawing her lower lip in to bite hard as his hands ripped her jeans down her thighs.

This was *basic*.

Primal.

It'd been too long. She just wanted him to give her what she wanted, and then they could talk *later*. The rest was pleasantries, and she didn't care for those at all. Not when he looked ready to *ruin* her. She didn't know how it had happened because everything moved *so fast* when they were like this, but he got her bent over the arm of the couch before she even had time to admire the room or look around.

His kisses dotted up her spine.

His hands followed the same path.

Gabbie's breaths came out *shuddering*. Her whole body felt him *everywhere*, and he wasn't even inside of her yet. Like the way her arse clenched when he palmed her backside, and clenched hard against the supple flesh before spanking her so damn good. Or how shivers chased his hands when he drove them up her back.

She heard the rip of foil, and then felt him behind her as he fitted between her thighs. That first thrust was heaven—it was when he pulled out that she thought it was *hell*. And then he quickly gave her that heavenly feeling back when he slammed in all over again.

His kiss had been brutal.

And so was his pace, now.

This was frantic, and *dirty*. She didn't need his words whispering in her ear to get her higher, or his teasing touches to light the flames inside her body. She was already there, and working toward the cliff that would throw her straight off the edge of bliss.

What a wonderful trip that would be.

Michel found her hips to yank her harder into him as the rhythm between them came a little faster. It made his cock hit the deepest spot inside of her pussy as his groin slapped her backside with every snap of his hips.

It ached.

And it felt *so good*.

"Right there," Gabbie gasped. "*Right there, oh, my God.*"

It was the feeling of him leaning over her back, and his teeth finding the junction of her shoulder that sent her *spinning*. Because that's how it felt when the orgasm crashed over her senses. Like she was a coil coming undone—spinning and twisting, unfurling a million miles a minute until she hit bottom, and crashed to the ground. She was sure her body was in a million little pieces, but it couldn't possibly be because Michel pulled away, and in the next blink, had her wrapped in his arms to cradle her.

The softness of a bed met her back before he was crawling in between her thighs. All she could do was open up to him, and let him in. Too sensitive, and trying to recover, she felt him enter her again.

Softer, this time.

Easier.

He wasn't so frantic, then.

Wasn't so *rough*.

And she liked it, too.

Loved how he loved her. Sweet touches against her body, and his kisses drifting over her chest and throat as he used her body to make himself fly, too. She didn't think she was going to come again—wasn't her body already spent?

It felt like it.

Michel proved her wrong.

She came when he did, too, because just hearing his pleased, thick moan when he came was enough to shove her over the ledge again. This time, she didn't feel so broken as she tried to catch her breath, her fingernails digging into the hard muscles of his shoulders as she trembled all over.

It still somehow *broke* her, though.

He always did that.

He'd ruined her for other men.

There could be no other but him.

"They follow me all the time," he muttered against her lips.

Gabbie stiffened on the bed, her naked body moving against his on the sheets. Just like that, her high was gone. It was time for them to talk, it seemed, and she didn't know if she liked that, or not. "What do you mean?"

"The Italians. It's ... they're *watching* me."

"I mean, my father's people watch me, too, Michel."

He shook his head, and she knew then that he was trying to tell her something else. Something *important*, but she wasn't hearing it correctly.

"Why does it bother you, then?"

Michel leaned away from her, using his elbow to keep him propped up on the bed. In the dim lighting, she still had a good view of his face, but he wouldn't meet her eyes. "Because it means they don't trust me. And since they won't let me in on their plans, and I don't want to be associated with my ... *friends* here anymore, I'm in the dark. But it puts me on edge to know they're watching me like they *have* to."

"Oh."

"Yeah."

"Were they following you to—"

"Lost them downtown," he replied quickly.

Gabbie blinked. "They're that close to you that you can see them?"

"Exactly."

She quieted in the bed, and just as quickly, his weight was covering hers again. The blankets on the mattress were pulled over them, and the rest of the world disappeared. For a second, it was just Michel and Gabbie hidden under the blankets, naked and together. The way she *always* wanted it to be.

No one would understand, though.

It wasn't this easy.

She couldn't have him.

"Gabbie?"

"Yeah?"

Peering up in his embrace, she found Michel watching her in *that* way. Intense, and pensive. Like if he looked away, then she might not be there when he glanced back again. She knew that feeling too well.

"What?" she asked when he stayed quiet.

"I was thinking ..."

"About?"

"Me and you."

She tensed. Because he knew this was a dead end for them? Because it was likely this thing between them was going to end nowhere good, and the only thing she would be left with was a broken heart to show for it?

That's how it felt sometimes.

His hand on her hip flexed almost painfully. "Don't do that—don't *ever* second guess what I feel about you, or what I want, okay?"

She swallowed hard. "It's hard not to. Everything is bad right now and … it's always on my mind. I can't *not* think about it, Michel."

"Except I want you. And I'd do anything to have you. *Anything*, Gabbie. I've had a month to think about the shit going on, and I tried to play by their rules. I thought stepping back might calm it down, and they would realize this war with the Irish is foolish, but it didn't work. Because that's *not* what they want. They want a war, and I'm starting to think it's not about me and you at all. I just haven't figured out *why*. But I plan on figuring it out, and soon."

"You shouldn't meddle, that's *dangerous*."

"So is not knowing their endgame, Gabbie."

Fair point.

It still left her unsettled, though.

Michel let out a bitter laugh, and one of his hands left her hip so that he could scrub it down his face. "My father would tell me to get the hell out of this city, you know? If I called him today and told him what was happening, that would be the first thing out of his mouth. And he's not wrong …"

She stilled again, fear slicing through her heart. A part of her wondered if he would leave, but just as quickly, it was quashed by the side of her that heard what he'd said not a minute before loud and clear.

He wants me.

He wouldn't leave without her.

His next words confirmed it. "I'm here for you—do you hear me?"

She nodded. "I got it."

"But would you leave?"

"What?"

Michel's hands found her body again, and he rolled her over on the bed. Once again, she was on her back, and he hovered above her. His hands splayed across her rib cage—so strong, and expansive. He could squeeze her body, take her breath away, and she would *beg him for more*. She wanted everything he gave her.

Including *him*.

"If we could leave, would you come with me?" he asked.

"Is it that simple?"

"Probably not. It might be a last resort."

"Okay, and *yes*."

Her heart was with him. Her soul, too. What good was a woman without a heart and soul? What would she possibly do with herself if she was left without him, and he had taken those parts of her with him, too?

No, she would have to go.

She would rather die, otherwise.

Michel's throat jumped at her reply before he dropped a quick kiss to her lips. She smiled under his mouth, but the truth was simpler. In a way ... it wouldn't *be* that easy. Nothing ever was in this life.

She learned that lesson well.

• • •

Gabbie woke up in the bed to chaos. At first, she wasn't even sure what was going on as she was yanked from her slumber next to Michel with viciousness. She wondered if the scene playing out in the hotel room was a nightmare, or reality.

She wasn't sure she was even *awake*.

And then it became painfully clear that yes, she was awake. The men storming the hotel room had familiar faces—one bad sign. Their words as they dragged her out of the bed from the right, and Michel from the left was the second sign.

It happened so fast.

Seconds, really.

Even still, she fought against the hold of the person keeping her away from Michel. She slapped and scratched and spat while the men on the other side of the room slammed Michel against the wall with no care or concern.

"*Enough, lass!*"

That *voice*.

That voice she knew so well.

She was still focused in on Michel, but the hands that suddenly landed on her arms squeezed tightly enough to leave bruises behind. She was forced to stare into the eyes of a familiar face instead of the man across the room like she wanted.

"Let her go!" Michel shouted.

His next yell was stopped by one of the men slamming a punch to his gut. Gabbie felt like she had taken that punch, too.

"Stop," she mumbled.

"Then you *leave*, lass," the man holding her said.

Out of the corner of her eye, she found the door had been kicked in. That was likely the noise that woke her up. Still, she felt hazy and confused. Unsteady even as she was pulled to her feet, and a handful of shite was pushed into her hands.

Gabbie blinked at the items.

Her clothes.

Humiliation filled her to the brim.

She was still naked.

So was Michel.

It was then that she realized who exactly had beaten down their door to get her. Oh, sure, she understood perfectly fine that it was her father's men. But the one who just handed her the clothes to get dressed and was now looking at her right in her eyes?

Brennan.

Her father's right-hand, and best friend.

Charles was *not* playing now.

"Your father wants you to know this won't happen again," Brennan told her as she slipped on the shirt to cover her breasts. She was still trying to wake up. What

112

time was it? How had they even found her here? "He'll make sure of it, Gabbie. Do you understand me? Are you feckin' listening, lass? If you pull this shite again, he's going to take care of the issue *permanently*."

Fear cut through her heart.

Nothing had ever hurt so badly.

Yes, she heard him.

She heard his threat perfectly fine. Michel's life was now determined by her behavior. It was a simple threat, sure, but effective.

"Don't hurt him," she whispered.

The man glanced Michel's way. Struggling with the two men holding him against the wall, still naked, his wild gaze met hers.

She knew this was risky. It was only a matter of time before her father found them.

"Gabbie—"

"It's okay, Michel," she told him.

He shook his head. "It's *not*."

She knew how this worked.

How this could *end* ...

Gabbie turned to Brennan again. "You won't hurt him, right?"

"Not if you leave right now ... no fighting, lass."

Done deal.

She would do what she had to.

Michel would do the same for her.

"Okay, let's go."

"*Gabbie!*"

"He will kill him," Brennan murmured to her, shaking her resolve a little more. "He is not going to play these games, not after this stunt. Is that what you want— for the man to *die* because you won't stay away from him?"

No.

"It's time to leave," she was told.

Gabbie nodded, saying nothing. She left the hotel because she didn't have a choice. Not when the only options for her were staying there only to know it would mean Michel's death, or leaving to give him one more chance.

They'd figured it out *this* far, right?

Surely, they could do it again.

She didn't look back as she left, either. Not even when Michel called out for her again. She couldn't—her heart just wasn't strong enough.

Stupid heart.

FIFTEEN

It was only once Gabbie had left the hotel room that the men keeping hold of Michel let him go. *With* a punch to the face. He hadn't been expecting the hit, or he might have been able to prepare for it a bit better. At least, it might not have hurt nearly as much had he been able to see the fist coming right for his mouth.

Instead, it sent him sprawling to the floor. He snarled under his breath, an ache like nothing else spreading over the side of his face. *Great.* He bet that was going to bruise, and he'd be the stupid fuck brushing it off all week when people asked about it at the college. Blood bloomed in his mouth, coating his tongue and telling him they'd busted *something.* The throbbing in his bottom lip didn't really fucking help, either.

Jesus Christ.

What had he gotten himself into here?

He didn't have much time to think on the fact Gabbie was *gone.* Oh, sure, it hurt like nothing else. His chest felt like someone had ripped it open and tore his heart right out of his body with a laugh, but he couldn't spend time on it.

Not when these idiots were still looming over him, and he didn't know what in the hell was going to happen next. With them, it could be anything. Michel didn't trust them to let him go alive, certainly not after *all this.* They'd come for what they wanted, and yeah, they got it by taking Gabbie away from him. That didn't mean the assholes weren't planning something extra for Michel, too.

How did they find them?

Had *he* fucked up?

Michel refused to even consider that it had been Gabbie. And if it had been her, by chance, he didn't think for one second that she would purposefully *do this.* She wouldn't lead them to the two of them here—he knew that for a fact. So how in the hell did they find them when he was certain they had both been careful about this meet up?

"Stay down there, lad," one of the old men said when Michel put his hands to the floor, ready to push himself back up to his feet. He didn't plan to fight, but he didn't want to stay on the floor when he had a handful of men above him. The least they could do was let him get to his feet and try to … do *something.* "Ye forget the Irish be like dogs when we dig for the bone—*savages.*"

Michel hadn't forgotten *anything.* Hadn't he been the one to be hesitant when the Irish came up as an issue the first time? Well, for the rest of them, anyway. He'd never for even one second thought Gabbie was dangerous.

For his heart, maybe.

Not the rest of him.

Michel spat his mouthful of saliva mixed with blood to the floor, wanting the taste out of his goddamn mouth. He let out a bitter laugh, and shook his head because this was *ridiculous.* "Couldn't *knock,* assholes?"

That probably wasn't the brightest idea he'd ever had. One of the Irishmen confirmed that thought by kicking Michel right in the ribs. The force of the hit sent him rolling over, and sprawling to his back on the floor.

His mouth kept bleeding.

Now, his chest hurt, too.

Stop running your smartass mouth, his mind snapped. Like he needed a reminder that it was always his attitude and arrogance that got him in trouble more than anything else. He knew how this worked.

Didn't mean he could change it.

Besides, he'd much rather die giving them the shit he could than crying on the floor like a damn baby. He was a *Marcello*—they didn't give anything; they only took. This included, and Michel refused to shame his name for anyone else.

"You're not a very smart lad, are you?"

Michel eyed the man looming over him now. He wasn't nearly as old as the others. If anything, the man looked younger than Michel by a couple of years. And maybe a bit familiar, too, although Michel couldn't place his face for whatever reason.

"I'm quite smart," Michel replied.

Even to his own ears, his voice was hoarse.

He'd not gotten nearly enough sleep, and then to be woken up only to have Gabbie yanked from the hotel room before they kicked the shit out of him ... well, it wasn't looking like it would be a great day.

He was *tired*.

Of everything.

"Aye, tell him, Aidan," one of the older men said.

Michel's brow dipped.

Aidan.

Suddenly, he remembered where he knew the younger guy from. At the club that first night when he was fixing Gabbie's arm up, Aidan had come to the doorway with the girl ... Aine. Weren't they ... cousins of Gabbie?

What did it even matter?

"Last warning from the boss," Aidan said, "because he won't feck around a second time, Italian. Stay away from his daughter ... all you Italians want is a war, and he won't have you using her as another pawn to get what you want. You feckin' hear me?"

Michel blinked.

He didn't want a war at all.

"*Are you deaf, lad?*"

Michel glanced up at the guy still hovering above him with fists ready to rain down on him once again. Like every other man that still remained in that room. He really didn't give much of a shit about any of them.

He had other things to consider, now.

Both sides still thought he was ... playing for the other side. The truth was a hell of a lot simpler than that. Michel was fucking *Switzerland*, here. He respected the life his father brought him into, even if it was from the outside looking in, when it came to the Italian side of things. And he loved Gabbie like nothing and nobody else, so he had no interest in causing her or the people she came from any harm, either.

But they thought he did.

Michel's decision was set, then. He couldn't *be* Switzerland anymore, and expect to come out of this thing a winner. And to him, being a winner meant having the thing he wanted more than anything else.

Gabbie.

He was going to have to do whatever he needed to do to get her—pick a side, make it easier for someone to win ... or something else entirely.

Michel didn't know yet.

He needed a plan.

• • •

Gabbie's phone was either destroyed, trashed, or hidden away somewhere. It had to be—otherwise, why two weeks after being pulled out of the hotel room would she still not be answering his calls or texts? And she had made no effort to attempt to contact him in any way, either.

Michel didn't think that was *her* choice. There was no way his girl would purposely keep a distance from him unless she was being forced to do so. Which only pissed him off even more.

So, he put those two weeks to use.

Or ... *tried.*

Something was happening that Michel didn't understand at all. Just a couple of months ago, he could have called any number of Italians—including Sal, and people in the man's crew—and they would have picked up his calls in a heartbeat. If he asked for something, they would make sure he had it. He'd been invited into their spaces and allowed to be near when business was happening.

Now?

Fuck.

Now, he couldn't even get a phone call through. No one was picking up. Which, in a way, Michel would have brushed off because he knew all the places where he could find Sal and any other number of Italians with connections to the Capo.

The problem with that?

Simple.

"You're not coming in," the enforcer at the front of the restaurant said. "Besides, Sal ain't even around today, man."

Bullshit.

He wasn't stupid, despite what these idiots might think about him. And there was no way in hell he was going away *again*. There were questions he needed answered, and he bet Sal was the only one who could do it.

If he couldn't get to Gabbie, or an Irishman, then he was going for the Italians first. Depending on what he got from them, or what he thought he could use, then Michel had more choices to make. Possibly more options.

Except, he didn't know what he could do at all when he knew nothing and could speak to *no one*.

Michel's jaw ached from how hard he was clenching his molars in that moment. This was the third time in a week that he had been turned away from Sal's restaurant. The man's usual meeting place. In fact, he knew Sal was here for sure because the enforcer was watching the door, and Sal's black town car was in the parking lot.

"I know he's here," Michel returned, "and the place is open for business, so—"

"You're still not coming in."

Goddammit.

Michel was *very* close to letting his anger spill over which wouldn't be a good thing for him, or the people here. Acting out of anger never led to anywhere good, so he tried to tamper the reaction down a bit.

At least, for a second.

"At least go *ask* him if he'll see me," Michel argued.

The enforcer rolled his eyes upward. "I don't have to ask. I know what I was told."

"You know I can stand here all day, right?"

Not that he had the time. He was missing out on a day of classes for this, and he couldn't afford that. It didn't matter—eventually, Michel would get back to what was important in his life once he got the other important thing back.

Gabbie.

"It's gonna be a boring day for you, then," the enforcer replied.

Michel's gaze narrowed, and he had the greatest urge to punch the cocky fucker right in his throat. "If you don't go ask Sal—"

"Michel."

The smoothly cool, yet still annoyed, tone coming from deeper within the entrance of the restaurant had the enforcer sighing. Then, the man stepped aside to allow Michel to see Sal had come to stand just beyond the doorway. The woman who usually worked the podium was gone, leaving just the three of them standing there alone.

Probably smart.

"You're making a scene," Sal told him.

Michel shrugged.

Was that a problem?

Good.

Sal was there.

That was the point.

"Maybe," Michel said, pointing a finger at the man because he was just feeling that kind of mood now, "had you answered any one of my phone calls, or allowed me to see you earlier in the week when I came around, it wouldn't have come to this today. Right?"

Sal's lips flattened into a grim line. "I don't owe you *anything*, Michel. And I also don't answer to you. If you've forgotten that this still isn't New York after all this time, that's not my problem. That sounds like an issue *you* need to work on."

Michel let that comment roll off his shoulders like it was nothing. Because frankly, now it was *nothing* to him. These fucking Italians here kept using that statement to throw at Michel like it was supposed to be an insult. He no longer took it that way—he couldn't. He knew this place wasn't New York. No one in New York would behave the way these people did.

"I have questions about—"

"I don't *care*," Sal interjected sharply. "You no longer have anything I need, Michel. I got what I wanted from you, and now here we are."

Michel stilled on the spot, confused.

What in the hell was Sal talking about?

"You *got what you wanted*," Michel echoed.

"That's what I said."

Except it didn't make sense, did it? What had Michel *really* given Sal? He worked for the man as a dealer for a couple of months, but that was it. It wasn't like Michel had any real hand in the man's business, or anything of that nature. He'd rarely been allowed a seat at the table when business was happening.

It just didn't click.

And then all at once … it *did*.

The Irish kept saying it, didn't they?

The Italians only want a war.

Michel knew enough about the families in Detroit to know there had always been a tenuous relationship between the Casey and Vannozzo families. They barely tolerated one another on their good days, and the Italians always felt like the Irish had a little too much control in the city. A complaint they often voiced whenever the Irish came up in conversation.

Yet … there were rules in this world.

Peace was *peace*.

No one disrupted peace without a reason.

Had Michel been the reason?

Gabbie, too?

Had he given them a reason—as stupid and as petty as it might be—to cause a problem with the Irish that would eventually lead them into war? Because wasn't that exactly what they were heading to, now?

Michel thought so.

The Irish wouldn't budge. They refused to feed into the violence the Italians kept throwing at them. Michel might not be on the front lines, but he knew just enough people to get details about the current happenings in the city. He could also watch the news on any given day, and see the escalating violence playing out on the streets day in and day out, although they tried not to *name names*.

He didn't need names.

He knew how this worked.

Michel grew up in this life.

"Are you talking about … the Irish?" Michel asked, arching a brow because he was silently *daring* this motherfucker to deny it. "Are you saying you used me as an opening to get to the Irish—you thought, *oh*, there it is, and you what, fucking *took it*?"

Sal chuckled darkly. "Michel, don't be offended. It's really not about you. I just saw the opportunity because I knew the girl's father would be uncomfortable with an Italian from our side of things being so close to her … and so I took it. I got what I wanted."

"Yeah, you want a fucking war."

The man smiled. "And we're *almost* there."

But not quite.

The Irish were still holding back.

For now.

What would happen when they answered?

Who would be waiting at the proverbial door?

It scared the hell out of him because he knew how wars worked, and *everybody* was nothing more than collateral. He'd known it for a while, but the fact was, he tried to ignore it. He hoped it wouldn't get this far.

Yet, here they were.

Gabbie on one side.

Him on the other.

Michel was going to correct that.

Starting now.

If he couldn't figure out a way to get Gabbie back by going through the Italians, then he would go to the source that was keeping her away. After all, if what the Irish needed was to get rid of their problem with the Italians ... then who better to give them every bit of information they needed to do it than the son of a Cosa Nostra boss?

Michel knew how *la famiglia* worked.

And he knew how to ruin it.

To his own legacy, that would be the greatest betrayal. What choice did he have?

SIXTEEN

"What are you reading, lass?"

Gabbie refused to look up at her father's voice. Instead, she continued flipping to the next page in the thriller. Charles sighed at her silence, but he shouldn't be surprised. Awkward silence or all out shouting could sum up the last weeks of their lives under this roof.

Her *father's* roof.

Because she wasn't allowed to leave.

Or have her phone.

… go to school.

Charles thought he was teaching Gabbie a lesson, but all she learned here was just how controlling her father could be when he wanted to. And she didn't like it one bit. Sure, at first, she had been willing to play along. Like every other time when he got a little too overbearing, she figured he would get it out of his system quickly enough. He'd let her go back to her place and be *normal.*

Or as normal as she could be.

Nope.

Here they still were.

"Will you at least look at me?" her father asked, not unkindly.

Gabbie continued reading her book. Some might consider her behavior childish, but she no longer gave a shite. That was the problem—*this* was the only way she had to show her father how unhappy and disappointed she was in him for the things he was doing to her. She had tried literally everything else.

Shouting.

Talking.

Begging.

Nothing worked.

So, if he didn't want to hear her, then she had little to no desire to hear him, either. Besides, if he wanted to treat her like a child by taking away her freedom, hiding her phone, and deciding who she could and could not be with, then she might as well prove him right and *act* like the child he thought she was.

He wouldn't hear her when she tried to explain that Michel wasn't the bad guy Charles thought he was—to her father, he was just that *feckin' Italian gobshite.* Just another Italian for her father to see as a problem to his business, and life.

Certainly not the man she loved.

It was *killing* Gabbie. It killed her that she didn't know what was happening outside her father's house. Not with his business, his men, or the people on the other side. Including *Michel.* Charles was so careful now about what he said around Gabbie, and he no longer allowed his men to freely come in and out to discuss the current happenings in the city.

She didn't know *anything.*

Was Michel even okay?

Charles wouldn't entertain Gabbie's questions, either. Not when they came to what was happening between the Italians and the Irish, and certainly not about Michel. If she did dare to ask him a question about one of those two topics, he quickly shut her down and made it clear that it wasn't for her to be concerned about.

She was a woman.

Not one of his *men*.

She was to remember that.

Oh, it had never been clearer.

Apparently, her father's patience was running particularly thin with her at the moment. Maybe the lack of conversation, and awkward dinners was finally starting to get to him.

Who knew?

Grand.

Maybe he'd finally get the feckin' point.

"*Lass.*"

"You know, the more annoyed you get … it's not going to change the fact I don't want to speak to you," she told her father, finishing the last bit of her chapter. Setting the book aside, she finally did look at her father then. Not because he wanted her to, but rather, because she was done with the pretenses. "You can't actually hold me here *forever*, Da."

Charles arched a brow. "On the contrary, Gabbie, I can do exactly that if I want to. I have managed just fine for these last weeks. Please, go ahead and tell me how you think if you throw enough fits and say more horrible things to me that it will get you what you want when so far, that hasn't worked out for you. Go on, I will wait."

She scowled.

Her father remained cold.

That was the whole problem.

Since this conversation was clearly going to get her *nowhere*, Gabbie picked up the book she'd discarded earlier, and flipped to the page where she left off. Her father let out another heavy sigh at her choice, but she didn't give a damn.

It was hard to care about him.

After all, he didn't care about her.

Not really.

Charles proved that again and again by doing things that hurt her. Before, Gabbie was more than willing to overlook the things about her overbearing father that bothered her because he was literally *all she had*. Sure, she had uncles and aunts … cousins, too. Friends from school, and things like that.

But those closest to her?

No.

Just her da.

He was the man who used to tuck her in night after night as a young girl, and would play tea party with her no matter how many times she asked. He was the man who she remembered *vividly* next to her bedside in the hospital when she was five, and her sugars were so out of control that they thought it might do organ damage because they couldn't get it stabilized. He cried for her then, too.

But he was also the same man who wouldn't let her grow up. He was the same man who made choices for her when she was perfectly capable of making them herself. He was her father, and she *loved him entirely*, but she couldn't love the part of him that wanted to control every aspect of her life more than he wanted to see her flourish on her own.

And right now?

He was hurting her in a new way.

She wasn't okay with that.

"Gabbie—"

"Unless you're going to give me my phone so that I can talk to Michel, or let me go home, then I don't want to speak to you, Da."

Silence echoed.

She got her answer.

Gabbie went back to reading her book, all the while, quite aware that her father was still lingering in the doorway of the living room. He stayed there, too, as she read through a whole chapter of her book. He didn't move or say anything the entire time. She almost wondered if he was just going to stay there all day because she had no plans to speak to him again.

Not now, anyway.

"I only want what's best for you," her father murmured. "That's all I have *ever* wanted, Gabbie."

Dammit.

She didn't want to talk to him, but ... "The problem with that is you think what's best for me are things *you* chose for me, and that's not how it works."

"I think you're wrong. I don't think you understand the dynamics I face day to day with a single child ... a woman who people constantly look to because I have not yet chosen a path for you in this life."

Gabbie stilled on the couch. "What?"

"See, I tried to let you be as normal as you could possibly be, lass. You deserved as much freedom as you could have, and I gave you that, didn't I? But that does not change the fact that we both live a life where expectations come along with it. I was fine to let you go on like you were, until you stepped out of line, and people looked to me for the answers as to *why*."

"You can't really mean—"

"Had you just picked an *Irish* lad," her father said, his tone thick with something she couldn't decipher. Glancing up, she found her father's gaze to be dark and pained, but he was still cold in every other aspect. The same way he was to the rest of his people, she knew. And now, it was her turn to see this side of him and face it. He had to be *this man* to her now, too. "But you didn't ... and I couldn't *let you* pick when you wouldn't pick someone that was appropriate to our people, too. You forced my hand."

She didn't think so.

Those expectations he talked about had never been a prominent figure in her life because he didn't make it so. And now he expected her to just ... *fall in line*?

It wouldn't happen.

"And I know you have this wee idea in that crazy mind of yours that the Italian man is the person for you—that you *love* him—but he is a phase," her father said, clearly not realizing how much he hurt her with every word that passed his lips. He was wrong ... *so wrong*. "After a period of time, you will realize how silly this all was, and you will be grateful that I forced your hand to keep you from making another mistake."

Gabbie shook her head. "It's not a phase, and he isn't like my diabetes, Da. You can't treat him like he's a piece of food I might shove in my mouth, or a missed sugar check. He's not something you can *control*. My feelings aren't something for you to decide whether or not they are valid. *I* make those choices."

"Except you aren't right now, are you?"

She quieted.

He wasn't wrong.

Charles cleared his throat, and turned to leave the living room. But not before tossing over his shoulder, "I have done my very best not to go to the last resort on this issue, Gabbie, but if you continue to push my line here … I will remove the man from your life permanently so that it's clear. *There is no choice.* There is only my choice."

That killed her more.

Because he would do it.

She knew it.

Gabbie was left with only one option. Just like her father said, really. *His* option. Because otherwise, it meant sacrificing Michel's life simply because she wanted him.

That was the thing …

She couldn't do that.

Not when she loved him.

• • •

"Don't *move*," the man at Gabbie's back hissed. His fingers tightened around her arm, forcing her to stay hidden in the shadows just beyond the entry hallway to her father's home. Every part of her was screaming to *fight*, to go to the man in the doorway just ten feet away, but she couldn't move at all. "Stay right where you are, lass. You heard the boss."

Right.

Charles wasn't even her da anymore.

He was just *the boss*.

"You have a death wish, lad," her father said.

For the first time in a month, Gabbie heard Michel's voice. She had no idea what brought him here to her father's home. They'd been in the midst of yet another awkward dinner when one of the men watching the house came rushing inside. His gaze had darted from her at one end of the table, to her father at the other side.

Then, he uttered, "*Michel.*"

Just like that.

Her immediate thought was simply *no*. There was no way in hell Michel had come to her father. Not to look for her, or otherwise. He was not a stupid man. At the same time, she couldn't say for sure if that was true.

Because love was crazy.

It made you do crazy things.

Gabbie inched closer to the hallway, but the man kept his grip firm to keep her back. "Let me *go*."

"No way, Gabbie."

She closed her eyes, and willed the pain in her heart to go away so she could *think*. It was physically painful to be this close to Michel, yet not be able to look him in the eyes or speak to him. She'd had a whole month of worrying about him, and considering every single possible scenario that could be going on with him.

Every bad, horrible thing.

"Not a death wish," she heard Michel say to her father, "more like a … an offer. Information, even. And you can do with it what you want, but I think you also have something *I* want, and I would like to talk about that. Because that's the problem here, isn't it? You think I picked the wrong side, when in fact, I haven't taken *any* side. *Yet*."

Charles cleared his throat. "What kind of information?"

"Your men—they said all the Italians want is a war. They weren't wrong, but it's got fuck all to do with what I was doing with your daughter, even if they want to spin it that way. It's all about what they can get from *you*."

"That's all it ever is with your kind of mutt."

Gabbie flinched at the insult.

Michel kept talking like it didn't bother him at all. "I was simply a reason they could use to cause an issue. And when that issue continued to spiral into a worse situation, well, what would be the harm of feeding into it? If it meant they could finally get a stronger hold on the city when it's always been the Irish who had it before them?"

"Your information isn't something that helps me, lad," Charles replied, unaffected, "but I suspect you already know that."

"Salvestro Vannozzo—goes by Sal."

"What about him?"

"He's the cousin to the Cosa Nostra boss, and the brains behind this whole … shitshow," Michel explained. "And I know just enough about him, and his business to cause a real fucking problem for him. I have access, and know people around him to get close enough that he could be gone before anyone even knew what happened. He assumed just because he won't see me or take a call that it's the only *in* I have to his people and business, but he's wrong. For a year, I followed him around and had access to his people before I even took up dealing for him on the side."

"Your point?"

"It goes beyond getting rid of him … being as close as he is to the boss, it's one stepping stone, if you get what I am saying. His work and loyalty is intricately tied to the head of the Italian organization in Detroit. He's a domino—kick one out, and the rest of them will quickly follow the same path. Cosa Nostra isn't like *other* Italian mafias. When you cut out at the head of it, the rest falls apart."

Gabbie inched closer to the hallway, but this time, the man let her go a little further. Not enough that she could be seen by Michel, but it was something. Her heart calmed for a split second at the idea she might be able to go to him, but then quickly realized she was still too feckin' far away.

And that *hurt*.

"My father ..." Michel made a noise under his breath, something harsh and painful. "My father would be sorely disappointed in me to know that I am using what I know about Cosa Nostra and their ways to help someone outside ruin a whole organization, but I don't have a choice. I have to do what I have to do, so here I am. Is it a risk? Could you kill me before I stepped out of this house? Absolutely."

"Right on both accounts," her father replied dryly. "And something I am seriously considering at the moment."

"Except, I have things you might want. The information on Sal, which will lead you right into the heart of the family to cull the organization. They're so protected, it's how Cosa Nostra works, that you'll never get to the boss to cut the head from the snake without causing enough of an uproar that you'll never be able to leave your home again. Police attention—the *feds*, too. And that's before the rest of the Italians that will come after you from outside of Detroit. *My family*, for example. It's a risk if you do it your way ... not one I would want to take."

Michel sighed, before adding, "But *my* way, with the influence I could have outside of Detroit and the information I have to help you *in* the city ... it would be cleaner, and far easier. That's what you need, isn't it? To get rid of *all* of them, and then you'll never have this problem again?"

"That's interesting enough to make me listen to you instead of put a bullet in your brain, aye. The problem, Michel, is that you are under some assumption that this is a *tit for tat*. You think if you give me something, then I will give you another thing. Am I right?"

"You're not wrong," Michel returned.

"My daughter, you mean to say. You want *her*."

"I love her."

Gabbie's heart clenched again.

Her father made a dismissive noise. "It doesn't matter *how* I go after the Italians because it all means the same thing in the end. A war I don't want, Michel. Maybe a smaller war, sure, but there will still be one. I know who they would come after first—I know what they would try to take from me, and while she might hate me right now, I'll never put her in danger. The Italians want a war, but I don't."

"So, you plan to keep letting them attack you and ruining your source of income for your organization? What good does that do?"

"It keeps her alive. They're focused on instigating me, not *hurting* me. Do you see the difference?"

"That could ruin you—ruin your entire *organization*."

"Men have done worse for blood, lad. I assure you."

She never considered that was why her father refused to go to war entirely with the Italians. She just thought ... he was waiting for the final straw, and it had not yet come to break the proverbial camel's back.

She was that straw.

For her father.

And for Michel.

The difference was ...

One of them reached their breaking point.

Michel, that was.

"Tell me what you want from me," Michel said, "and I will—"

"Nothing," Charles replied quietly. "I want nothing from you."

A second passed.

Then, *two.*

Enough for her heart to pound hard in her chest, and make her stomach do flips. She was straining in the grip of the man holding her back again, but her eyes were blurry from the tears that she refused to let fall.

She wanted *him.*

God, she wanted Michel.

More than anything.

"Gabbie, come out here, lass," she heard her father call. "Let her come, Conor."

The man who had been holding Gabbie back the entire time finally let her go. She was still straining to get out of his grip, so the second his fingers unfurled from her arm, she all but stumbled right into the hallway.

Lifting her gaze, she found Michel ten feet away.

There he stood.

She had no doubt that the two of them were a mirror to one another in those moments. That pain she felt was reflected in him, and her racing heart seemed so loud, she almost wondered if he could possibly hear it.

Her soul …

It, too, *screamed.*

She was so close to him.

And not nearly close enough.

"Lass, tell the young man what you've decided about him," her father said, "and then maybe we have saved him from a worse fate, aye? No need for the man to go making an arse of himself over a woman who isn't interested."

Then, Charles looked Gabbie's way. His gaze narrowed, and she saw the warning flash in her father's eyes. It was his silent reminder of their conversation a week before—his threats against Michel if she couldn't drop him from her life.

It was a war in her mind.

Her heart, too.

"Tell him," her father said, "so this is one more thing I can finally put to rest before I move onto another, Gabbie. Unless, of course, you want to go the other way we discussed."

No.

No, she didn't want that.

It meant Michel *dead.*

She looked at Michel again, her hands twisting into the wool skirt of her sweater dress because she needed to do something with her hands when she *lied* to him. If she was going to lie to the love of her life—because it meant saving his—then she needed to make sure her hands were busy, or they might just reach out to him.

"Gabbie?" Michel asked.

Why was life like this?

Why?

SEVENTEEN

This had been a risk.

And maybe a mistake.

Michel wasn't willing to admit it had been a mistake, though, not even as Gabbie stared at him from where she stood at the end of the hallway, her eyes lined with unshed tears like she didn't want to say the next thing that was about to come out of her mouth.

He knew what she was going to say.

Knew it in his soul.

It still fucking hurt.

The risk in approaching her father was simple—Charles could have killed Michel before he ever even got the chance to tell the man about the things he knew. He'd thought that if he made it clear which side of the lines he stood on, then no one could question his motives here. No one would think he was playing both sides, and maybe it would get him what he wanted in the end.

A pipe dream.

That's what it was.

Still, Michel had to *try*.

Now, he was paying for that attempt. And as far as he could see, this was the last option he really had to make use of. Everything else, he had already done. What more could Michel do now to get Gabbie back with him?

Nothing, apparently.

This was it.

And she was about to ruin it.

He stared at Gabbie the same way her father did, waiting for her to finally force that lie out of her mouth. Yeah, he knew she was lying. He could tell by the way her hands shook at her sides, and she kept glancing away from him as her throat jumped with every swallow.

Because she was swallowing her lies, too.

It's okay, he wanted to tell her. More than anything, he wanted her to know that he didn't blame her for the choice she was about to make. He wasn't going to pretend like he knew the shit going on behind these closed doors, and he didn't doubt that she had her reasons for this mess here. That didn't make it easier on him.

Not at all.

"Lass, get on with it," Charles said, his tone firm.

Gabbie nodded, and her gaze drifted to Michel again. Still full of tears that had yet to fall, and cutting him when she blinked, and *finally*, one of those tears slipped down her cheek. She was quick to wipe it away when her father's head was turned so that he didn't see the emotion.

Michel saw it, though.

He saw.

It only confirmed what he already thought, regardless if this was killing him inside, and it was going to hurt even more to walk away from her ... she didn't want this, and she was about to lie to him.

127

"Da's right, Michel ... it's for the best if you leave me alone," Gabbie whispered.

He blinked.

Yeah, she was lying.

It still fucking *ached*.

"All right," he heard himself mutter.

Because what else could he do?

"I'm sorry," Gabbie said quickly.

Michel shook his head. "Don't be, *bella*."

Charles cleared his throat, and his gaze swung back to Michel. "Have you gotten what you wanted, then? If so, I think it's about time you take your leave before the rest of your lot figures out you made a trip down to speak with me. I hear the Italians are watching us. I hope they're enjoying the show they're *not* getting from me."

"I wouldn't know," Michel replied.

He wasn't lying.

Not that it mattered.

The Irishman scoffed. "I doubt that. See yourself out, lad."

Michel did.

But not before looking back to see Gabbie still staring at him. Now, though, her father was distracted by watching *Michel* leave his house.

She mouthed, "*I love you.*"

He only nodded.

Because yeah, he knew.

• • •

"Son, how're things?"

Michel's gaze drifted to the phone on the edge of the pool table. He'd put it on speaker simply because he didn't want to talk at all, but that would be the first sign to his father that something was wrong. Once Dante found a bone to dig, he'd keep going until the entire skeleton was revealed under the dirt.

He was in just the right state lately—one of pure desperation—that he very well might spill his guts to his father about everything happening here in Detroit, and how this last year had fucked him *straight up*. Everything from the snakes running the Italian organization here to the Irish family that didn't seem to give a single *shit*.

Michel didn't understand how to fix this.

He also knew he couldn't tell his father. Dante would have one, and only the one, goal where Michel and Detroit were concerned. It would be a simple one, too. *Get Michel as far away from that city as possible*. His father knew how this kind of thing worked, and there was no way Dante, even heading an organization as large as the Marcellos, would make his way here just to insert himself between the war of two families.

It wouldn't happen.

Because Dante was smart.

Fuck.

Michel used to be smart once, too. Or he thought so, anyway. Last year, he'd been at the top of his class at the end of the final semester. Top *five*. And now, even his schooling was suffering because of the hell that was going on all around him. He couldn't focus, and his grades showed it. Sleep was an evasive bitch, and his professors were pointing out his distraction more and more often.

He mostly ignored the issue of school simply because he knew at some point, he could fix that. If he needed to do a year over because things got to be too much, and he let his grades slide terribly, then that was fine. He didn't like it, but he would do it.

School was something he could *fix*.

Gabbie being out of reach was not something that was as easily corrected. It had never been more apparent than now. He was *dying*. There had never been another time in his life when Michel felt so entirely useless.

"Are you coming home at the end of the month?"

Michel looked up from the shot he was prepping to take, and stared out the window of the bar. Heavy, white flakes drifted down in front of the glass, and he let out a sigh. December came before he even knew what happened—he'd spent almost a whole month in a daze that he couldn't break free from no matter what he tried to do.

He stared at his phone.

No call from Gabbie.

He watched the news.

More violence from the Italians.

He went to school.

He thought about *her*.

Michel couldn't get her face out of his head as he left her house that night he went to speak to her father. That *pain* staring back at him from where she stood at the other end of the hallway, and how he just knew it was reflected back in his eyes.

She'd been lying.

And yet, she still said what she said. She *stayed* with her father. He was quite aware that it was likely because she wasn't being given a choice, but that didn't change anything for Michel. It didn't change the fact he couldn't get her the hell out of there. Not to mention, he still hadn't figured out a way for them to be together.

A whole month wasted.

Fucking *useless*.

"Michel, you're not even listening to me, are you?"

Shit.

He gave the guy at the other end of the pool table a wave as if to silently ask for a minute before he went back to their game. Apparently, he couldn't even hold a conversation and play a game of pool at the same time, lately. His head was just *too full*.

With his mistakes.

With his inabilities.

With her.

With too much.

"I'm listening," Michel lied after he'd snatched up the phone, and took it off speaker to make the conversation a little more private. "I was just ... busy."

If his father heard that brief pause as Michel searched for another lie, Dante didn't call him out on it. He was grateful.

"I thought maybe you were avoiding the question because you *don't* want to come home for Christmas, and assumed I would be angry," his father replied.

"I'm not coming home for Christmas, but I didn't think you would be mad when I let you know. Besides, aren't you and Ma coming up next month, anyway?"

Didn't his mother say they were thinking of stopping in on their way to California in the New Year? How long did that give Michel before his father was in this city, realized the chaos happening all around his son, and yanked him out of Detroit?

A month ... ish?

Fucking *great*.

"Michel, I am sure you can afford a week off school," his father said. "I know they give you a month break, son."

Dante wasn't wrong.

His break started mid-December.

"I'm not coming home for Christmas," Michel said, not offering any more information and refusing to argue further. "I have to catch up on things for school."

Not entirely a lie.

He also wouldn't be studying.

Michel was *not* leaving this goddamn city unless Gabbie was going with him, or she *couldn't*. He really didn't want to consider the reasons that would make it impossible for her to come with him if he found an out for them both, but he knew it was still a possibility. Nonetheless, it didn't change his opinion or decision. He was going to be here until the very end, and he would not be leaving without *her*.

Simple as that.

He still couldn't explain it to his father.

"Fine," Dante murmured, bringing him back to the conversation. "I'm starting to think you love Detroit more than you love your own family considering you've only come home all of *one* time since you moved there."

"I hate this city and most of the people in it."

The words slipped past Michel's scowling lips before he could stop them. It was hard not to notice the absolute silence that filled the other end of the line as soon as he said it, too. *Shit*, that's not what he meant to do. He didn't need his father thinking something was wrong here. He had to do this alone.

"Is there a particular reason why that is?" his father asked.

Michel pinched the bridge of his nose, willing his frustration away. "It's many things, but mostly, the people here aren't like the people back home."

"The Vannozzos."

How did his father just *know*?

Well, Dante partly knew.

Michel would not fill in the details. "They're part of it, sure."

"I never did like that faction of my organization, but they bring in decent money, and mostly keep business clean. There isn't much more a boss could ask for, honestly."

His father wasn't wrong.

They were also *snakes*.

"Just stay out of their way," Dante said, his tone stiffer than was normal, "and let them do their business, Michel. You made friends with a few, didn't you?"

"It didn't stick."

Dante chuckled. "I won't say I am disappointed. I know you think every made man is going to be like the rest of your family, or even your cousins, but it's a different dynamic everywhere you go, and I would rather you didn't integrate too much in families I don't feel are … trustworthy."

Jesus.

That would have been great for his father to tell Michel a year ago. He had the greatest urge to turn around, and beat his forehead on the edge of the pool table because he felt like such an idiot. How he managed to find himself in this situation, Michel would never truly understand.

Oh, no.

That was a lie.

He knew exactly why.

For love.

"I hear they're having some trouble with the Irish there as well," Dante added after a moment, making Michel's heart stop for a split-second. Did his father know the truth about just how much *Michel* was involved in the business with the Irish, too? That it wasn't *just* the Vannozzos? "You are quite aware of how our family always handled any Irish organizations around us, and it was with *great* care and concern, Michel. If they are foolish enough to take the Irish to war, as if the past hasn't taught us Italians anything about them, then let them sign their death warrants."

"From what I understand, the Irish haven't entertained the Vannozzos' trouble here."

"*Yet.*" His father made a harsh sound, saying, "Yet, Michel. It is only because the Vannozzos have not done something so egregious to the Irish organization there that they have not answered them back yet. But when they do, they *will not care*. It will be so brilliantly violent and chaotic in that city, no one will feel safe to even walk down the street. That's the thing about the Irish … they don't care of the consequences. A lifetime in prison is worth their pride and legacy, son. Do not mistake their stubbornness and patience for weakness. They are *waiting* for the Vannozzos to step out of line, and only then will they end them."

Michel blinked.

Was that it?

Had the Italians simply not pressed the *right* button for the Irish yet? What would happen if someone did push that button?

It was only his father's voice that brought him out of those thoughts when Dante said, "You are *not* to be caught up in it. Do you understand me?"

Michel swallowed hard. "Yeah, Dad, I got you."

"Good." Dante made a noise under his breath, adding quieter, "and if you do feel like you need to get out of that city *for any reason*, you do that. Do not waste time, I will be waiting for you here, son."

"Yeah, I know."

"And call your mother later. She misses you."

Michel nodded, though his father couldn't see it. "Will do."

After a quick goodbye, Michel hung up the call. He rubbed the heel of his palm against his forehead, and wished shit wasn't so … *confusing.* And difficult. It was all hard, too. Nothing could ever be simple for him when he needed shit to just be one clear path.

But he was the one who worked best under pressure, right?

That's when he did his best work.

Or it used to be.

Michel leaned back a bit on the table, his hand resting against the felt top. Mistakenly, he hit one of the balls on the table, causing the other player who had been silent during his conversation to give him a look.

"That's dirty pool, man," the guy said, "moving balls like that."

Michel didn't even answer the man back. He was too busy running through his previous thoughts, and the conversation with his father.

Dirty pool.

Michel had assumed the button for Charles Casey was his daughter—the man said it, essentially, and he believed it to be true. But was there more than one? After all, the man was running a *whole* family. And not every person in that organization cared for Gabbie the same way Charles did.

They had other priorities. Like themselves, and the men they were protecting. Those are the ones at the top, and the ones keeping them safe.

Was there another button to push for the Irish family *besides* Gabbie that would force Charles Casey into a war? Could Michel *find* it? What would happen if he punched that button as hard as he fucking could? What if he did something that *made* them react?

He bet the city would be in such an uproar, and both the Italians and Irish would be so busy with one another … they would entirely forget about him. Maybe Gabbie, too. At least, for a time.

Michel was going to find out.

• • •

Sal had bad habits.

It was also one of the first things Michel tended to notice about the people around him—he found quirks, or oddities to be something that made people *more* interesting. He also found that their bad habits were sometimes the things about a person that spoke to deeper beliefs or explained certain choices someone might make day to day.

Sal was paranoid.

Constantly.

It was the second thing Michel realized about the man. Sal didn't like to shake hands with strangers. The shaking hands thing was an oddity, sure, but not uncommon in the world of *Mafiosi*. Made men were often careful when shaking hands with someone they weren't familiar with lest they touch the hand of a cop, or worse, a rival that wasn't—as a proper made man would say—of their standard.

The paranoid thing?

That's where it got interesting.

That's what Michel could *use*.

Sal was so paranoid, in fact, that when he was inside one of his many businesses, he kept the security cameras turned *off*. He told Michel once, that should something happen when he was inside, and the authorities asked what happened to the footage on the security cameras, Sal would simply say it must have been a glitch. Shit happened all the time with electronics, and it was a perfectly acceptable excuse.

To Sal, anyhow.

Michel could have poked a half a dozen holes into the man's theory, but he'd quickly learned that when it came to Sal, it was better to just keep his mouth shut. The man wasn't interested in the opinions of others, he just wanted people to agree with him, and be done with it. So, that's what Michel did.

Usually.

Tonight, though, he planned on using Sal's paranoia and bad habit against him. The cameras in the club Sal frequented every Friday and Saturday night to do his business, never failed, would be turned off. Sure, Michel expected there to be a handful of Sal's associates inside the club as well, but they were always at their *posts*.

At the same time, Sal drifted between his office, the VIP section, and the bathrooms in the far hallway that everyone used. Michel never understood why the man didn't have a private bathroom installed in his office, or at least closer to it, so that he didn't have to use the public one, but again …

Bad habits.

Normal for Sal, even if bad.

Good for Michel tonight.

The bouncer at the front of the club didn't even give Michel a second glance— he was a new guy because Michel didn't recognize his face at all. He didn't have an issue with stepping aside to let Michel enter the club without standing in line as soon as he greeted the man in Italian.

He didn't even check Michel to see if he had a weapon on him, but he doubted the bouncer checked *any* of Sal's men when they came into the business. The bouncer likely thought Michel was part of Sal's crew, and didn't think it would cause any harm to let him in.

He had been part of the crew once.

But not for long.

Inside the club, Michel stuck to the shadows and the crowds of people so that he couldn't be easily picked out. On the dance floor where everyone was moving fast, the music pumped louder, and the lights overhead flashed in such a way that one couldn't properly focus on anything around them, Michel looked for the cameras.

He had to check.

Just to be sure …

Sal's bad habits followed through. Michel found three of the cameras easily enough, and the lack of blinking red lights told him that yes, they were all turned off, and probably would be for the rest of the night. Or at least until Sal was out of the building.

Perfetto.

Not wanting to waste anymore time, or risk the chance that one of Sal's men might notice Michel lingering on the dance floor, he headed into the shadows of the far end of the club. Slipping down the back hallway that led to the bathrooms and a few storage rooms, Michel ducked into the storage room directly across from the men's washroom. He didn't bother to close the door, but he did stay just beyond the line of light that filtered in past the threshold. Here, he couldn't be seen at all.

Which was the entire point.

A long time ago, Michel had decided that he didn't want to be ... like every other man in his family. It wasn't because he thought he was better than them, or that he couldn't *handle* the way they chose to live. He'd simply wanted to be different, and do *more* than just the mafia.

There was still a part of him, though, that would never change. A part of him that had been raised by a Cosa Nostra boss, with uncles who were made men, and cousins that he watched work their entire lives to *be* that man he chose not to be. That part of him was just like them—just as volatile, and dangerous. Just as cunning, and quick on his feet.

He simply didn't show it.

He couldn't when he wasn't them.

Until now.

Michel wasn't sure how long he waited in the darkness of the storage room—it could have been an hour, but it was probably more. Eventually, though, he heard the familiar voice shouting from the other end of the hallway that said his plan was about to come together. Oh, there were still a lot of variables, and shit could go wrong, but he didn't think it would.

Not tonight.

"Yeah, yeah," Michel heard Sal say to someone else, "give me a minute here to take a piss, and we'll take a look at the details for that deal. Grab the folder from my office, yeah?"

"You got it, Sal," someone else replied.

Michel waited.

He didn't move.

The footsteps came closer until he could see Sal passing by the doorway where he was hiding. The man turned to enter the bathroom, and Michel smirked a bit. He knew there was no one else in the bathroom at the moment—he'd been watching it for a hot minute, now. Still, Sal opened the door and shouted for anyone in the room to get the fuck out.

When he didn't get a response, he headed into the bathroom. Michel waited all of five seconds, just long enough that the door swung closed behind Sal, and he figured the man had crossed to the urinals to do his business.

This was low, in a way.

It didn't offer the man *any* pride. He'd be found with his cock in his hands, likely. An embarrassing thing to have to explain to those who would need to be told about his death, and all. This wasn't the way Michel would typically choose to do this kind of thing, but at the same time, it felt oddly appropriate for Sal.

After all, the man had never cared for Michel's pride.

Certainly not his dignity, either.

Michel stepped out of the shadows of the storage room, crossed the hall with two long strides, then slipped into the bathroom, and locked the door behind him just as fast. If someone had blinked, they would have missed him making the move. The door of the bathroom didn't make a single sound as Michel let it close, or when he locked it.

Sal was still looking down at the urinal he was standing in front of when Michel's gaze did a quick sweep to find the man. As he crossed the bathroom, he pulled the switchblade he liked to keep on him from his back pocket.

Rarely did he use that knife.

It was always his *just in case.*

His mother taught him to appreciate a good knife, and the wickedness it could do. He was going to have to remember to thank her for that when the time felt right.

Sal glanced up at the same time Michel came up behind him.

"What the fuck are—"

He didn't get to finish his question. Not before Michel had reached around with one hand to grab Sal by his forehead, yanked his head back, and drew that switchblade across his throat. Blood arched against the mirrors lining the wall, and the urinals, too. A heavy, dark red spray that painted *everything* crimson.

A beautiful sight, really.

Do no harm, Michel thought.

That would be his oath.

One he would follow as best he could.

He'd simply not spoken it yet.

It didn't count.

Sal dropped to the floor, and Michel let the man fall. He grabbed helplessly at his throat, trashing against the bloody tiles as more red slipped past his useless fingers that were doing nothing for the throat wound.

Bending down, Michel used the tip of his gloved-finger to draw a messy shamrock right in the middle of the bloodstains on Sal's forehead. Then, he met the dying man's eyes.

"You're just a means to an end," he said, shrugging. "Like I was for you, so it's only fair, right? The rest of your people will find you. They'll think the Irish did it." Michel pointed at the shamrock on the man's forehead, even though Sal couldn't see it. "That'll help their suspicions along, of course, and I'll make sure to make another on the mirror just to *really* drive the point home."

Sal's eyes widened, and he tried to make a sound, but all that came out were gurgles, and bubbles of blood. Michel scowled at the mess he was making.

"Oh, and tonight, I'll take out Brennan Brady, too. That's Charles Casey's right-hand man, but you don't need me to tell you that, right?" Michel chuckled, resting his gloved hands over his knees, and letting the switchblade dangle from his fingertips where he spun the weapon in a slow circle. Sal was almost dead, now, and Michel really needed to leave. "Every Friday night, he likes to drink himself stupid at a pub close to his house, and then he stumbles home like the idiot he is. The Irish will find him tomorrow … they'll think you did it."

Michel smiled, knowing he only had a few seconds to drive this point home for Sal before the man was so gone, that he wouldn't understand at all. "You see, the Italian boss's cousin was killed tonight—*you*—by who they think is the Irish. And the man next to the Irish boss will be dead, too, and they'll assume it was the Italians. You just didn't push the right button to make the Irish react the way you wanted them to, Sal, but no worries … I have you covered. You simply won't be able to watch what happens now."

And neither would Michel.

He'd be too busy getting Gabbie the fuck out of this city.

"See you in hell," he told Sal before standing up.

EIGHTEEN

"Our Breaking News this morning brings us further escalation of the violence on the streets of Detroit between rival criminal organizations. Late last night, Salvestro Vannozzo was found murdered in his club in the lower end of the city—no official statement has been released, but a source close to the investigation has said they believe this incident to be tied to the other recent issues brought on by organizations."

"Feckin' shite, get his stupid arse on the phone right now!"

Gabbie's father's roar all but shook the walls in the house, and yet, she couldn't look away from the television in front of her. On the screen, the latest drama played out as the anchors discussed the breaking news alongside the reporter who had been at the scene the night before when Salvestro was pulled from his club in a body bag.

But that wasn't the worst of it.

No.

That wasn't even *half* of it.

"I don't *care*," Charles barked at a man as they passed her by in the living room, "you tell those feckin' bastards I'm not going in for *any* interviews today. *Wagons*, the lot of them. The police won't be pushing any of us around."

Yeah, the *police.*

Because—

"Following the murder last night, a high-ranking member of the Irish Casey family was found beaten to death this morning just a half a block away from his home. The victim has been identified as Brennan Brady, and again, while no official statement has been released from the police, our source believes it to be retaliation for the killing of the Vannozzo man at the club the night before ..."

The reports went on and on and *on.*

Gabbie was barely blinking.

What time was it, now?

She looked at the digital time on the box under the television. A little after noon, apparently. It was almost hard to believe, but she had sat on the couch after waking up, and once the news started playing, she literally couldn't *move.*

Her house became more chaotic.

Her father grew louder.

All of the sudden, the forced peace that Charles had made every effort to keep in his house and organization was suddenly ripped apart. He seemed to forget about the fact that Gabbie was still there, listening as he ordered men on the streets—*men on the Italians.* He wanted blood for Brennan's death, and he planned on getting it by the bucketful.

"I'll paint this feckin' city with it; it's what they want."

Gabbie should have been thinking about her father, and her family. She should have considered the fact that the streets were dangerous, and it wouldn't be getting better for a long feckin' time. She should have been sad for her father's best friend, a man who was also her godfather.

That wasn't what she was thinking.

Or feeling, for that matter.

A part of Gabbie was numb. Cold all over, and immovable. Like a statue that didn't have any feelings or thoughts at all. Sitting there on the couch, she felt like she was fading away into the background of the people around her. All the men coming in and out of her father's house, the cell phones that continued to ring nonstop, and the hum of the television in front of her as the reporters kept going … she saw it all and heard every second of it, but she still felt removed.

Watching it.

Not a part of it.

The other part of her that *did* feel something and *was* thinking wasn't focusing on her family, the dangers, or anything else for that matter. All that kept drifting through her mind was that this might be her chance.

This could be *it.*

Her one chance to get away.

No one was looking at her in those moments. Her father was so busy with his men, his rage, and the choices he had to make that not once all day had he even looked her way. He'd not said one single thing to her since she came out of the bedroom that morning.

And the others?

Charles' men?

Same thing.

She felt like shite in a way. Because how awful of a person did it make her that when her father and his people were dealing with the most tragic of circumstances, she was trying to figure out a way to get *away* from them all?

"Get in me feckin' office!"

Gabbie jumped on the couch from the way her father shouted down the hallway. The men in the house didn't even question Charles' order, though. A half of a dozen boots hit the floor like galloping hooves as they headed up the stairs. She glanced upwards at the ceiling, listening as men walked over top her head, directly inside her father's office. Then, she heard the distinct sound of a door closing, too.

The house was quiet.

Mostly.

Gabbie's heart raged.

Like her mind.

And her soul, too.

There was a war going on inside her head. The part that told her it was crazy to consider anything but staying right where she was, and waiting for this hell to blow over. And the other part of her … the one that had spent every single night *crying.* Because she was alone and without the person she wanted the most, and she knew how much she hurt him that night he stood inside this house.

Was Michel even waiting on her anymore? Did he still care?

Did he still love her?

Those were the questions that terrified her, and the fact that she didn't have answers to any of them. Her fingers twitched in her lap as she glanced to the side, finding the landline cordless phone sitting in the cradle to charge. She wasn't allowed to use the phone, and her own cell phone had been taken away a while ago.

A thump hit the floor upstairs.

She looked that way, and stilled on the couch.

Nobody left the office.

Gabbie breathed easier. It was almost funny how she felt like if she picked up that damn phone, someone was going to come around the corner, and catch her. She didn't want to be controlled by fear any longer.

She reached for the phone. Shaking fingers dialed a familiar number. Putting the phone to her ear, she eyed the entryway to the living room as she listened to the call ring and ring and *ring*. Silently, she begged for him to pick up.

Just feckin' pick up.

On the fourth ring, he did.

"*Ciao*," Michel greeted.

"Michel ..."

Silence answered her back.

And then, a sharp, "*Gabbie*."

She didn't have time to waste, so the only thing she could think to ask was, "Does it still stand—if I want to, and I can get to you, we leave?"

"As soon as I can get a flight out of this fucking city. Do you have access to your ID or—"

"Da makes me keep every piece of identification and my passport in my bag just in case we have to leave fast." Gabbie glanced upward again, praying the men in the office stayed there for just a little while longer. "I could probably get a car right now and come to you."

By *stealing* it.

Did it matter?

"I'll be wherever you want to meet up," he said just as fast.

She rattled off a street name mid-city, close to city hall, and the police station. Probably safest right now, all things considered.

Michel let out a heavy breath. "I'll be there. Fucking love you, huh?"

"I know. I love you, too."

She hung up the phone.

The house was still quiet, too.

Now or never ...

• • •

Gabbie ditched the car—one of her father's men that had left the keys in the ignition—two blocks from where she was supposed to meet Michel. She knew what car to look for because she was sure he would have told her if he was driving something different. Tightening the coat around her throat, she tried to blend into the people walking down the busy street.

She was just another woman.

Detroit was *full* of those.

And yet, she still felt like she had to keep checking over her shoulder to see if someone was coming after her. Surely, her father must have realized she took off by now, and there was no doubt in her mind that Charles would know the first person she went to, as well. He'd be looking for her, or at the very least, he would have sent his men out after her.

Gabbie was almost directly in front of the city hall building—although, on the other side of the street from it—when a horn beeped. She jumped in the running shoes she'd pulled on before leaving the house and spun around fast only to realize she had walked *right past* Michel's car.

The relief was sweet.

She almost laughed.

Almost.

For a brief second, Gabbie forgot about *everything* as she met Michel's gaze behind the windshield. His fingers tightened around the steering wheel, and she was finally okay again. Her world righted itself, and started turning again. Because that's how it felt for so long ... like the world just stopped because he wasn't there.

She no longer felt like she had to look over her shoulder as she darted forward to open the passenger door of his car. Slipping into the vehicle, she wasn't thinking about anything except for getting as close to Michel as she possibly could.

He was already reaching for her.

She reached back.

The second his hands were cupping her face, and she was close enough to kiss him, Gabbie did just that. The rest of the world disappeared, then. It didn't even matter any longer. All those nights spent on tear-stained pillows because she was *without him* were a distant memory. This was so much fucking better.

Michel kissed her hard enough to take her breath away. Her fingers curled into the fabric of his jacket because she just couldn't seem to get him close enough even as their tongues warred. He tasted like *heaven* on her tongue—perfect and *hers*. She'd never felt quite so desperate before, but he was right there to coax her through it with every sweep of his lips against hers, and each strike of his tongue along her own.

All too soon for her liking, he was pulling away. Not far, of course, as his lips still grazed hers when he spoke, but it was still a little too far for her.

She hiccupped.

When had those tears started?

Michel let out a soft noise, and used the pad of his thumbs to quickly wipe away the wetness from her face. "Don't cry ... *God*, don't cry, Gabbie."

"Sorry, sorry ... I'm just—"

"Overwhelmed, yeah. I get it."

Still, he wiped away her tears.

He waited her out.

Out of the corner of her eye, she noticed the bruises dotting his knuckles. Every single one them. Like he'd beaten the hell out of something. They looked *painful*.

"What happened?" she asked.

Michel's gaze darted away from hers. "Nothing, babe."

"But—"

"You're here, right? I'm *here*. That's what matters."

Gabbie nodded because yeah, he was right. "You're right. It's just ... everything happened so fast, didn't it? *Everything changed.*"

Michel's jaw tightened. "It had to. It had to change, or I was never going to get you back with me, you know?"

She sucked in a shady breath.

He was as still as stone.

"What does that mean?" she asked.

"Gabbie—"

"Just tell me, Michel."

"One side wanted a war. The other side didn't. I thought … if I forced their hands, then they both might be too busy to notice what I was doing. With *you*."

Oh.

Her heart thundered.

Michel cleared his throat, and then quickly kissed her again. "If other people can do what they have to do, then why can't *I*?"

He wasn't wrong.

"But what about after?" Gabbie glanced out the windshield where the people were still blowing by their vehicle parked along the side of the street. No doubt, they were in a no parking zone, but she just didn't care. "So we leave, and then what happens once things calm down here? You think my father won't come after me? He *will*, and then what will happen? He won't stop. You know that, don't you?"

"We'll deal with it when—"

"I want to be with *you*."

Michel's hands on her face tightened a bit. "I know. First this, though. We'll figure out something else later."

"I don't want to worry about it at all."

She loved her father.

She loved Michel more.

Gabbie's gaze caught the building across the street from where they were parked, and a thought drifted through her mind. It was so quick, she almost laughed it off. It was absurd, in a way, but she'd heard the thought nonetheless.

Michel hadn't missed her silence, either. "What's going on in your head?"

"I just thought about something foolish, that's all."

"*Nothing* you think is foolish."

He would say that.

"This probably is," she muttered.

He kissed her again—desperate and hungry like that first time, but now, sure and *strong*, too. God, she loved this man.

She would love him forever.

"Tell *me*," he uttered against her mouth.

Gabbie smiled. "But it *is* stupid, so don't say I didn't warn you."

"Gab—"

"I thought we could get married."

He stilled.

Her gaze drifted to his, and held strong. "See? *Stupid*. I just thought if I made it clear how I felt with something like that, then what could he really do? I would be somewhere else with you, and I couldn't make my position any more obvious if I wasn't even a *Casey* anymore. It's … foolish, isn't it?"

"Gabbie."

"What?"

"*Gabbie*."

"What?" she asked, sharper.

Michel laughed, but it was dark and beautiful. Like sin had come to coat her in all of its wickedness, and she just couldn't get enough. "If you wanted to marry me today—like none of this was happening—it's the first thing I would do."

She blinked.

He just smirked.

"No, you wouldn't," she said.

"I would."

"Michel, that's *crazy*."

"And either way, today or ten years from now, I am still going to be yours. You're *mine*. That's how this works—it's how *love* works, Gabbie. So yeah, if you wanted to really marry me, I would do that in a heartbeat."

She just blinked again.

Michel stayed quiet.

"Okay," she whispered.

His stare darted away before coming back to her. "I don't know what that—"

"It means *okay*. City hall is right there."

Michel made a noise in the back of his throat.

"What was that for?"

"Three-day waiting period after getting a marriage license in Michigan."

"How do you even *know* that?"

Michel shrugged. "Not important. New York, though … it's a twenty-four hour waiting period, and since we'll already be there, it'll be safer for us."

"You think?"

"Home is *always* safe. Even if they might kill me for doing this."

Gabbie smiled. "Home, huh?"

"New York has always been home for me, but it'll be better with you."

"New York, then?"

"We have to get the hell out of here."

Gabbie nodded. "*Now*."

• • •

"You sure this is what you want to do, man?" John asked. "Because you two are up next."

Gabbie looked over at Michel's cousin—she didn't know much about the guy, but he asked *no* questions when Michel called him the day before. All she knew was when they went in to get their marriage license, a day *after* arriving in New York, someone had pointed out to them that they were going to need a legal witness for the marriage. Michel swore up and down there was no damn way some random witness would work for this.

He needed *family*.

"You should call your mother or father," John added.

Michel's hand tightened around Gabbie's leg. "After, John."

"Yeah, that's gonna fly over well."

"I could have called Andino, you know."

John scowled. "Low blow."

"Yeah, well …"

The two cousins shared a look between one another, and then they grinned. Gabbie had no idea what in the hell she just missed, but she had a feeling Michel would eventually explain it. She didn't mind waiting. There was a lot about Michel, and his life *here* that she didn't know anything about.

She wanted to learn it *all*.

John cleared his throat, bringing their attention back to him again. He nodded at Gabbie as his gaze drifted to Michel. "So, are we going to pretend like the marriage license in her hand doesn't have her last name down as *Casey*, because I'm pretty sure Detroit has been on the news for the last forty-eight hours since the city might as well be burning down from the shit happening there, and all. But you know, totally up to you if you don't want to share and all."

"You didn't ask questions last night."

The man shrugged. "I'm bored now, indulge me."

"I really should have called Andino."

John outright scoffed at that. "*Right,* fucking Andi, who follows the rules of this family even more than I do, Michel. I am sure that would have blown over exceptionally well for you. He'd have had your mother, father, *and* sister here. But sure, you can keep living in that delusion."

"I fucking hate you."

"No, you don't." John smirked, asking, "And how is the whole … becoming a doctor thing going for you?"

Michel sucked air through his teeth, his frustration clear. "I'm probably going to fail my second year, but you know, shit happens."

"*Yikes.*"

"What can you do?"

"Uh, *not* get involved with the idiots in Detroit who are apparently warring with that woman's family … shit, is she like … *the* Gabbie Casey?" John raised a brow when Michel said nothing. "You know I've spent time in Detroit before, right? I know who people are there, Michel."

"Michel Marcello and Gabbie Casey, you're up!"

Michel passed his cousin a look, and Gabbie stayed quiet beside him. She was quite aware that there was more happening between these two men than she understood. A whole family dynamic that she had never been privy to, likely.

"I *know* I'm not doing it the right way," Michel said to his cousin.

"As long as you understand that."

"But it's the only way, John."

John grunted under his breath. "I'm just saying that if I came home married to a woman without telling my parents … but especially my *ma*, someone would have a great time pickling my balls for it. And *my* ma, Michel, she's the sweetest thing on the block. She won't hurt a moth when it gets into the house. You ever see Lucian running around the living room with a net to catch a moth because Ma won't let him kill it? *Yeah.* That's my ma. Yours, though … she's going to cut your heart out for doing this, and then she's going to wear it as a necklace for the rest of her life as a reminder of how you broke hers."

"Wait," Gabbie muttered, looking between the two. "*That's* what this is?"

"Sorry?" John asked.

"It's because he's not told his parents?"

John's gaze narrowed at the wall right beside Gabbie's head. "I mean … yeah? You don't know much about Italians, do you?"

Michel chuckled, but said nothing.

Gabbie smacked him with the back of her hand, right in his gut. "Stop it, I thought he was going on like that because of what is happening in Detroit. I was panicking here, Michel. And he's going off like a feckin' *stook* because of your *family*? Bollocks, all of it, and then you sit here and take the piss out of me by *laughing*. Shite, that is."

John stared at Michel, then. "Did she insult me … or you?" His gaze darted around as he muttered, "*What* … because I don't understand a thing she just said."

Gabbie scowled.

Michel laughed harder. "This is going to be great, really."

"Until your ma finds out," John returned.

That quieted Michel.

"Still fucking hate you," he told his cousin.

John smirked. "But you did pick me to be your *witness*."

"Regretting that."

"Liar."

"Are we getting married today, or what?" the clerk's receptionist snapped at them from the opened doorway. "Because there is a whole line behind you waiting. Someone else can go instead."

Gabbie was the first to stand, and Michel quickly followed. Even with the idea that someone—mainly Michel's mother—was going to be *very* unhappy that this had happened without her knowing beforehand, she didn't feel any regret walking into the office with Michel's hand woven with hers. Detroit was a background thought for her now … as silly as that might be. Mostly because they were moving forward, and leaving it behind.

This—getting married—was one more step forward. It might be a shite way to start a relationship with her mother-in-law, sure.

Some things couldn't be helped.

NINETEEN

There wasn't anything *amazing* about being married at the City Clerk's office. If anything, it was very legal and final. Other than the clapping from the people in the office bearing witness to the weddings while doing their jobs, and John who stood in as the legal witness for Michel and Gabbie, it all happened rather quietly.

And quickly.

Michel thought … he liked it better that way. He never thought he would have said that. Being Italian, and growing up in such a large family, weddings were part of the culture. Loud, messy, and all night long. That was the typical Catholic, Italian wedding. He'd never given much thought to his wedding or how it might happen, but now that it had happened, there wasn't any other way he cared to do it.

This had been perfect.

"… I now pronounce you man and wife," the clerk said.

Michel blinked, losing his train of thought in the process. Not because of the clerk's words, but because Gabbie's sweet smile deepened at the woman's proclamation.

It was done.

"You may kiss your wife," the clerk added.

Michel's hands tightened around Gabbie's. It was the only warning he gave his wife before he tugged her closer to him in one fast, hard motion. He kept his fingers tangled with hers as his mouth crashed down on her own. He was pretty sure the clerk intended for them to have a quick kiss, and make their way out as fast as they came in.

Was that typical?

Michel didn't know.

All he cared about in that moment was the way his wife's lips worked against his. How her fingers tightened around his, and then a sweet smile curved her mouth because she knew it, too. It was such a primal urge, he thought, just to *do this.*

To kiss his *wife.*

Because that's what Gabbie was now.

His wife.

A *Marcello.*

For life.

* * *

Gabbie sat in the rental as Michel leaned against the passenger side to talk to John. He decided they would take the evening to themselves before making the trip out of the city to visit his parents.

That should be fun.

Michel wasn't really thinking about it right now. He had a million other things on his mind, and while he knew it was sure to be a shitshow with Dante and Catrina, in the end … they were going to be fine with what he did. They were his parents, and they loved him to the ends of the earth and back. That's what counted.

So, he just pushed it out of his mind.

"I'm calling Andino as *soon* as I leave here," John warned.

Michel chuckled. "Tell him not to be *too* offended. And make sure he doesn't call my father first. I have to be the one to do that, John."

"Yeah, yeah."

"Seriously, make sure he knows."

"He's going to kick your ass."

Michel nodded. "He can try."

John barked out a laugh, and reached out to smack Michel hard on his shoulder. "We really fucking missed you, yeah? Detroit wasn't made for you, man."

Didn't he know it?

Michel only shrugged as his response to his cousin, but John seemed to understand. Somethings were just better said without *words*. He didn't need to confirm John's statement verbally for it to still be true, and for both of them to know it.

New York was home.

It had always been.

In fact, he felt better already simply because he *was* on these streets. This was where he grew up, and these were his people. He'd wanted to get out of New York for medical school—despite there being perfectly fine medical schools in his home state—because he thought he needed to put as much distance between him and his surname as possible to become something *other* than just his surname.

Michel had been wrong.

He didn't have so much pride that he couldn't admit it, too.

"Better get back to that *wife* of yours," John said, nodding at the car.

Michel had to smile at the way his cousin twisted the word *wife* like it was some sort of foreign concept to him. "Who'll be next out of the three of us cousins? *You* maybe?"

John's cheek twitched. "No woman can handle me, I think."

"Right, right. You keep telling yourself that."

"I will."

"Until she knocks you on your ass," Michel said, "because that's how it'll happen, John."

Out of all the things Michel learned about love since finding Gabbie, *that* was the one thing he was most sure of. Love came when one was not expecting it because one could not *plan* for love. That wasn't how it worked. Love was not meant to be a thing you went out and found for yourself, because it was the thing that found *you*.

John eyed Michel from the side. "As long as it was worth it, man."

Out of the corner of his eye, Michel watched Gabbie in the rental. She toyed with a phone that rested in her lap, and then leaned over to fiddle with the radio station. She let her fingers drift through her hair to smooth back the wild, red curls he loved so much.

It was simple—even *mundane*—things for her to do, and nothing particularly special. He'd seen hundreds, if not thousands, of people do the same things throughout his life. Yet, watching her do those same things were not the same to him at all.

It was an *experience*.

It was her.

He could watch her do mundane, everyday things for the rest of their life, and he would never get bored with it. He wanted nothing more than to be the person watching her do those simple things, and apparently, she wanted the same things, too.

Like his wife knew he was looking at her, Gabbie turned in the seat to look out the window. Her green eyes met his, and a smile bloomed over her cheeks. It reached her eyes, and lit her whole face up.

She smiled for him all the time.

She smiled *because* of him.

What more could he want?

"More than worth it, John," Michel murmured.

"I'll take your word for it, man."

He could.

For now.

Someday, John would know, too.

· · ·

"I ... should call him."

Michel glanced over at his wife, but Gabbie was still staring at the phone in her lap. *His* cell phone, actually. She'd taken it from him at the City Clerk's office to hold onto it while he signed some paperwork, but he didn't think to ask for it back.

"Who?" he asked.

Gabbie's tongue peeked out to wet her bottom lip. "My da."

He'd be a fucking liar if he said he didn't react to that statement by stiffening in the driver's seat. Even his fingers flexed around the steering wheel tight enough that his knuckles turned white from the pressure. It wasn't even *Gabbie*, or the fact that she wanted to speak with her father, but more ...

The threat.

He felt the threat, and recognized it for what it was. Because that's how he saw her father, now. Just one big fucking threat. To him, and to *her*. He wasn't so stupid that he believed he had removed all the threats from their life, of course, but that was a big one he'd left behind.

What else could he do?

Michel wouldn't have *ever* touched her father—and he wouldn't now unless Charles Casey thought to do something that threatened Gabbie—because she didn't want him to. She adored her father; she loved him entirely because for a long time, Charles was all she had. He didn't think for one second that she would forgive him for something like that.

"Just to let him know," Gabbie said, glancing up at him.

Michel raised a brow. "So, then do that."

"But—"

"Babe, if you want to call him, then you should do that."

She pressed her lips together, whispering, "But what if he comes here, or something?"

"He won't."

Of that, Michel was most sure. Charles was a lot of things, but stupid was not one of them. The man had to know he didn't have any real allies in New York by way of major families to help him go against the Marcellos, if he wanted to try and take his daughter back. That was before they even factored into the fact that Gabbie was now Michel's wife.

He just wouldn't do it.

"Call him," Michel said as he pulled into the garage of the hotel where they would be staying. The Astoria had always been a favorite of his; sometimes, having expensive taste was more than worth the price. "You won't feel okay until you do, so just get it over with."

Gabbie nodded. "Okay."

Michel parked the car as Gabbie dialed on the phone. He thought she would put the phone to her head, allowing him access to only her side of the conversation, but she put it on speakerphone for him to listen in.

It rang three times.

Each ring, his anxiety spiked.

He almost thought the phone would go to the voicemail, which might be for the best, but he couldn't be so lucky. Charles picked up on the fourth ring.

"Aye, I'm *feckin' busy here*!"

"Da," Gabbie said softly.

A silence answered his wife back, thick and *loaded*. Michel didn't miss it, and even their car became so quiet that he could hear her swallow in the seat next to his. Wordlessly, he reached across the car to place his hand on her thigh. His fingers curved around her body, and he squeezed tight. His silent show of support, if she needed it. Gabbie gave him a small smile, but this time, it didn't reach her eyes.

He didn't need to ask why.

"*Gabbie?*"

"Yeah, Da, it's—"

"Where the *feck* are you, lass?"

"I'm—"

"You took off with that Italian cunt again, didn't you?" Charles let out a dark noise. It sounded like disappointment and anger all rolled into one. Michel felt the tremor that worked its way through Gabbie's body as it vibrated against his palm, but he just squeezed her leg again. It was the best he could do if she really felt a need to do this to herself. "Just tell me where you are, and make this easy on all of us, Gabbie. I'll send someone to come get you—do you want me to promise I won't kill the Italian? *Fine*. I will leave him alive. Is that better?"

Gabbie cleared her throat. "Da—"

"I don't have time for this shite, girl. Do you understand me? This entire city is in an uproar, I have police banging on my door, and too many men dead to *count*. And you want me to play *tag* with you all over Detroit while you chase after a man you *can't have*?"

"I'm not in Detroit, Da."

That silenced Charles.

For all of one second.

"What did ye just say to me?"

"I'm in New York with Michel. We just got married. I'm not coming home, Da. It's not where I want to be, and it's not where I belong. I love you, but I need to be where—"

"Say that again."

"What?"

"What you *did*, lass ... *say it again*."

Gabbie cleared her throat. "We just got married."

"You're dead to me."

His wife stiffened.

Michel went to grab the phone out of her hand, but Charles got in the last word before he could hang up on the asshole.

"Don't you ever step foot in my city again—I'll kill every single feckin' one of you. You want the Italian so much, do you? Then, you have him. *You are dead to me, Gabbie.*"

He hung up the phone, so she didn't have to.

Not that it mattered.

Gabbie was already crying.

• • •

His wife was too quiet.

Michel didn't like that at all.

Inside the hotel room, he wanted to see her wide-eyed and excited at the beauty and history surrounding her. He wanted her to ask him why he picked this hotel, so he could explain that his father rented a permanent room in the Astoria *just* so that Michel's mother had a place to escape to when she needed, often with her husband.

Instead, he watched Gabbie as she stared out the window. Entirely silent, she stood there while rubbing her arm with the palm of her hand as the people crowded the street from all different directions down below.

Yeah, *way too quiet.*

Stuffing his hands in his pockets, Michel cleared his throat. It did nothing. Gabbie didn't turn away from the window, and there was no flicker in her distant gaze to say that she had even heard him make any noise.

Damn.

"Gabbie," he murmured.

Still, nothing.

Michel sighed.

He was seriously regretting that phone call, now. It wasn't his choice, though, and he was never going to do that to this woman. She could and would make her own decisions, and whether he thought they were good or bad, he was going to be there to support her through it. Simple as that.

Since she didn't seem to be hearing him from all the way across the room, Michel figured the easy solution to that problem was for him to go to *her*. He closed the space between them until he was close enough to reach out and enclose her in his arms from behind. Resting his face in the spot between her shoulder and

149

neck, he pressed a lingering kiss to the skin just above her neckline. He physically *felt* the tension drift from her body as she relaxed in his embrace.

That was slightly better.

"I know that wasn't what you wanted from your dad," he said quietly.

She shrugged. "It was inevitable, maybe."

"No, it wasn't." That was his hard line—she should not *expect* that kind of thing from people who loved her, *ever*. No one should ever expect people who proclaimed to love them to hurt them. That was not how love worked. It might hurt occasionally, but only to make it better. "People always have a choice, Gabbie, to do what is right, or to do what they *think* is right. It might not always be obvious or easy, but that's what it is. He made the wrong choice, and I'm sorry."

A sniffle echoed in the room.

He kissed her skin again.

"My da was all I had ... my mam's been dead for years, and—"

"You have me," he said quickly. "And I promise there's a whole family of people here who are going to *love* you. They will love you so much just because I love you."

She sunk a little more into his embrace.

Michel held her tighter.

"Promise?"

"Until the day I die."

"Hmm," Gabbie said.

"What?"

"I was just thinking."

Michel's lips grazed higher on her neck until he came to the shell of her ear. Letting his teeth nibble on the flesh, he muttered, "*About?*"

Gabbie laughed, but he didn't miss the way her body shivered, either. "You."

"Oh, keep going. I do love it when people talk about me."

"*Vain.*"

"But is it really, though?"

"A wee bit, but I like it," she whispered. "I was thinking I don't know where you came from, or what put you in my path, and I don't think I deserve you ... but you're mine, I'm keeping you, and I love you, Michel."

"I love you, too." He grinned against her ear. "But you already knew that, right?"

Gabbie pressed the side of her head against his. "I suppose. So, what do we do now?"

Oh, there was a lot of things they had to do. He still hadn't called his parents despite being in the city for two days, now, and he hadn't ate since that morning. Although, he did manage to find something healthy and appropriate for Gabbie to eat during their long wait at the City Clerk's office.

But right now?

"I really just want to fuck my *wife*," Michel told her.

He saw her grin grow sinful in a blink.

"You should probably get on that, then."

Oh, most definitely.

It was silly, maybe.

Kind of stupid.

But Michel still picked Gabbie up in a cradle embrace to walk her to the bedroom. Because wasn't that what husbands were supposed to do with their wives on the night of their wedding? Walk over the threshold to start their life while *carrying* their life at the same time?

It was silly, sure.

It still felt right.

Once Michel had Gabbie on her back in the large king-size bed, he took his time to pull every piece of clothing keeping her body from him away until she was bare on the bed in nothing but her sin and *skin*. His fingertips traced the dots of her freckles—he still loved those the very most. The spattering of freckles across her breasts, and the ones coloring her features. His mouth followed the same path as his hands, too.

Kissing.

Tasting.

Biting.

Not hard, though.

Not tonight.

Gabbie made the sweetest sounds when she was being *loved*. Breathless, and high, he thought. Her soft moans echoed in his ears as he kissed down her clenching stomach, stopping only long enough to let his tongue trace her navel.

Then, he was lower.

Widening her thighs …

Finding *heaven*.

His heaven was wet, and pink, and *hot*. She tasted like candy on his tongue, a tart sugar he couldn't get enough of no matter how many times he got to indulge. The second his mouth encased Gabbie's pussy, her back lifted from the bed. Her hands fisted into the sheets when he sucked on her clit, drawing the little bud between his lips to *really* give her that shock she seemed to like so damn much.

"*Please, please …*"

Michel replaced his mouth with his fingers—not that he would be able to hold himself back from getting another taste of her, but for now … He worked her clit with two fingers, rubbing tight little circles into the nub as another two fingers slid into her tight sex.

"What do you want, Gabbie? *Tell me.*"

"Make me come. *Please, make me come.*"

He loved when she begged.

Loved it more when she sounded so desperate for it, too.

Nothing got him hotter.

"*And then?*" he demanded.

She let out a whine. "*Love me.*"

Yeah.

That's what he planned to do.

His fingers kept fucking her, but he replaced his other hand on her clit with his mouth again. A steady, hard beat with his tongue took her over the edge faster than he thought it would, but he wasn't about to complain.

"*God,*" Gabbie mumbled, her face turning into the pillow. "Love you."

More than she would ever know.

Michel couldn't shed his clothes fast enough, but once he was naked, and his cock was covered in the condom he found in his pant pocket, he was back between her thighs again. Pushing in deep and taking her slow. Instead of fingernails scoring down his back, he got her fingertips making lazy circles over his shoulders as he loved her. The gentle rocking of their bodies wasn't the roughness that usually accompanied their sex, but it didn't need to be, either.

He had all the time in the word for fast and hard later.

Right now, he just wanted to *love*.

• • •

It was only once Michel was sure that his wife was out for the rest of the evening that he finally crawled out of the bed, and away from her. Although, a part of him was still there, tucked into her side and feeling her heart beat under his palm. He'd get back to her soon enough, and she wouldn't even realize he'd left the bed at all.

Michel snatched the phone up from the bedside table and slipped out of the bedroom with quiet steps. In the darkness of the connecting room, he stared at the screen of his phone before turning it on, and scrolling through the contacts.

It was too late.

A little after eleven, now.

His parents *hated* late calls.

Michel put the phone to his ear, and waited as it began to ring through. Like an echo reverberating through his very bones, he swore it sounded like it was whispering *now or never, boy*. He shouldn't be this nervous, but here he was, feeling exactly that.

"Michel, it is *way* too late for you to be calling me," he heard his father grumble as soon as Dante picked up the call.

"Sorry, but this couldn't wait."

Dante made a noise under his breath, and something shuffled on the other end of the call. Was his father in bed already? *Probably.* "Well, what is it?"

"Is Ma awake?"

"She is *now*."

"I raised him better than *this*," Catrina snapped, making Michel chuckle.

"Tell her I'm sorry."

"Yeah, yeah. What is it?" his father asked.

"I'm … uh, in the city," Michel said.

Silence answered him back before his father gained his bearings enough to respond with, "Since when?"

"Yesterday."

"What—"

"We needed to wait twenty-four hours before we could go into the Clerk's office after we got the marriage license, that's all."

It took his father entirely too long to respond.

And then, when he did, all Dante could do was *splutter*. Michel couldn't remember a time when his father had been as equally upset and confused at the same time, but apparently, he got to be the lucky fuck who did it for him.

"*What?*" his father finally settled on barking.

Michel cleared his throat, adding, "I did some stuff."

"*I fucking guess, Michel.*"

"Give me the phone—you give me that goddamn phone, Dante!"

Something crackled, and then, his mother was on the phone, too. Michel thought to move the speaker away from his ear because he was pretty sure his mother was about to get *very* loud. Like the idiot he was, he kept the phone pressed tight to his ear, and just about got his eardrums busted out for doing it, too.

"*You got married and I wasn't there?*"

Michel blinked. "Hey, Ma."

"*Why would you do that to me?*"

She was hysterical.

Her words, a *shriek*.

"I have spent *years* loving and raising you, and *this* is what you do to me? How *dare you, Michel Dante Marcello!*"

Oh, full name.

He was sure Dante hadn't been his middle name *before* his parents adopted him, but as he didn't know his middle name from that time, this worked just as well to get his mother's point across.

Michel said the first thing that came to his mind, hoping it would calm his mother down. "You're going to love her, Ma. She's fucking amazing, and I just want … I just want you to love her like I do, okay?"

Catrina quieted.

He breathed a little easier, then.

Finally, his mother asked, "What's her name?"

"Gabbie. Gabbie Casey."

He must have been on speakerphone, because in the background, he heard his father ask, "Gabbie Casey, daughter of *Charles* Casey?"

Michel made a noise under his breath. "So yeah, that's uh … the *stuff* I did, Dad."

"Oh, my God, Michel."

Yeah, that's how he felt, too.

TWENTY

The first thing Gabbie thought when Michel parked the car in the driveway of his childhood home? It seemed *welcoming.*

The second?

Is that his mother?

Standing on the front porch, like they knew exactly what point Michel and Gabbie would drive up, were a man and a woman. The man, dressed in a silk dress shirt, black slacks, and a tie that had been loosened around his throat smiled briefly. Michel's mother, on the other hand, wore a long dress that draped her body, and maybe it was the appearance the woman exuded, but Gabbie thought the clothing had the privilege of being on Catrina, and not the other way around.

Rings adorned her fingers. It was closing in on supper time, and the woman's makeup looked like it had been painted on with such skill that it wouldn't move an inch throughout the rest of the day. Her hair, a few shades of a deeper red than Gabbie's, had been let loose in soft waves.

Catrina, who was simply standing next to her husband, seemed *regal.* That was the only appropriate word Gabbie could think of, and yes, it intimidated her. She had never met a woman who displayed the same air of authority that a man did simply by *being,* but what she knew about Michel's mother … she wasn't surprised that Catrina seemed this way, even from afar.

"Oh good, they came out to welcome us."

Michel's sarcasm did nothing to help settle her.

So, yeah.

Dante and Catrina.

Gabbie tried to calm her nerves, but it really didn't work. *At all.* Unfortunately, she didn't have time to think on it when Michel was already out of the car, and coming around to her side to help her out. He was the *get it over with* type, and Gabbie had figured out she was more of a *let it die a slow death while she avoided it* type.

Yup.

"Smile," he said, kissing her cheek as he helped her from the car. "They're going to love you."

Right.

Before or after they explained everything that went down in Detroit?

Gabbie didn't bother to ask.

Besides, she had other things to consider now, like the fact they were getting closer to the man and woman waiting on the front steps of the large, three-level home by the second. Michel slipped an arm around Gabbie's waist like he thought she might bolt, and frankly … he wasn't entirely wrong. She felt like a deer about to meet a Mack truck, but she didn't know *why.*

"Ma, Dad," Michel greeted as they climbed the steps.

Catrina, his mother, hadn't looked away from Gabbie once since she stepped out of the car. She wasn't quite sure what to make of that, but here they were.

"Michel," Dante replied, "and … Gabbie, yes?"

She smiled. "It is. It's very nice to meet you."

Dante looked to his wife, saying, "And us for you."

Catrina cleared her throat, and for the first time, looked away from Gabbie as she turned toward the front door. With a wave, she said, "We have coffee in the pot, if you two want to come in and ... get this started."

Get this started.

That was a great way to describe *this.*

"That sounds grand," Gabbie said, "I take mine black."

Catrina cracked a smile. "Me, too. It's an acquired taste."

Dante chuckled next to his wife. "Something Catrina can relate to being herself, I assure you."

"That's quite enough of that, Dante."

"But also, not a lie," Michel murmured in Gabbie's ear. At the same time, she smiled at his whispered secret, Catrina turned to look back at them. Her stance softened momentarily at the sight of the two together, but she quickly spun back around. "Come on, babe, let's get comfortable for this."

• • •

Gabbie palmed the mug as Michel finished explaining to his father just how they had gotten to *this* point. Coming to New York, being married, and finally, sitting at this very table. He'd skimped on some details, leaving out the fact he had been the one to drop the final straw that broke the proverbial camel's back in Detroit, but she didn't mind.

She understood why.

Dante exhaled heavily and rested back in his chair. "Give me a second, Michel. To *digest.*"

Michel nodded. "Yeah, I know. It's a lot."

Catrina, on the other hand, eyed her son pensively. "You stopped calling as much as you used to this last year."

"I'm sorry, Ma, I just—"

"Is this why?"

Michel shifted in his chair. "I mean, part of it, yeah."

Gabbie had never felt *more* awkward than she did in those moments. Maybe it was because the conversation had quickly turned serious, and she realized just how much of her private moments with Michel were being laid out bare on the table for basically *strangers* to dissect. Oh, sure, they were his parents.

But she didn't know them.

Not *that* well.

It didn't help that whenever Catrina spoke, she did so shortly, and with little emotion to her tone. Yet, the woman's eyes blazed. Gabbie understood why, sure, but it didn't make it anymore comfortable to sit there at the table like nothing was wrong.

"The Irish ..." Dante trailed off, giving Michel a raised brow. "Will I need to handle that?"

"I don't think so," Michel returned. "Charles made his position clear."

Catrina's gaze flicked to Gabbie, then. "Yes, shame, that."

She didn't know what to say.

So, she said nothing.

It was only the roar of a car's engine somewhere outside the house that stopped their conversation. Soon after, the front door slammed closed, and footsteps echoed down the hallway leading to the dining room.

"I thought you weren't coming home for Christmas this year?"

Everyone, including Gabbie, turned to find a young woman standing in the entryway. Catherine, Gabbie thought … Michel's one and only sibling. He'd never talked much about her, but the two siblings looked fondly at one another all the same.

Michel smiled. "Nice to see you, too, little sister."

Catherine stuck her tongue out in response. "Seriously, no one thought to tell me?"

Well, there was that awkwardness again. Silence coated the table, because clearly, no one wanted to explain to Catherine the same things Michel had just gone through before she arrived. Gabbie looked to Michel, but he glanced his father's way. Dante, to his benefit, was staring at his wife like she might like to be the one to explain.

"Well, you see …" Catrina started, making a face as though she couldn't find the right words to use. Gabbie wished she could just *shrink* away into her chair, and be done with it.

"It was a surprise for us, too," Dante finished for his wife.

Catherine seemed like she didn't care at all as she turned to Gabbie with a wide smile. "Hi, I'm Catherine."

She smiled back. "Gabbie."

The first thing Gabbie thought about Catherine was that she didn't look a lot like her brother. She shared her father's green eyes, his dark hair, but her mother's *entire face*, essentially. But the way she tilted her head to the side as she regarded her brother … Gabbie found familiarity there because Michel did the same thing when he was considering something.

"Holy shit," Catherine said to Michel, "you brought home a girl."

Michel relaxed next to Gabbie. "Yeah, I guess I did, Catty."

Dante chuckled across the table. "Sort of."

Heat rose to Gabbie's cheeks at the implication in the man's words.

"What did I miss?" Catherine asked.

The silence echoed.

Catherine, again, didn't seem to care as she turned to her brother for an answer. "You didn't, like … knock her up or something, right?"

Michel barked out a laugh.

Gabbie had the strangest urge to smack him for it, too.

"No," he said.

Okay, this was grand, but Gabbie had just about enough of being the brunt of the joke. As if this wasn't awkward enough, it was only being made worse. Maybe this hadn't been the best time to do this.

She didn't hide the roll of her eyes as she said to Michel, "Well, this has been fun, but maybe it's time to go."

Catrina quickly stood from her seat, and her gaze locked on Gabbie, then. "Please stay; this was just a bit of a shock, that's all."

Dante nodded. "Yes, stay."

Gabbie looked to Michel.

She would … if he would.

He winked.

"Seriously, what did I miss?" Catherine asked louder.

Michel cleared his throat, gave Gabbie a small smile, and then lifted his hand for his sister to see the gold band on his ring finger. A new addition to his hand, but permanent. At least … if he wasn't in a hospital working. They'd picked up matching bands that morning after breakfast because Michel didn't want to wait. And frankly, neither did she.

"Meet my wife, Catherine."

• • •

"Gabbie, would you like to help me make some bread?"

On the couch, Gabbie stiffened.

Beside her, Catherine let out a light laugh. Michel's sister was *nothing* like him, and yet, Gabbie still felt herself drawn to the young woman. There was something haunting in her eyes, and yet, a strength, too. Like nothing she had ever seen before in someone else. Catherine was also easy to like.

She needed to make friends here, didn't she?

"I don't know what that sound was for, Catty," Catrina said from the doorway, "but you better correct it."

Catherine rolled her eyes and stood from the couch. "You're a little intimidating, that's all, Ma. Don't have a stroke."

"Catherine."

"I'm not wrong, though." Catherine winked down at Gabbie and smiled. "Her bark is *way* worse than her bite—watch out for the claws, though. They're the *real* killers."

She could tell Catherine was just trying to poke at her mother, and it was amusing. Not to mention the way Catrina fumed in the doorway.

"Stop making up lies about me," Catrina said, a smile starting to grow. "I don't *bark*, Catherine. I enunciate words like a proper fucking lady, and use them like knives to cut people down, as anyone would. And if someone isn't doing that, well that's a damn shame, because they *should*."

Jesus.

"I would love to make bread with you," Gabbie said, standing from the couch as well. "A wee bit late for it, though, isn't it?"

Catrina gave her daughter a look. "See, she's going to be *fine*."

"Mmhmm. Watch the claws, Gabbie. That's all I'm saying."

Catherine drifted from the living room soon after, which left Gabbie alone with Catrina.

Waving a hand for her to follow, Catrina turned away from the entryway as she said, "Making bread is how I decompress, and think. No one around here complains when there is always fresh bread to eat."

"I do like bread, but …"

"Hmm?"

"Do you have a good whole wheat recipe? I'm a type two diabetic, and—"

Catrina turned fast, almost making Gabbie bump into her at the same time. "Are you?"

"Yes."

"Oh." Catrina rubbed her hands together. "I'll check what I have, but if I don't have what we need, then we can call one of my sisters-in-law. They'll have the rest."

"You don't have to do that."

"Of course, I do. Now come on, let's go cook."

Catrina didn't need to call for more ingredients; they ended up finding everything in the home's *very* large pantry. Gabbie was still a bit overwhelmed at how large the home was, and she thought her childhood house was huge. Not to mention, from the outside, the place looked like an upscale family lived here, but inside?

That's where the wealth was.

And it was *everywhere.*

"Yes, those are real gold-plated spoons," Catrina said as Gabbie eyed the utensils that had been haphazardly thrown in a cup to make coffee. "They don't get any use unless I put them there, and people still hesitate."

"Because it's gold, maybe?"

She was not unaccustomed to wealth.

They lived a good life.

This was not the same.

Catrina made a noise under her breath as she pushed a bag of flour across the island to Gabbie. "Possibly. Get it opened, hmm?"

Gabbie laughed, and did as she was told. Before long, Catrina had the dough made, and was working hard to knead it to what she called *perfection*. Was there even such a thing? She didn't know, but she wasn't going to ask the woman to go into further detail. As it was, making bread with Catrina was already a whole *experience*.

"My mother-in-law welcomed us women into the family by cooking, too," Catrina said, "and this was also, over the years, how she would bring us back down to earth. Cecelia never had an issue with dragging one of us into the kitchen, so she could bark orders at us on how we should cook, while at the same time, telling us the meaning of marriage and life."

"Oh?"

The woman nodded. "I was never more grateful. I didn't have a mother ... not for a long time, anyway. And when I needed one the most, I didn't have that influence. It felt, in a way, as though I met my mother figure later in life. You see, she wasn't very happy with me coming into my husband's life in the way I did, and it was rocky for a while, but this ... *cooking* ... was often how Cecelia and I worked through it."

Gabbie frowned.

Catrina didn't miss it. "What was that for, now?"

"I was just thinking ... well, I'm sorry if you're angry about me being here, or if you feel like you're being forced to like me because of everything. I—"

"Oh, that's enough of that."

Her head snapped up from the flour in her hand.

Catrina was smiling again. "Of course, I *like* you." She clicked her tongue, and passed Gabbie a look from the side as she quickly added, "I would dare say *love*, actually, but I wouldn't want to scare you with that. He loves you, after all. And you love him, don't you? That is all I need to know. I may not have been the woman who brought Michel into the world, but I still gave him life, and I am still the only woman he calls his mother. All I need to know is that he loves you, and you love him. That is enough for me. I may be angry at him, but I am blessed to meet you."

Gabbie blinked.

That had been a lot to take in.

There were a lot of things she wanted to reply to in Catrina's statements, but she kept rolling back to the same one thing. A *specific* thing. Something she hadn't known about Michel until this moment.

"Michel is adopted?"

Catrina's smile stayed firmly in place. "He doesn't act like it, does he?"

"No, and isn't that something someone might mention? You know, that they're adopted?"

Although, it made sense. Michel did not share his mother's blue eyes, or her red hair. He did not take his father's dark shade of brown hair, or Dante's dark green eyes. The dimples that peeked out whenever Michel grinned didn't come from either of his parents, either. He did have *some* similar features to Catrina, like the shape of her eyes and the sly look in her gaze as she looked at someone from the side, but the latter could be explained by nurture over nature.

"He's never felt like it, either, maybe that's why he didn't say anything. I can't say that makes me unhappy. All I ever wanted was for him to know that he was *so* loved."

"I can see you love him," Gabbie returned.

"I do, very much, as if he came from my body—I love him the same." Catrina shrugged one shoulder, and put her hands back into the dough to continue kneading it. "He was born to my half-sister. She died very soon after his birth, and I took him out of the country to bring him with me to America."

Huh.

"Ma."

The low voice coming from the kitchen entryway made Gabbie look up from her own work of dusting the counter with flour. There, she found Michel leaning against the entry wall, a small smile playing on his lips. Just how long had he been standing there?

His gaze drifted to her for a quick passing before cutting back to his mother. Catrina raised a brow at him, but he only chuckled in response. Gabbie swore she could hear the woman silently chiding her adult son for *spying* on their conversation.

"Ma," he said again, giving her a look.

"Yes, Michel?"

"I have always known that I am loved."

Catrina kept her gaze on her work, but one couldn't miss the smile playing on her lips. "I know, *ragazzo*. I know."

• • •

Gabbie flipped a decorative pillow off the bed, and onto the chair in the corner. Michel tossed her another from his side of the bed, too. For now, they would stay at his parents' home until they figured something else out.

"Are you still set on the lawyer thing?" he asked.

"Why not?"

Michel shrugged. "Because here, you can do anything."

Gabbie winked. "And that's what I want to do."

"All right. We can head to the college tomorrow and start the process to get everything transferred for you. If your grades are good enough, we shouldn't have any problems." Then, he smirked sinfully, adding, "And just in case they are a little iffy ... I have enough money to pay your way in."

She didn't even think before picking up a normal pillow from the bed and whipping it at him. He barely managed to catch the pillow before it hit him right in the face, which probably would have been a grand sight to see.

"*Hey*," she joked, "my grades are *perfect*."

"I have no doubt."

"You do—you just said so!"

"In case, I said ... *in case*, Gabbie."

She threw another pillow at him.

He blocked that one, too.

"And," she added, "I can't be too mad at you because I love that you want to take me there *tomorrow*. Like it can't wait a day or a week."

Michel's gaze met hers, and love shined back. "I want you to be happy, Gabbie."

"With you, I am."

"Yeah, I know."

"What about pre-med for you?" she asked.

Michel shifted on his feet before leaning over on the bed. He used his palms against the sheets to keep him steady as he grinned. "I had acceptances from colleges all across this state—they'll *jump* to take me, so I'm not worried."

"Arrogant," she tossed at him.

He just laughed. "You know it."

"Why didn't you tell me you were adopted?"

"It's not important to me," Michel said. "I never knew my real parents, and I didn't find out about the adoption until I was a teenager. It just ... I know some people expected me to make a thing about it, but I never cared. I know who my mother and father are, and it showed me that sometimes, blood doesn't make a family."

She could tell he wasn't lying.

"Is your sister also adop—"

"Catherine is the spit from my mother's mouth, and the apple of my father's eye. If there was *ever* a perfectly terrifying combination of the two of them, it is *her*. She is their biological child, can't you tell?" Michel shook his head, adding, "They are *so alike*, in fact, that it has become a running joke to the rest of us, one they aren't aware of because then we would have to listen to all of them go on about it together. *At the same time*, Gabbie."

Gabbie pressed her lips together to keep from grinning. "Oh, you have a sibling complex, huh?"

"You didn't have Catherine as a teenager growing up next to you, let me just say. She purposely seeks out trouble … it's what she does. I love her, but facts are still facts."

"And so do you, apparently." Michel stilled across the bed, and Gabbie arched a brow to challenge him to deny it. "But am I wrong, though?"

"I don't want to talk about it," he said.

"*Right.*"

Gabbie threw another pillow.

Michel let that one hit him.

Their laughter colored up the bedroom with the sound—it felt like love, really. She knew they still had so much to figure out, like where in the hell they went from here, and what they were going to do.

That was fine.

That was okay with her.

Because they were *together.*

Just like they were forever meant to be.

EPILOGUE

Eight years later ...

"This isn't *right*."

Michel glanced upward, the ceiling staring back at him, and he swore if it could taunt him, it would be saying, *keep looking, fucker*. Warm ceramic met his lips as he tipped the mug up for another drink. Bitter heaven coated his tongue, the coffee sliding down his throat and waking him up even more.

And upstairs?

Chaos *reigned*.

Michel was not a dumb man, nor was he a stupid husband. Being just two years shy of a decade in marriage to Gabbie taught him a single lesson, one that was simple: the worst thing a man could tell his wife was to *calm down*.

Now, most times, men didn't even *think* before saying it. They just did. The dumbness slipped out of their mouth because the first thing normal humans thought to say to another human when they were in a panic was the obvious thing—*to calm down*.

No, that was foolish.

And a death wish.

So, as Michel thought he was quite smart because so far, he'd not died from being dumb, he knew better than to go upstairs and step in his wife's path. Every morning for the past week, she woke up the same way.

Confused and then chaotic.

His first need was to make his wife happy—*always*. But she was not going to be happy when Michel did the dumb man thing when all else absolutely failed.

He knew how this worked.

Gabbie's footsteps pattered above Michel's head as he quickly finished what was left of his coffee. He needed to get that into him now if it was going to do him any good when he finally arrived back at the hospital. With only ten months left to his residency, Michel was looking forward to *really* starting his career as a doctor.

He had options. Continuing in the trauma bay was high on his list, but so was not spending every waking hour at the hospital. Despite finding all his life that he worked *best* under intense pressure, Michel knew it couldn't last forever. Someday, he was going to burn out, and he didn't want that to be the day he lost a patient not because nothing had worked, but because he made a mistake.

He planned to spend two weeks in the hospital working trauma, and two weeks in the clinic he wanted to open up as a private practice for ... well, he'd not decided on that quite yet. Possibly a second, shorter residency was in order if he wanted to focus elsewhere.

He had options.

That was the thing.

People asked him often what he planned to do once he was finished with his trauma residency, and Michel liked to joke *private practice*. Even to his own mother and father when they asked, followed up with a statement about *more money*. Which wasn't entirely a lie, but really, he was just telling people nothing.

Because *options*.

And he'd never been one to do what others expected.

It was Gabbie's footsteps echoing in the stairwell of their three-level Long Island home that finally drew Michel's attention away from the only thing keeping him awake after two weeks of twenty-four-hour shifts in the trauma bay. His wife came to stand in the entryway of the kitchen, but she didn't look happy to be there.

She was still wearing that over-sized sweater, too.

One she stole from his closet the night before.

Because it hid what she thought was—

"Another pound this morning," she said.

Michel arched a brow at that. "Does that make ten, now?"

"*Total*, Michel."

His gaze shifted to the cabinet in their kitchen where Gabbie kept all her diabetic supplies to manage her disease. Just as fast, he looked to the fridge where her exercise and diet plan for the next *month* was pinned there by a magnet.

She never diverted.

She took her heath *most* seriously.

"Ten pounds in three weeks?" he asked.

Gabbie gave him *that* look. The one that said her emotional side was about to come out and take a bite out of his stupid man ass if he didn't cut that shit *fast*. Although, she'd call it *shite* and when he got a chuckle out of her Irish accent still showing itself after almost a decade living in New York, she'd add on that he was a *feckin' gobshite*, too.

All in love, though.

And he loved her for it.

He needed that sass in his life, and her fire. Some people might raise an eyebrow at a woman like Gabbie, but he *adored* her most of all for her quick wit and dark humor. Not to mention, the way she sometimes showed affection.

This was not one of those times.

"Gabbie—"

"Don't *even*," she snapped, ready to turn around and leave him alone in the kitchen.

"I'm asking as a *doctor*, not because you think I've noticed the weight gain in a bad way, before you try to bite my fucking head off, here."

She tensed all over.

Maybe that'd been a little strong.

"I have noticed it," he added, shrugging, "but it's not been a bad thing. I love you at two pounds underweight, or when you're at the best you've ever been, and I love you like this. I will love you at your worst, too, but I would rather you not get to that point at all. *Not* for your weight or the way you would look, but because I fucking love you, and we both know what could happen if your diabetes goes out of control."

The tension softened.

Michel breathed easier.

It was funny.

But it wasn't, too.

"Something is wrong," she said. "It's been six years since I had a significant weight gain like this, and we *know* that was because I went a little off track because of everything going on with college and—"

"Something is wrong," he agreed.

"You're not going to ask at all?"

"Ask what?"

"If I ate like I was supposed to, or kept up my exercise routine?"

"No."

Because he knew she did.

Simple as that.

She was an adult, and he didn't need to chase after his wife when she knew very well how to take care of herself. Unfortunately, she was so accustomed to someone checking over her shoulder all the time that they still found themselves like *this* ... her, out of habit, thinking he was going to question her because he didn't trust she could handle her business.

Michel checked the watch on his wrist, and scowled. "*Cazzo.* I have to get out of here, or I am going to be late at the hospital." He didn't want the lecture for it, either. Moving to his wife in the doorway after discarding his mug to the sink, he pressed a fast kiss to Gabbie's forehead, murmuring, "It could be anything—a hormonal shift, a developing allergy, or even your cycles changing, right? We'll figure it out."

She stiffened.

"What?" he asked.

Just as quickly, Gabbie shook her head and glanced up at him. "Nothing. You should get to the hospital, and I managed to get that appointment with my doctor today."

"Oh, good. Maybe we'll get an answer, then."

"Maybe."

He kissed her mouth next, giving her a lazy smirk as he said, "And get that fucking sweater off—I love you in my clothes, babe, but not when you're trying to hide something that looks great in *anything*."

Gabbie grinned.

Michel winked.

• • •

"GIVE ME THAT GAUZE!"

With his legs straddling a man on a gurney—who'd been brought into the parking lot by his friends who basically *shoved* him out of the back of their car with a fucking hole in his chest that looked like a bullet wound—Michel's hands trembled from the force that he was putting into keeping pressure on the wound.

"The gauze!" he snapped again.

They had four minutes going *full speed* to get this man from the parking lot, to the trauma bay so that he could get in and figure out what was causing the bleed to be as bad as it was. So bad, in fact, that they were leaving a trail of blood in their wake that looked more like a river than dribbles.

Everybody's hands were full.

Except the *new*, and young resident who had apparently never been faced with a trauma quite this violent and serious if her *very* white face was any indication, was lingering behind. He'd had that moment, too, once. Every trauma surgeon faced their moment. That one split second where *everything* fucking changed about what they thought regarding this career, and what they could handle. His had come when someone brought in a three-month-old baby that had been badly burned in a house fire and didn't have a pulse.

It was a burned *baby*.

A fucking baby.

He had nightmares for *weeks*.

He didn't remember snapping out of the moment, either, because the next thing he knew, he was doing chest compressions on the infant. Because that's what the trauma bay did to a doctor—everything became instinctual. Even if a doctor *wasn't all there* because something set them off balance, their brain and body still knew what they had to do. The world might feel like it had stopped, but the doctors kept moving.

They had to.

Or people *died*.

So, no, he didn't fault the woman for finally having her moment, he really just wished it wasn't right now when everyone else's hands were full, and he needed hers *on deck*. The doctor in question finally snapped back into reality, and tossed Michel the large roll of gauze to him. He began to stuff as much of the unrolled gauze as he could into the chest wound of the man who was now *choking out blood* under the mask the nurse was pressing against his face.

Staunching the wound was important, as much as pressure on it was, anyhow. And he just needed to get control of this goddamn bleed as much as possible.

"Three minutes to trauma bay," Michel snapped, his hands working faster than even his mouth. "Bay *three*. Call it down!"

"Got it."

"Michel!"

His head snapped up at the call of his name at the same time the gurney rocked when it rolled over the small ledge leading into the trauma center. They were finally leaving the parking lot—they hadn't even gotten in the hospital yet. He hadn't realized that until *just then*.

That ran through his mind at the same time the fact that his wife was watching him from just beyond where an ambulance was parking with its lights flashing. Her wide eyes drifted from him to the gurney, and his bloody hands at the man's chest.

All at the same time, he kept drifting further away from her.

It was just a split second.

The doors were closing.

Still, he heard her shout, "I'm pregnant!"

His first thought?

That explains a lot.

His second?

He's lost too much blood.

And that was how Michel found out he was going to be a father.

• • •

Antony Dante Marcello didn't have a concept of *bad timing*. In fact, he decided to make his way into the world when his father was working during one of the *worst* emergencies New York had faced in several decades. An improper discharge of dynamite on top of a bridge overpass that needed replacement before it was intended to detonate, and *while* vehicles were still driving underneath on the freeway.

Twenty cars.

Most had two people inside each vehicle.

Eight dead on arrival.

Three air lifted out.

The rest … under the rubble.

So was Michel. Because if they couldn't bring the injured to the *hospital*, then he was going to *them*. Along with the rest of the trauma team. They would do what they could on the road under the sections of rubble that had been lifted enough to find the injured. If they could be treated on site, then they were. If they could be brought out *safely* without causing death, then they planned to do that.

Assessment was crucial.

That was when he got the fucking call, too.

"Gabbie's in labor."

Michel's whole world stopped.

Except it didn't.

That was the thing about being who he was—nothing *stopped* for him. He couldn't walk out of a disaster where his skills were needed simply because his private life stepped in the way to throw him a curveball.

"Why are you not in your car right now?" Dante demanded.

"Because *I can't*. She'll understand."

"Michel—"

"I'll be there," he barked into the phone at his father, "tell her I'll fucking be there, Dad."

It was a first birth—so the labor could take *hours*. Days, even, for some women. Michel knew that, so he didn't rush, not that he could have, anyway. He worked with the trauma team and the rescue crew to pull the victims out of their crushed cars without losing their life.

It didn't work for all.

They lost three more before it was said and done.

Michel was on route to the trauma center with one victim who had been flattened under a large piece of cement that fell directly on top of his car—his body was *crushed*, and somehow, the man was alive. They couldn't say the same for his wife, but they hadn't told him that yet. It was better he didn't know in the current state he was facing, and everything was literally *second by second*.

It all counted.

That was thirty-six hours after the first call about his wife.

"Michel, you've got an emergency family call!"

That was thrown at him as he slipped into trauma bay one to start one of *many* surgeries that would hopefully save the crushed man's life. It was a long shot, but nobody wanted to say it out loud. They had to *try*—it's what the patient asked.

"Michel!"

"Put them on the speaker for the bay," he shouted behind his mask, hands up and safe from touching anything as he backed through the door being held open for him. "That's the best I can do right now."

Time was still crucial. The more seconds they wasted, the more likely it was that they would lose the man on the table.

The speakers for the trauma bay crackled as Michel glanced at the monitor tracking the man's vitals—the numbers weren't great, but that's about what he expected. It was going to be touch and go for this first surgery, and it would determine if they would be capable of taking him in for the second, too.

Then, the room went quiet as the speakers suddenly got *loud*.

Michel glanced upward.

So did everyone else.

A baby cried.

Strong, and beautiful, and *perfect*.

He didn't need anyone to tell him. A part of him just knew—deep in his fucking heart, so visceral and raw—that it was his son's cry. He made that child; that boy came from *him*, and he knew the cry belonged to what was *his*.

Quietly, Michel said, "Tell my wife I will see her soon."

And then, to the rest of the room, he added, "Let's get to work—call cardio *again*. They should have been down here already. I want Jessi on this man's heart while we have his torso opened. *Two minutes*."

• • •

Twelve hours later ...

How long had Michel been awake?

He didn't know.

Too long, maybe.

The smart part of his brain knew this was *bad*. He couldn't function on so little sleep that he was almost falling over as the elevator continued climbing. Somehow, he managed it, but he wasn't at all sure how.

It felt like he blinked, and he was standing in front of his father. A door was opened, and despite the light shining in from the windows inside the private hospital room, it still seemed like he was in a sleepy daze.

And then he saw her.

And *him*.

His son swaddled in light blue, and his wife holding the baby close to her chest where she sat on the edge of the hospital bed. He didn't remember how he crossed the room, but the next thing he knew, little Antony was in Michel's arms, and he was kissing the top of his wife's head.

"I'm sorry," he heard himself say.

Gabbie shook her head. "Don't *ever* be sorry for that, Michel."

167

The patient was still alive. After twenty-four hours, Michel had to go back in for another twenty-four-hour shift. He knew he should put those thoughts aside, so he did for the moment. It allowed him to focus on the baby in his arms as he settled into a chair in the corner of the room.

Antony slept on.

God, he was small.

Peach and cream skin.

"He looks like you," Gabbie said in the background.

He did.

Michel whispered, "I know. He's perfect, Gabbie."

And then he fell asleep like that, reclined on the chair with his newborn son tucked safely into his arms. He didn't wake up again until the baby needed to feed, and it was only long enough to hear his father tell someone that a visitor would be arriving soon.

Who the hell was coming?

It could be anybody.

Their family was huge.

It was *not* who Michel expected.

• • •

"Da," Gabbie whispered.

Michel's back stiffened at his wife's soft exclamation, and he spun fast on his heels to find a man he *never* expected to see again standing in the doorway of the hospital room. Another three hours, and Michel would have to head back to the hospital he worked at across the city.

Seeing Charles Casey standing there made him want to say fuck those plans in a *big* way. It was hard for Michel to feel like ... he could trust Charles, not after everything. The man had promised, as he said, Gabbie was *"dead to me."*

Exact words.

And yet, there he stood.

Next to Dante.

Michel gave his father a look, and subtly moved sideways to stand in front of his wife and child. "What is he doing here?"

"Michel, now—"

"No, I asked a fucking question."

Dante cleared his throat. "This is his grandchild, too. His *only* grandchild, and that woman is his *only* child, Michel. I extended the gracious offer when I first got the call that Gabbie was in labor for him to ... make his way here and share in this joy with the rest of us. *If,* of course, we were all willing to let the bygones be bygones. That's what *good* men do, son."

Michel was a good man.

He still didn't like this.

"It's been almost ten years," Charles said, "and I would like it if it wasn't one more, lad."

"Michel," Gabbie said behind him.

He felt her hand graze his back. It wasn't much. The soft sweep of her fingertips, but it was all she needed to do. It really wasn't about *him*, when it had always been about her. He didn't have to like it as long as she wanted it.

Michel nodded, and stepped aside a bit to let Charles see his daughter and grandson. "We named him Antony … for my grandfather."

"Strong name," Charles replied.

"I missed you, Da."

Charles swallowed hard as he took a step further into the room. And then another and another until he was in front of his daughter, and bending down to hug her. "More than you know, Gabbie. I have missed you far more than you know—I'm *sorry*."

Always the sweet one.

Always the loving one.

She was far too forgiving, his wife.

But Michel was grateful.

She was perfect for him.

"Let me see this wee lad," Charles said, taking the baby from Gabbie's arms to hold him high. Awake and blinking with hazy, dark eyes, Antony stared at his grandfather. The *Irish* side of him—the colorful bits that made him special, Michel thought. His son was not *one* thing, but many things. "You look just like your da, child."

Michel chuckled.

Charles passed Michel a glance before tucking the baby into the crook of his arm. He ran a fingertip down the slope of the baby's nose, still speaking to him all the while. "But that's grand to take after him, ain't it? I hear this father of yours, Antony, does amazing things every day. And I suspect you are one of them, child. I have time to make up for here."

Well, then …

Michel let out a breath he hadn't known he was holding in until just that second. Anxiety had a funny way of manifesting, but just like that, it was gone.

"*Grazie*," he told his own father.

Dante smiled.

Like he just *knew*. And Michel supposed he did considering he was the father of a daughter himself. How would Dante feel if he had spent close to a decade estranged from his only daughter because of his own mistakes? Would he take the chance to close the distance, even if it meant admitting his stupid pride?

Michel would bet *yes*.

"Forgiveness sometimes begins with taking the first step," his father replied. "Even if you weren't the man who forced the distance."

Yeah.

Michel would remember that.

ABOUT THE AUTHOR

Bethany-Kris is a Canadian author, lover of much, and mother to four sons, two cats, and three dogs. A small town in Eastern Canada where she was born and raised is where she has always called home. With her boys under her feet, a snuggling cat, barking dogs, and a spouse calling over his shoulder, she is nearly always writing something ... when she can find the time.

Find Bethany-Kris at her:

WEBSITE: www.bethanykris.com
BLOG: www.bethanykris.blogspot.ca
FACEBOOK: www.facebook.com/bethanykriswrites
TWITTER: @BethanyKris
INSTAGRAM: www.instagram.com/bethany.kris
PINTEREST: www.pinterest.com/bethanykris

Sign up to Bethany-Kris's New Release Newsletter here:
http://eepurl.com/bf9lzD.

OTHER BOOKS

Renzo + Lucia

Privilege
Harbor
Contempt

Andino + Haven

Duty
Vow

John + Siena

Loyalty
Disgrace

Cross + Catherine

Always
Revere
Unruly
The Companion
Naz & Roz

Guzzi Duet

Unraveled, Book One
Entangled, Book Two

DeLuca Duet

Waste of Worth: Part One
Worth of Waste: Part Two

171

Standalone Titles

Dirty Pool
Effortless
Inflict
Cozen
Captivated
Dishonored

Donati Bloodlines

Thin Lies
Thin Lines
Thin Lives
Behind the Bloodlines
The Complete Trilogy

Filthy Marcellos

Antony
Lucian
Giovanni
Dante
Legacy
A Very Marcello Christmas
The Complete Collection

Seasons of Betrayal

Where the Sun Hides
Where the Snow Falls
Where the Wind Whispers
Seasons: The Complete Seasons of Betrayal Series

Gun Moll Trilogy

Gun Moll
Gangster Moll
Madame Moll

The Chicago War

Deathless & Divided
Reckless & Ruined
Scarless & Sacred
Breathless & Bloodstained
The Complete Series
Maldives & Mistletoe

The Russian Guns

The Arrangement
The Life
The Score
Demyan & Ana
Shattered
The Jersey Vignettes

Find more on Bethany-Kris's website at www.bethanykris.com

www.ingramcontent.com/pod-product-compliance
Lightning Source LLC
Chambersburg PA
CBHW071436260626
47170CB00008B/2740